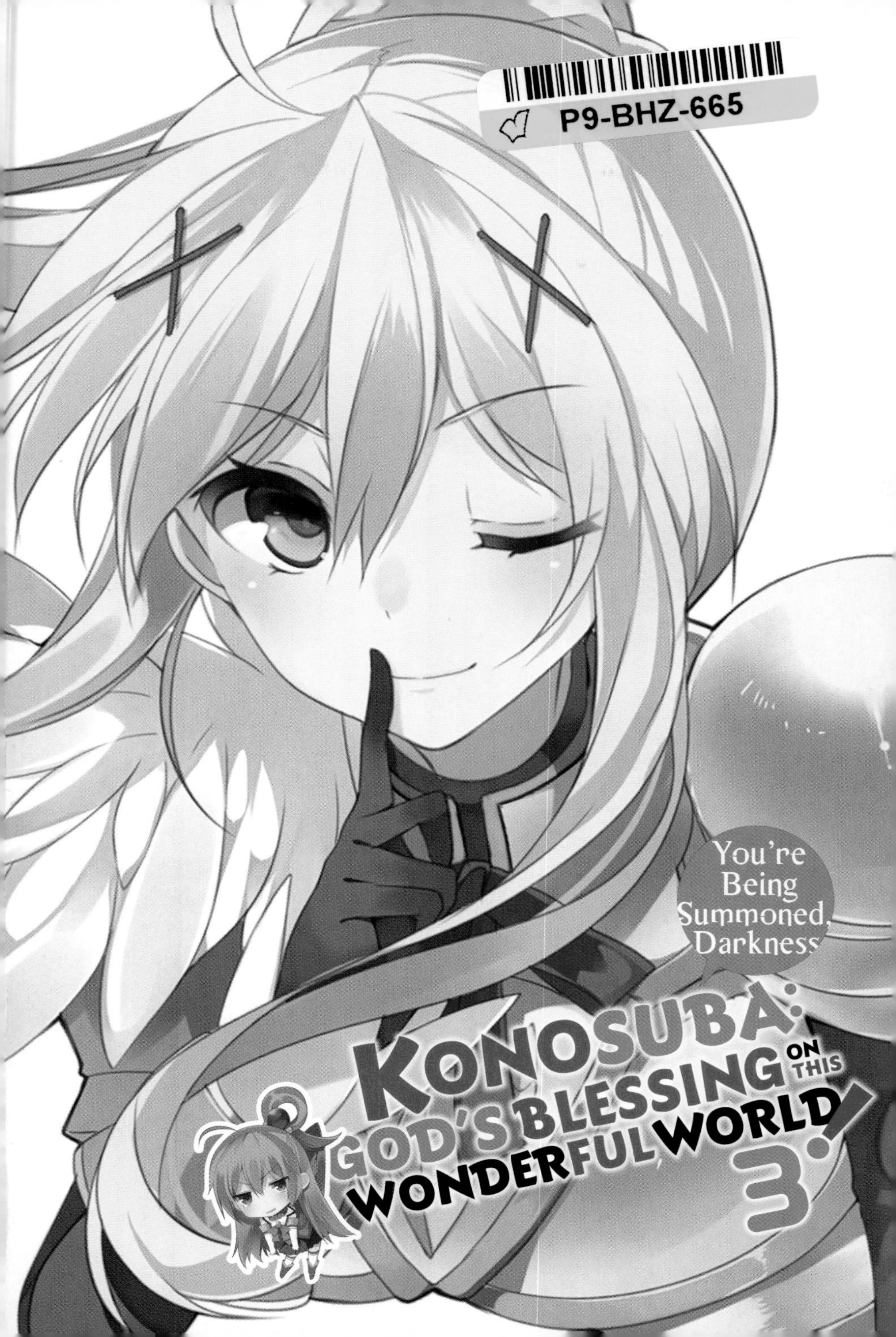
You're Being Summoned, Darkness
KONOSUBA: GOD'S BLESSING ON THIS WONDERFUL WORLD!
3

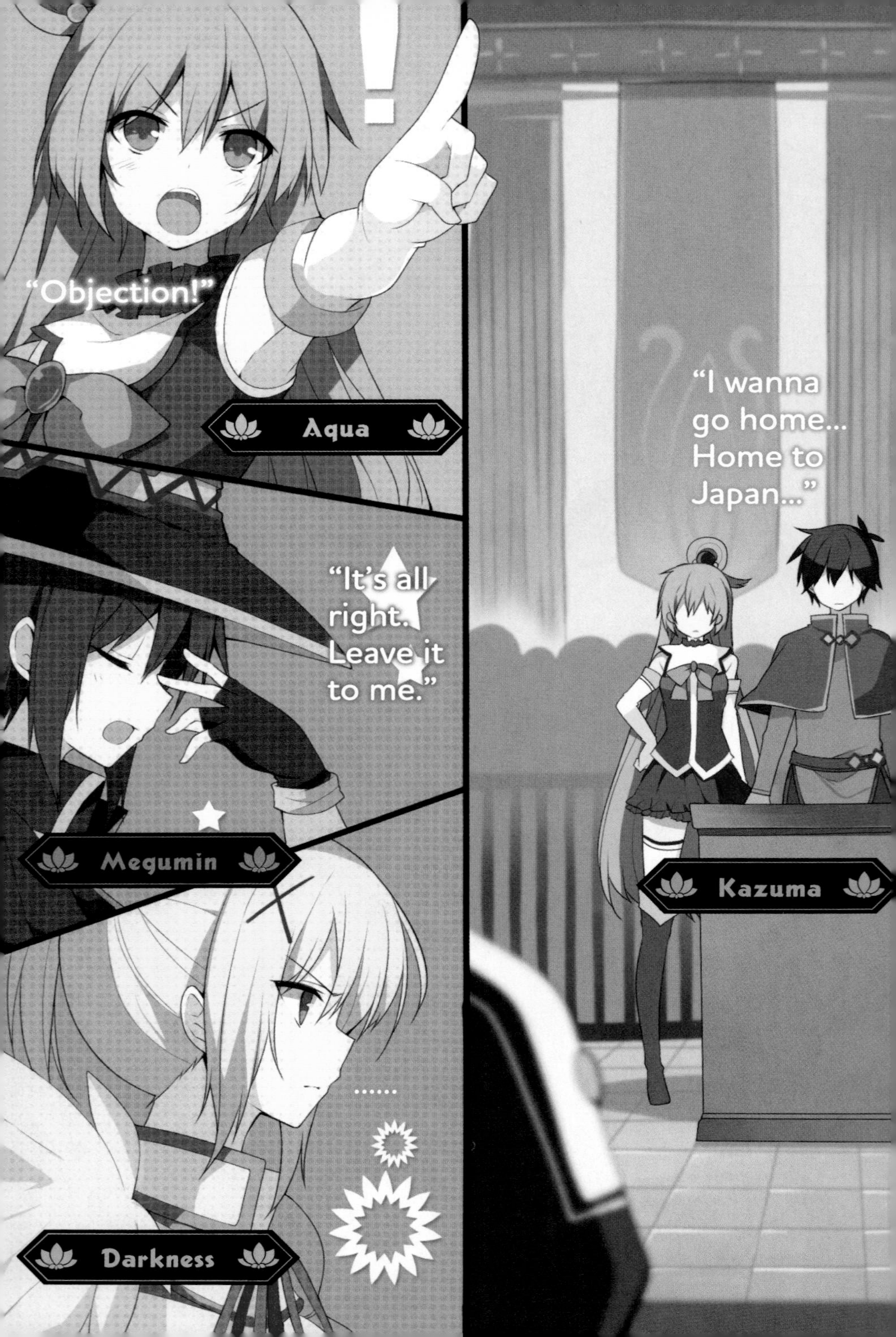
"I wanna go home... Home to Japan..."
Kazuma
"Objection!"
Aqua
"It's all right. Leave it to me."
Megumin
......
Darkness

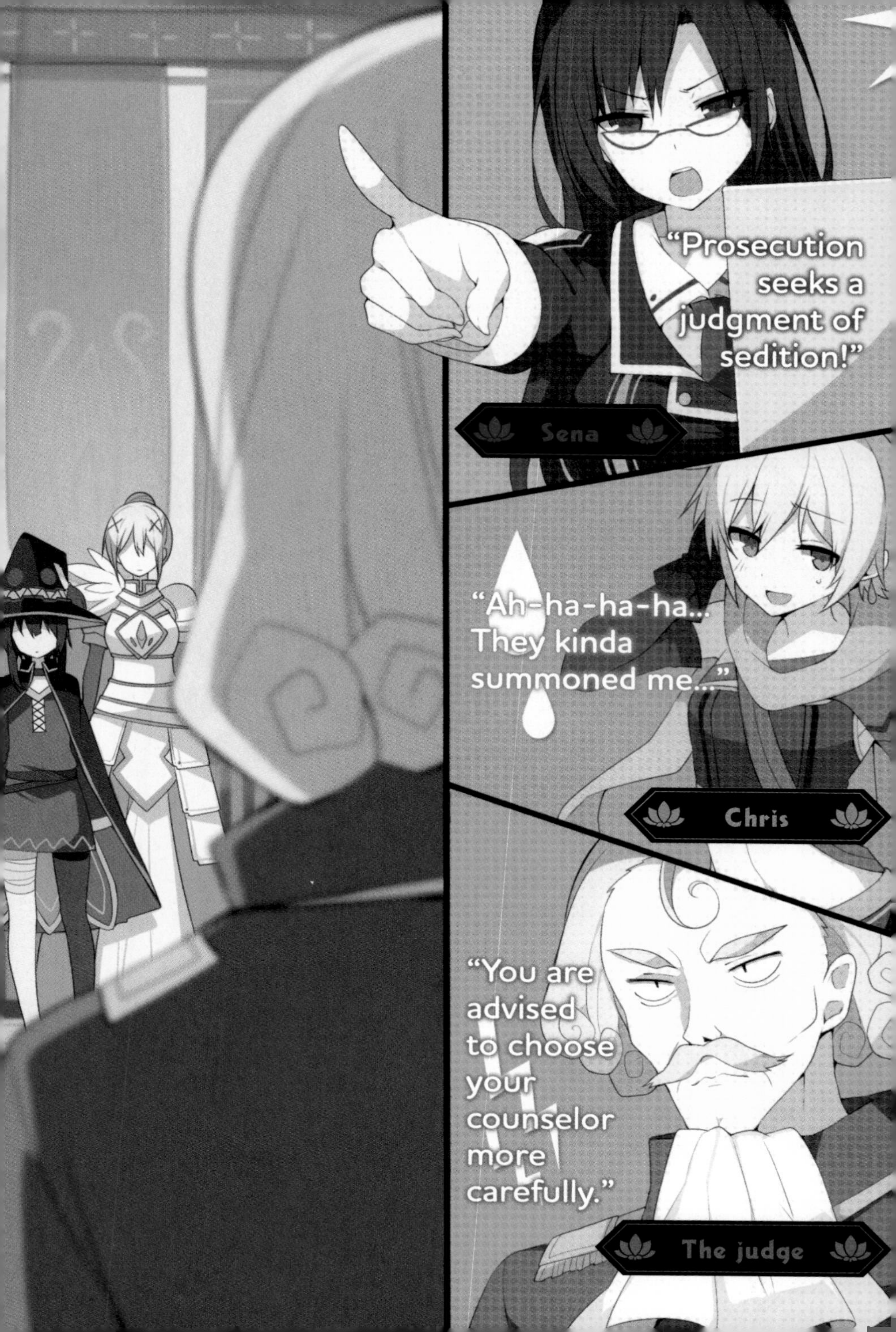
"Prosecution seeks a judgment of sedition!"
Sena
"Ah-ha-ha-ha... They kinda summoned me..."
Chris
"You are advised to choose your counselor more carefully."
The judge

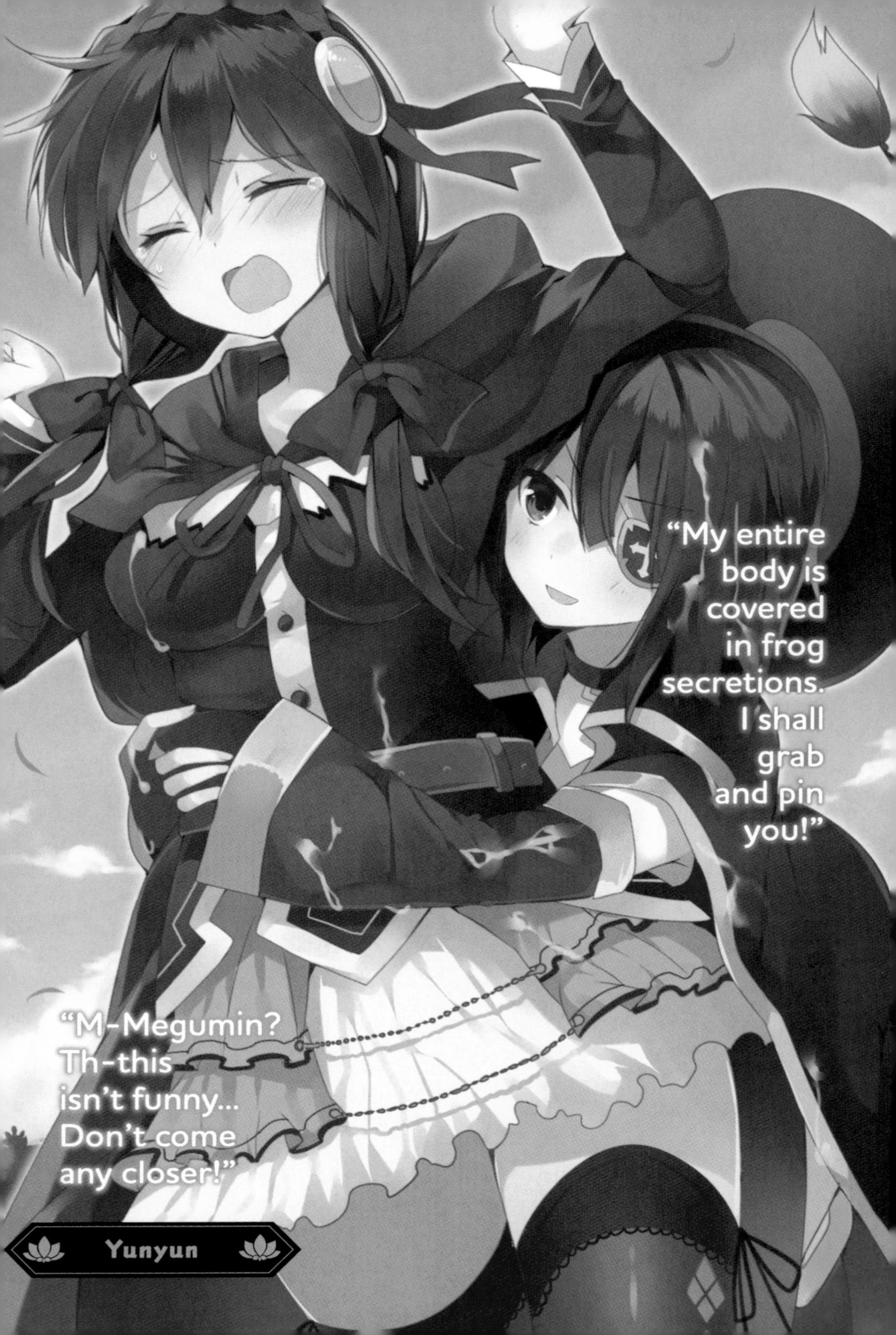
"My entire body is covered in frog secretions. I shall grab and pin you!"
"M-Megumin? Th-this isn't funny... Don't come any closer!"
Yunyun

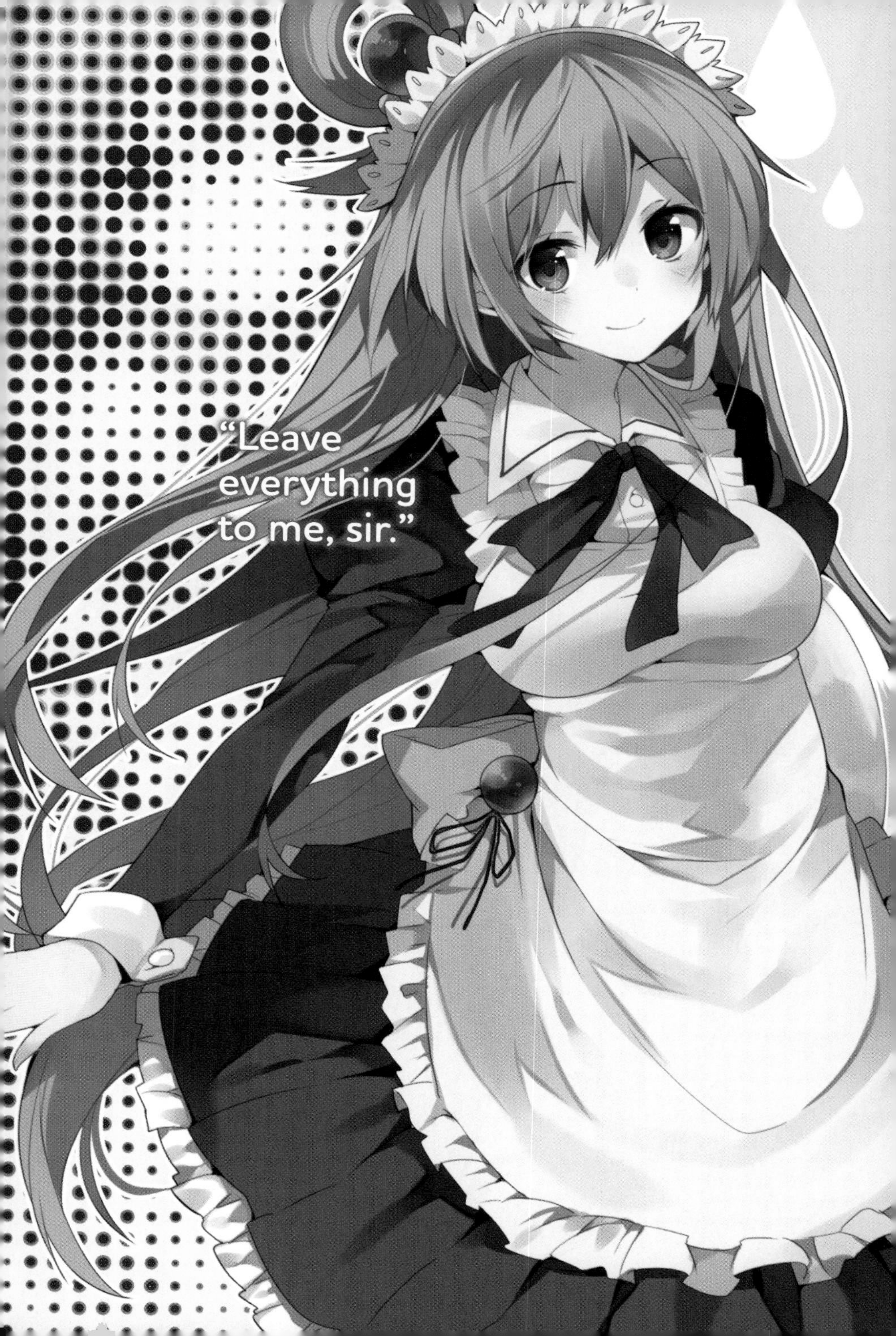
"Leave everything to me, sir."

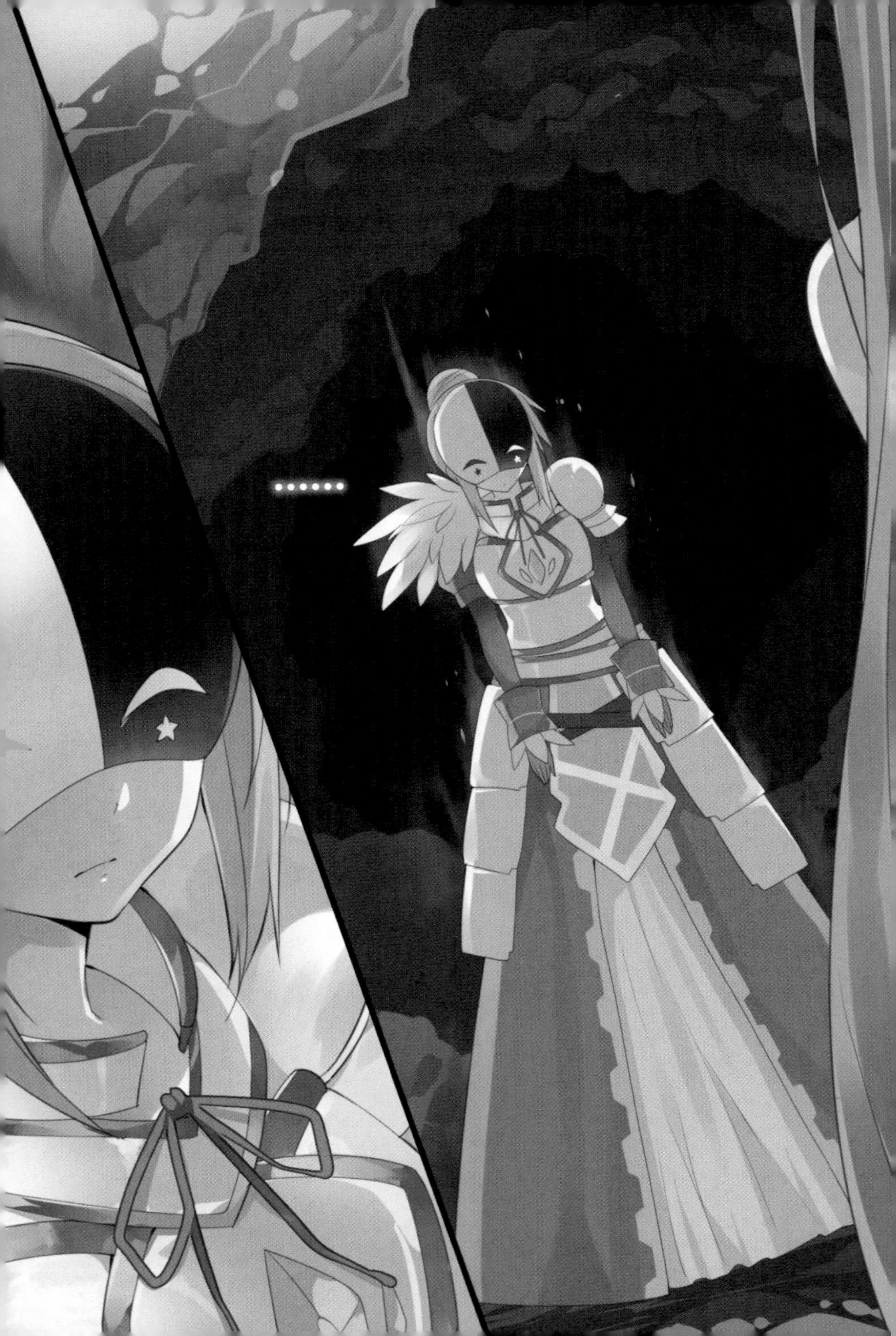
......

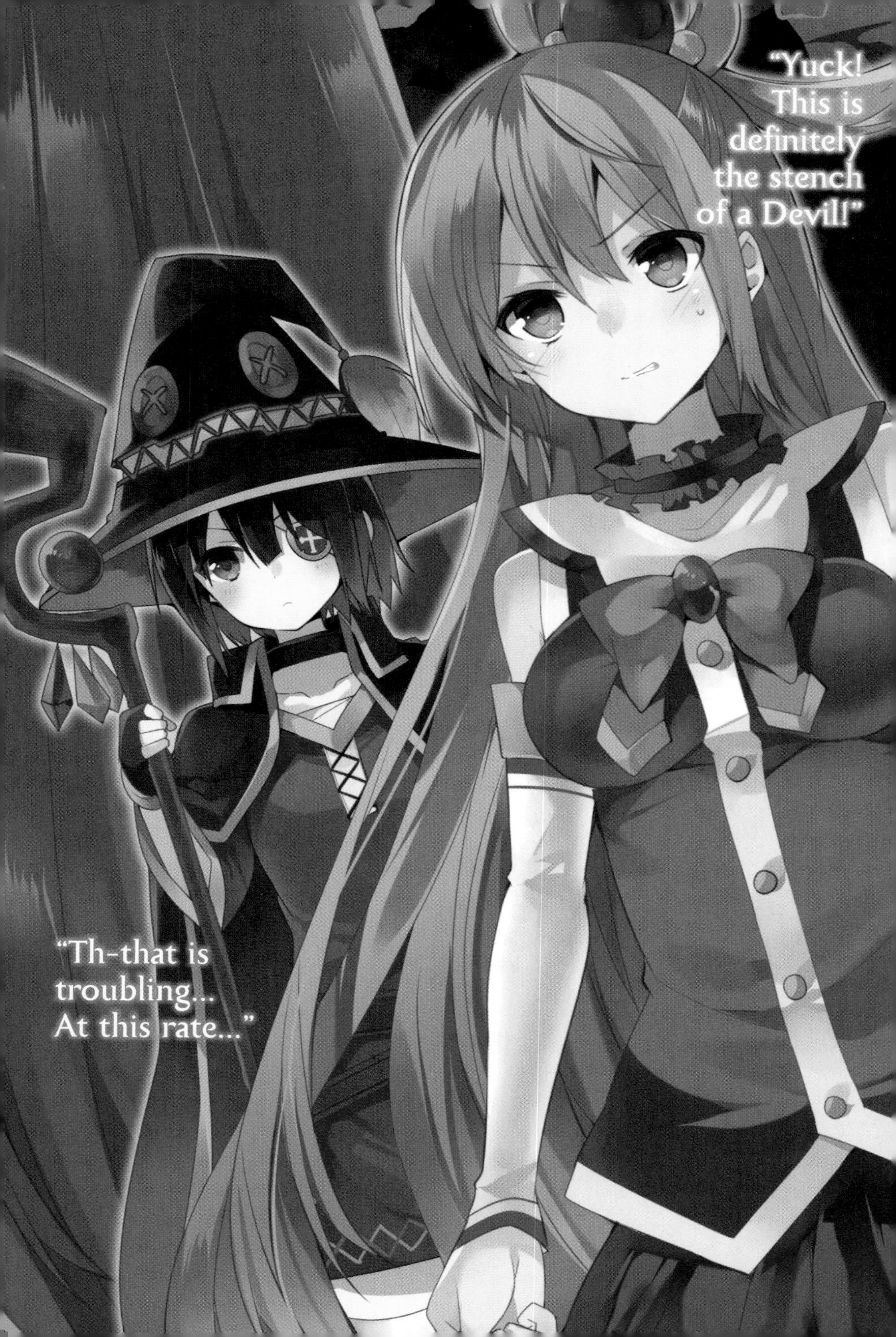
"Yuck! This is definitely the stench of a Devil!"
"Th-that is troubling... At this rate..."

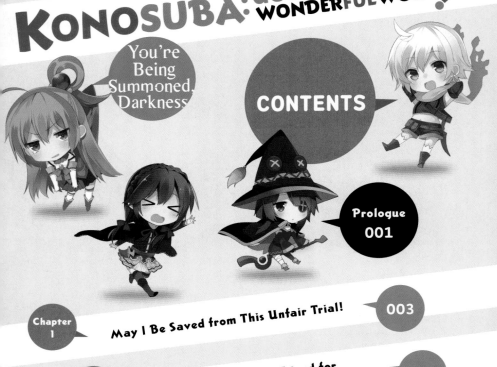

KONOSUBA: GOD'S BLESSING ON THIS WONDERFUL WORLD! 3

You're Being Summoned, Darkness

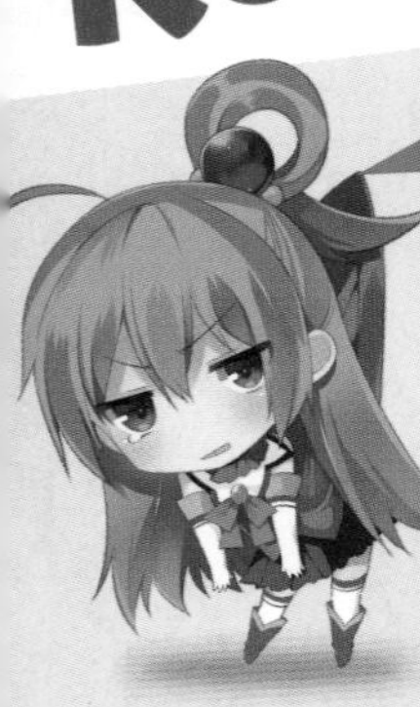

CONTENTS

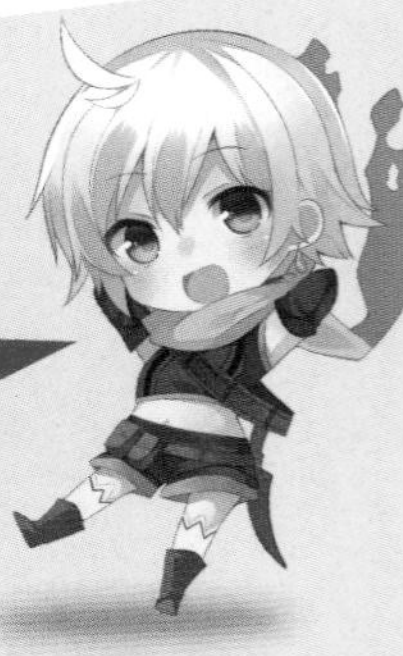

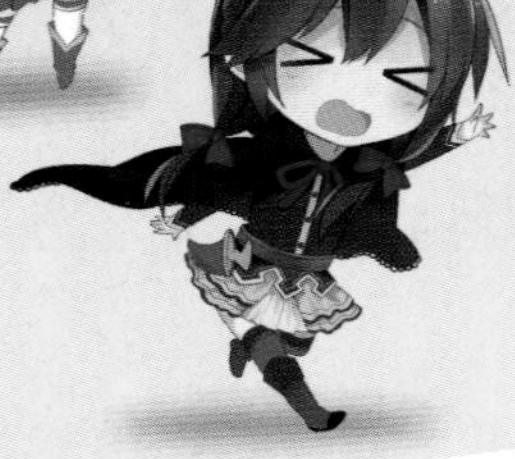

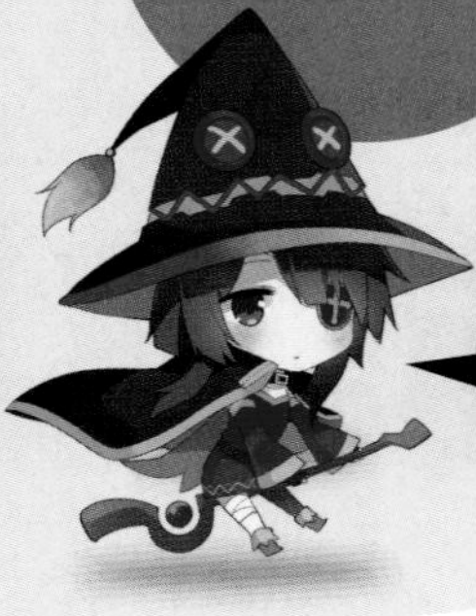

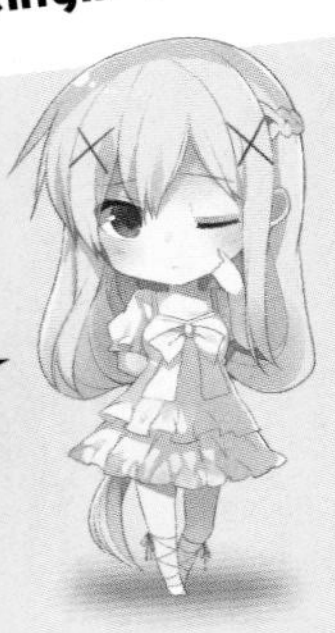

KONOSUBA: GOD'S BLESSING ON THIS WONDERFUL WORLD!

You're Being Summoned, Darkness

3

NATSUME AKATSUKI

ILLUSTRATION BY
KURONE MISHIMA

YEN ON
NEW YORK

KONOSUBA: GOD'S BLESSING ON THIS WONDERFUL WORLD! 3

NATSUME AKATSUKI

Translation by Kevin Steinbach
Cover art by Kurone Mishima

This book is a work of fiction. Names, characters, places, and incidents are the product of the author's imagination or are used fictitiously. Any resemblance to actual events, locales, or persons, living or dead, is coincidental.

KONO SUBARASHII SEKAI NI SHUKUFUKU WO!, Volume 3: YONDEMASUYO, DAKUNESU SAN.
Copyright © 2014 Natsume Akatsuki, Kurone Mishima
First published in Japan in 2014 by KADOKAWA CORPORATION, Tokyo.
English translation rights arranged with KADOKAWA CORPORATION, Tokyo, through TUTTLE-MORI AGENCY, INC., Tokyo.

English translation © 2017 by Yen Press, LLC

Yen Press, LLC supports the right to free expression and the value of copyright. The purpose of copyright is to encourage writers and artists to produce the creative works that enrich our culture.

The scanning, uploading, and distribution of this book without permission is a theft of the author's intellectual property. If you would like permission to use material from the book (other than for review purposes), please contact the publisher. Thank you for your support of the author's rights.

Yen On
1290 Avenue of the Americas
New York, NY 10104

Visit us at yenpress.com
facebook.com/yenpress
twitter.com/yenpress
yenpress.tumblr.com
instagram.com/yenpress

First Yen On Edition: August 2017

Yen On is an imprint of Yen Press, LLC.
The Yen On name and logo are trademarks of Yen Press, LLC.

The publisher is not responsible for websites (or their content) that are not owned by the publisher.

Library of Congress Cataloging-in-Publication Data
Names: Akatsuki, Natsume, author. | Mishima, Kurone, 1991– illustrator. | Steinbach, Kevin, translator.
Title: Konosuba, God's blessing on this wonderful world! / Natsume Akatsuki ; illustration by Kurone Mishima ; translation by Kevin Steinbach.
Other titles: Kono subarashi sekai ni shukufuku wo. English
Description: First Yen On edition. | New York, NY : Yen On, 2017– Contents: v. 1. Oh! my useless goddess! — v. 2. Love, witches & other delusions! — v. 3. You're being summoned, darkness
Identifiers: LCCN 2016052009 | ISBN 9780316553377 (v. 1 : paperback) | ISBN 9780316468701 (v. 2 : paperback) | ISBN 9780316468732 (v. 3 : paperback)
Subjects: | CYAC: Fantasy. | Future life—Fiction. | Adventure and adventurers—Fiction. | BISAC: FICTION / Fantasy / General.
Classification: LCC PZ7.1.A38 Ko 2017 | DDC [Fic]—dc23
LC record available at https://lccn.loc.gov/2016052009

ISBNs: 978-0-316-46873-2 (paperback)
978-0-316-46875-6 (ebook)

10 9 8 7 6 5 4 3

LSC-C

Printed in the United States of America

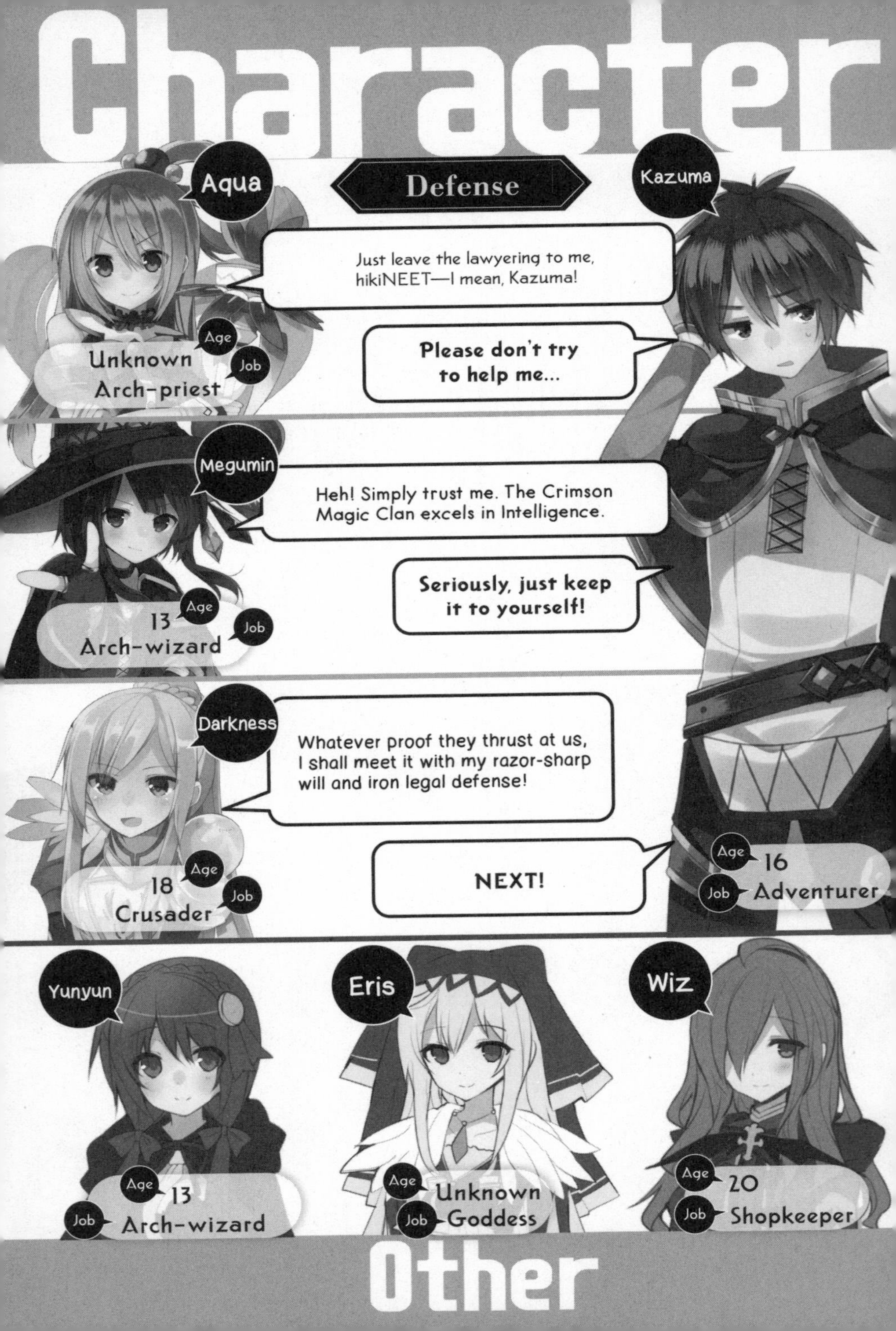
Character
Defense
Aqua
Just leave the lawyering to me, hikiNEET—I mean, Kazuma!
Age Unknown
Job Arch-priest
Kazuma
Please don't try to help me...
Megumin
Heh! Simply trust me. The Crimson Magic Clan excels in Intelligence.
Seriously, just keep it to yourself!
Age 13
Job Arch-wizard
Darkness
Whatever proof they thrust at us, I shall meet it with my razor-sharp will and iron legal defense!
NEXT!
Age 18
Job Crusader
Age 16
Job Adventurer
Yunyun
Age 13
Job Arch-wizard
Eris
Age Unknown
Job Goddess
Wiz
Age 20
Job Shopkeeper
Other

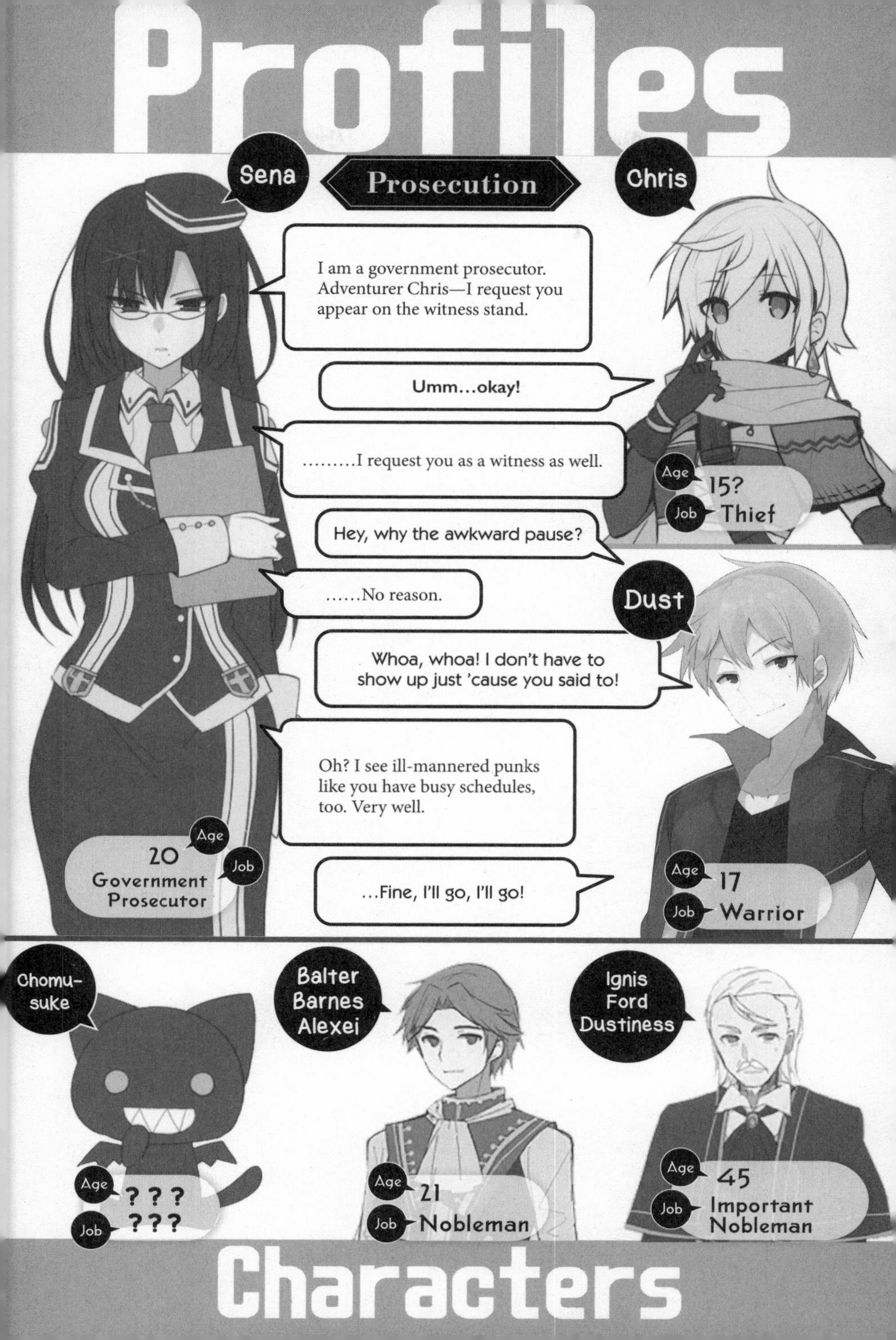
Profiles
Prosecution
Sena
Chris
I am a government prosecutor. Adventurer Chris—I request you appear on the witness stand.
Umm…okay!
………I request you as a witness as well.
Hey, why the awkward pause?
……No reason.
Age 15?
Job Thief
Dust
Whoa, whoa! I don't have to show up just 'cause you said to!
Oh? I see ill-mannered punks like you have busy schedules, too. Very well.
…Fine, I'll go, I'll go!
Age 20
Job Government Prosecutor
Age 17
Job Warrior
Chomu-suke
Age ???
Job ???
Balter Barnes Alexei
Age 21
Job Nobleman
Ignis Ford Dustiness
Age 45
Job Important Nobleman
Characters

Prologue

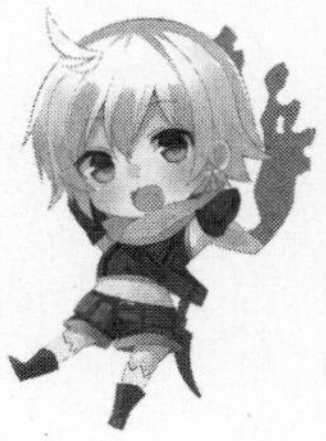

Hi Mom, hi Dad.

How are you doing? I'll bet it's pretty cold back in your world.

"Defendant Kazuma Satou. In light of your numerous immoral deeds, to say nothing..."

Or will the snow be melting for you soon?

How's my little brother? Same as always?

"...of your total—indeed, sociopathic—disregard for public safety..."

I know you guys. I'm sure you're all getting along fine.

"...I consider the prosecution's recommendation to be appropriate."

For the most part, I've been doing great in my new home.

"I find you guilty—"

* * *

So even though your son has shamed you forever in a court of law...

"—and sentence you to death."

...I hope you'll find it in your heart to forgive him.

Chapter 1
May I Be Saved from This Unfair Trial!

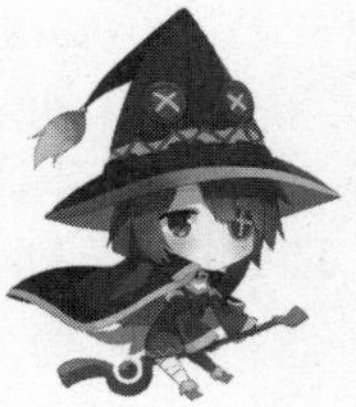

1

I don't know who named it, but behind its ridiculous moniker was an existence with a bounty on its head, feared the world over.

Mobile Fortress Destroyer.

And just the other day, we took it down, thanks to my exceptional leadership.

Then we came to the Guild to collect our reward, but…

"Adventurer Kazuma Satou! You are hereby accused of sedition. I will need you to come with me."

Things were getting a little weird around here.

"Umm, who are you? And what's sedition? I just came to collect a bounty," I said nervously to the woman, who had a dangerous glint in her eyes.

The pleasant chatter in the Guild Hall faded away as the woman, with two Knights escorting her, explained.

"I am Sena, government prosecutor. Sedition is the crime of attempting to undermine or overthrow the State. And you are currently under suspicion of being a terrorist—or perhaps an agent from the Demon King's army."

Long black hair framed the face of the prosecutor called Sena as she fixed me with her intense gaze.

At first glance, you could mistake her for some highly paid executive's secretary. Also, you might notice that she was drop-dead gorgeous.

Aqua exclaimed, "What?! Just a second, Kazuma—what did you do?! Can't I leave you alone for one minute? Apologize right now! I'll help you—just hurry up and say you're sorry!"

"You idiot! Why would I commit a crime like that? And when did you ever 'leave me alone for one minute'? You ought to know full well I haven't done anything!"

As the two of us shouted at one another, Megumin broke in.

"Pardon me, but is there not some kind of mistake? Kazuma may be constantly committing minor offenses such as sexual harassment, but he does not have the nerve for the large-scale lawlessness you accuse him of."

"Are you defending me or trying to start something?"

As I laid into Megumin, Darkness picked up the thread.

"Hmm, I agree, this man isn't capable of such grand malfeasance. If he had it in him, he would do more than just stare at me with animal lust when I walk around the house in clothes that barely cover me. But he can't even bring himself to sneak into my room at night!"

"I—I—I—I—I do *not* stare at you! You're just way too self-conscious! Just 'cause you're a little hot, don't let it go to your head! Am I not allowed to make my own choices?!"

Darkness flushed.

"Wh-why, you—! You made me do all that stuff in the bath, and now you…?!"

"We agreed I was under the control of a succubus then! You're the one who let yourself get caught up in the moment so bad, you just went ahead and washed my back! What? Maybe you hoped it *would* go somewhere! Just how easy are you, woman?!"

"I—I knew you remembered! A-and as a Crusader who serves Eris, my body is yet pure! Plus, are you calling me an easy woman?! I'll kill you!"

Darkness was attempting to strangle me when one of Sena's escorts broke in between us.

The prosecutor watched the whole exchange without batting an eyelash and said, "The Coronatite at the heart of Mobile Fortress Destroyer was teleported on this man's orders to the manor of the local lord."

At that, the Guild Hall got extremely quiet.

Coronatite. In the battle with Destroyer, we'd used Teleport magic to get rid of it moments before it exploded. And yes, I had been the one to give the word.

But how could it have…?

"Oh man! The lord died in an explosion *I* caused?!"

"Don't assume! He's not dead. Reports indicate that all servants had left the house and the lord himself was in an underground bunker. Hence there were no injuries, although the house itself was blown to smithereens."

"So zero casualties in the battle with Destroyer? That's great!"

"Great?! Do you understand the situation here? You transported an explosive device to the noble's manor and destroyed his home. As I stated previously, you are suspected of being either a terrorist or in league with the Demon King. We'll learn the details at the station."

The hall erupted into discussion as she finished talking.

Of course. All the adventurers here knew me.

And they knew all about what I'd done in the Destroyer fight.

"Hmph, and here I thought there was an actual problem. Kazuma is the hero of the battle against Destroyer. True, he ordered the teleportation of the stone, but that was a necessary emergency measure. Without his quick thinking, the exploding Coronatite might have claimed many lives. He deserves an award, not an arrest!"

All around the Guild, people murmured agreement with Megumin.

Y-you guys…!

While I was busy feeling warmth in my heart, Sena broke in with a retort.

"Incidentally, the charge of sedition can apply not only to the main actor but to any coconspirators. I advise caution in your words and actions until the trial is over. Though if you really want to join this man in prison, I won't stop you."

At that, the Guild went quiet again.

Then…

…Aqua suddenly piped up. "…I recall Kazuma saying at the time, *'It's a big world! There's gotta be a better chance of it landing somewhere deserted! Do it—I'll take full responsibility! I may not look like much, but I've got Luck to spare!'"*

…True, I'd said that. But why would our resident idiot choose to have a perfect memory this *one* time?

"Aqua. You can't seriously want to pin this…all…on…me…?"

She didn't answer, only looking away unhappily.

"I didn't go aboard Destroyer myself. I'm sure I could have stopped Kazuma if I'd been there. But I *wasn't*, so there was nothing I could do… *Nothing…*," Megumin commented loudly to herself.

"Hang on, Aqua, Megumin… How can you…?"

No way—they wouldn't…?!

Then Darkness stood between Sena and me as if to protect me.

"Wait. I'm the one you want. I gave the order. So, if you must subject someone to dungeon play… No! I mean, please take me with Kazuma and subject me to your brutal tortures as well!"

"Interesting," Sena said. "I heard you simply stood in front of Destroyer the entire time and did nothing of any use at all."

"?!"

Struck right in the heart, Darkness had tears leap to her eyes. She looked at me, but Sena was right, and anyway, now wasn't the time.

Finally, Wiz, who had been silent the entire time, raised a trembling hand.

"U-um! I was the one who actually used Teleport, so if you insist on taking Mr. Kazuma away, p-please take me, too…"

Aqua grasped Wiz's raised hand.

"No, Wiz! Only one person needs to sacrifice himself! I know it's hard, but try to bear it…! This isn't good-bye. We'll just wait for Kazuma till he's served his sentence, all right?"

You despicable woman! You've given me up already?!

No. I *did* give Wiz the order. I couldn't let her take the rap for me alone.

"Fine, you guys! Abandon me! I've got a whole Guild behind me!"

As I spoke, I looked around the Guild Hall. One by one, adventurers averted their gazes before our eyes could meet.

Et tu, entire Guild?!

"C-c'mon, guys! Show a little spirit! Help me out here!"

A Wizard girl spoke up quietly.

"When I first saw Kazuma, he was… I remember. He was back behind the Guild Hall Stealing the panties from a lady Thief. It's hard to forget a sight like that."

Hey—!

"Yeah, I always figured it was only a matter of time before he snapped."

"You're telling me. I heard he took that Priest in his party, put her in a cage, and tried to feed her to some alligators!"

"I heard he stole a magic sword from some guy who challenged him and then just up and sold it."

"You're the most fair-weather friends I've ever met! I know who spoke just now! Just you wait till I'm proven innocent…!"

The two Knights took my arms as I spit out my last words.

"You'll regret thiiiiis!"

2

We were at the police station in the middle of town.

As a law-abiding adventurer, I hadn't had much experience here, but now I was being led deeper and deeper into it.

"Get in there. Until the trial is over, this will be your home."

Sena, walking in front of me, stopped and indicated a dank, cramped cell.

"H-hey, I thought I was the hero who saved the whole town—you've gotta be kidding. Are you really putting me in jail? Hey, are you serious?"

Sena replied to my bout of dread in an accusatory tone.

"We'll talk tomorrow. For now, enjoy your stay."

She hadn't answered my question, but the Knights took this as a signal to shove me inside. Then Sena and her escorts spun on their heels and walked away.

"Hey! Wait a second! You can't leave me... You're...leaving me..."

I clung to the bars of the dim, cold cell, speechless with disbelief.

Just this morning I'd been lounging at home.

How did *that* turn into *this*?!

At a loss, I surveyed my cell. There were a few blankets on the cold floor, a small toilet in one corner, and a window with bars over it. That was all.

This was outrageous. How could the savior of the whole town end up like this?

I sat on my haunches in the dark cell and buried my face in my knees.

You know, I used to enjoy my life as a *hikikomori*.

I would sleep till noon; wake up in my nice, warm room; and play all the video games I liked.

I ate home-cooked meals, went to sleep when I wanted, woke up when I felt like it. Ah, the self-indulgence of it all!

And then I got here, and every single day became a struggle.

I didn't know how anything was supposed to work in this world, so I couldn't get a decent job or handle anything that involved interacting with customers. Instead, I did manual labor and lived in a stable every day.

I spent all my time babysitting a bunch of people I could barely understand, only to wind up in debt...!

I only got angrier and angrier. When I was out of this place, they'd all get theirs!

But...

"I wanna go home... Home to Japan..."

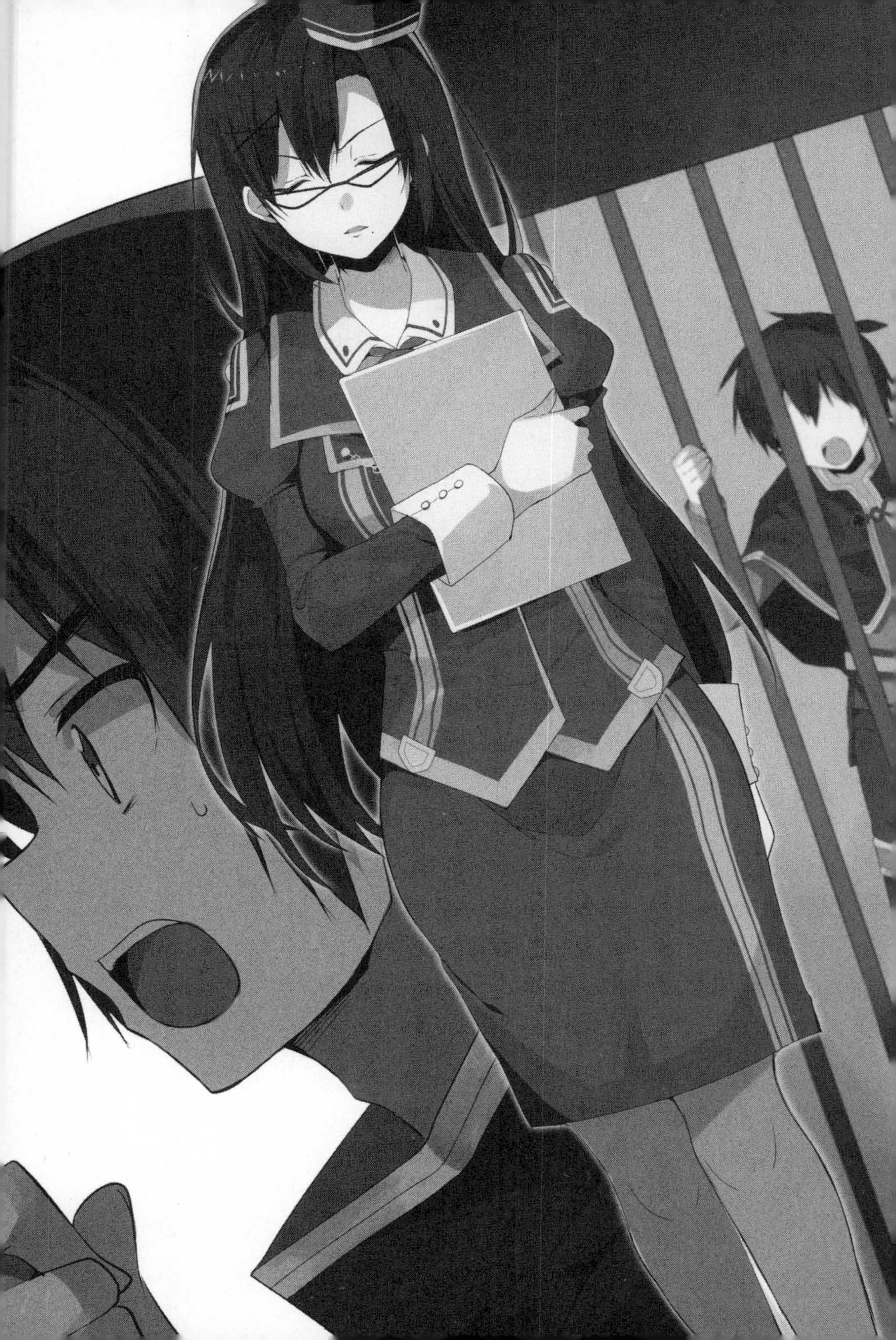

For the first time in a long while, I remembered my original goal: to get home.

I was on trial in a world where nobles and kings and stuff were normal. Considering who I was up against, it wasn't hard to imagine I might get the death penalty.

It began to dawn on me just how bleak my situation was. That realization, combined with the mustiness of my cell, made me very unhappy very quickly.

Surrounded by stone walls and on the verge of tears, I heard several sets of footsteps in the distance.

"Hey, I'm not struggling, so take it easy already!"

"Less talk, more walk, punk!"

I heard a rattling of armor and a thuggish voice.

Looked like they'd collected some company for me.

...Hold on. This is the only cell.

You've gotta be kidding. Some criminal stranger and I were gonna be crammed in this cell together?

"Get in there! How many times do we have to dump you in here? It's a jail cell, not your room! Someone else got here first today. Try not to kill each other."

"Yeah, yeah, whatever. Hey, someone else, nice to meet— Well! If it isn't Kazuma! How'd you wind up in a place like this?"

There was only one guy everyone in town knew as a punk adventurer, and here he was in my cell. Dust.

"Geez, fancy meeting you here! Whatcha in for?"

The Knights had left. Dust seemed surprisingly upbeat for a jailbird.

"Oh, you know, they...they think I'm a terrorist or something. When we took down Destroyer, I was the one who gave the order to teleport the Coronatite just before it detonated. I guess it landed in some lord's mansion and blew everything up."

Hearing my story, Dust nearly exploded himself.

"Bwa-ha-ha-ha-ha! You don't do anything halfway, do you,

Kazuma? Ha-ha! That damn lord's not worth the ass he sits on, is he? Way to go! Ha-ha-ha! You showed him!"

"Shut up. I didn't *mean* to! I don't have anything against that lord or whoever! ...Hang on, what are *you* doing here, Dust?"

From his conversation with the guard, it sounded like he was a regular here.

"Me? Aww, I heard they were giving out the rewards for the Destroyer job, so I had a little feast ahead of time—on a tab, of course. I figured there'd be plenty of dough, you know? So I gambled with some of it...also ahead of time. They just didn't give me quite as much reward as I expected. Couldn't pay off my debts. With no money, I have to sleep in the stables, but it gets pretty cold in there this time of year. So I figured, why not stay here? You get something to eat, and you're not gonna freeze to death. So I pulled the old dine and dash. If they toss you in here, it doesn't even count toward your debt!"

Living up to the name, there, Dust.

I'd been all torn up about going to jail, but finding out that Dust didn't care about being the most obnoxious punk he could be made me feel a little bit better.

3

I killed time by having pointless conversations with Dust, ate my dinner, and went to bed early.

How long have I been asleep...?

I woke to the sound of an explosion in the distance, small tremors shaking my cell.

Someone was whispering something, too.

"...zuma... Kazuma! Hey, Kazuma, get up!"

Moonlight streamed in between the bars on the window. It had to be around midnight.

"Hey, Kazuma, can you hear me? Hey!"

I recognized the voice outside my window.

I glanced around, making sure there was no one else nearby besides Dust, who was snoring.

Apparently, they didn't think they needed to keep too close an eye on a cell this deep in the police station.

The window was way too high for me to reach. I stood under it, and this time I could clearly hear Aqua's voice.

"Aqua, you—! Why are you here?"

"To rescue you, obviously. Megumin and Darkness are busy creating a distraction for the officers. Megumin used Explosion just outside town. Pretty much the whole force went to check it out. Right about now Darkness should be booking it out of there with Megumin on her shoulders."

So those tremors had been from Megumin's spell, huh?

"What's the deal, anyway? If you were gonna break me out tonight, why not just cover for me this morning?"

"If we'd done that, they might've arrested everyone. Anyway, it's not like we're really worried about what kind of revenge you might take when you get back."

That last part largely explained why she'd come to rescue me.

But...

"Should I really be running away? Won't that just make things worse?"

"What are you talking about? It can't get any worse. Sedition is a capital offense. According to Darkness, the lord whose house you blew up is a real jerk with a special talent for holding a grudge. And you're just an adventurer of questionable origins. He probably has the power to ignore the facts and just kill you no matter what."

Well, I had compared this world to the Middle Ages.

A human life here was basically worth garbage.

"Fine. But how are you gonna break me out? Can you cut through the window bars or something?"

Aqua gave a self-confident little chuckle and tossed something through the bars. It hit the ground with a soft metallic sound: a wire.

What was her plan? She couldn't possibly mean to...

"First, you take that wire and pick the lock on your cell, like in a manga or something. Then you use your Ambush skill to walk right out of the station undetected! You head back to the mansion and get ready to make a run for it. Got it? I'll be waiting outside the station!"

With that, she left.

I picked up the wire and looked at the lock.

...It was a dial. You needed to enter a combination of eight numbers to open it.

"...Maybe I'll just get some sleep."

And I curled back up on my blanket.

4

"Wake up! You're coming with us. It's time for the interrogation."

I woke, still wrapped in my blanket, to Sena smacking me.

"Geez, do you know how early it is?"

"It's almost noon! What kind of life have you been living?"

They led me past the gazes of the station staff to a certain room.

"All right, get in. We'll listen to your pathetic excuses. Then we'll decide whether to go to trial. I'd advise you to consider your words carefully."

I entered the room, quavering at Sena's intimidating declaration. Inside, I found a table and two chairs. Another small desk and seat were located next to the doorway. It could pass for the interrogation room of pretty much any police procedural.

One of the Knights who'd accompanied us sat wordlessly at the little desk and spread out some papers.

He must have been the—what was it again?—stenographer.

The other guard shoved me into the chair on the near side of the desk in the center of the room. He stood just behind me—wordlessly, too—probably so he could jump on me the moment I turned violent.

I was quaking even harder under the pressure of being in a narrow space with two fully armored Knights. Sena sat across from me and set a small bell on the table.

"Do you know what this is? It's a magic item that can tell when you're lying. It's quite common in courtrooms and police stations. In conjunction with enchantments on this room, it rings when someone says something untrue. I'd suggest you bear that in mind... Now, shall we begin?"

Her words only added to the oppressiveness of the atmosphere. And then she started to interrogate me with a brutally expressionless face. She had a habit of going *tap, tap, tap* on the desk, maybe just to keep up the pressure.

"Kazuma Satou. Sixteen years old. Job: Adventurer. Class: also Adventurer, I see. To start with, tell me where you come from and what exactly you were doing before you became an adventurer."

First question, and already I could barely answer.

How was I supposed to explain "where I'd come from" and what I'd been up to?

And if I lied, the bell would ring...

"I come from Japan. I was going to school there."

Riiing.

The bell sounded. Hey, I hadn't lied!

Sena ceased her *tap, tap* and knitted her brow.

"Misrepresenting place of origin and personal history..."

I could hear the stenographer dutifully writing down her words.

"Wait! I didn't say anything untrue!"

Riiing. What the hell?! Why'd it ring?!

I *was* from Japan! And I *had* been going to...school...?

"I'm from Japan. And every day I stayed shut up at home, leading a life of complete self-indulgence."

As I answered, Sena stared fixedly at the bell. So did I.

This time, it didn't ring.

"Why did you pretend you were a student?"

"I wasn't pre— Aww, never mind."

Dammit! Stupid magic bell...!

"I've never heard of a land called *Japan*. But never mind that. Next, tell me why you decided to become an adventurer."

"To help all the people suffering under the thumb of the Demon King's army, I wanted—"

Riiing.

"……"

"…I thought being an adventurer sounded pretty cool, and I figured you could make a bunch of money, no problem. Plus I assumed girls would love me."

"Th-that will do. Next. What do you have against our lord? I'm told you were often overheard complaining about debts you'd incurred…"

"We received a large reward for defeating a Dullahan, but after the cost of repairing the town was subtracted, it actually became a large debt. Saving the town means nothing if we also destroy the town; I fully accept that."

Riiing.

"……"

"*Sigh.* Honestly? That's the logic I've used on my friends when they get angry about it, but the truth is, I can't believe the heroes who saved the whole town got treated like that. Sure, it makes me want to kill somebody."

"I—I see… Then, next…"

"…I'm sorry, could I ask you something?" I said a bit hesitantly, jumping in before Sena could ask another question. "Couldn't you just ask me straight-out? 'Are you an agent of the Demon King's army?' or 'Did you give the order out of hatred for our lord?' or whatever. Because I keep telling you, I *did* say to use Random Teleport, but I *didn't* deliberately target this lord or whoever. I had no idea things would turn out this way. I said to do it in order to save the town. That's the truth."

Sena stared at the bell the entire time I spoke.

Of course, it didn't ring.

When she realized it wasn't going to, she heaved a sigh.

"It appears I was mistaken, on account of only ever having heard terrible things about you. I apologize for that."

Her tune had sure changed in a hurry. The prosecutor gave me a deep bow of her head.

I guess the way she'd sounded all this time was just how she talked to criminals. This was the usual her.

Then I, freshly cleared, had to go and get on my high horse.

"Geez! Throwing people in jail because of some rumors! I bet you could lose your prosecutor's license for that!"

"Hrk… P-pardon me… I really am sorry…"

She kept bowing her head.

"Do you know what I've accomplished? I was crucial in the defeat of the Demon King's general, Beldia. In the fight against Mobile Fortress Destroyer, I brilliantly took command and brought down the 'impregnable' fortress! You ought to be thanking me, not arresting me!"

I had leaned back in my chair so hard it began to creak. She had stuck me in prison for a night, and I wasn't about to let that go.

"P-p-pardon me. I was just trying to do my job… Of course I've heard about your achievements, Mr. Satou. It's just—"

"Just? Just what?! Forget it, don't they serve tea to visitors around this police station? And I'm not a suspect anymore, just a visitor. Or maybe you were planning to bring out a whole pork cutlet bowl?!"

"P-pork…?! I'm sorry, we d-don't have anything like that on hand. B-but I'll bring you something to drink right away…"

Sena rushed out and put on some tea, which she brought back to me.

"This is lukewarm! Doesn't anyone at this police station know how to make tea? Between that and your catty attitude, I'll bet you've never had a boyfriend in your life! Since we've got this helpful magic bell here, maybe I'll just ask. Is there a man in your life?"

"No," Sena said, looking straight at me, not flinching. "There isn't. With my terrible personality, I still don't have a boyfriend at my age. Are you satisfied? I would be wary of getting too carried away if I were you."

"Very sorry," I said in a sudden bout of fear as I looked at the silent bell. "But what are these terrible things you heard about me? Just stuff the other adventurers were saying yesterday?"

"W-well… I also heard you stole the panties off your underage companion in public, that you forced the Crusader you live with to wash your back in the bath, that you abandoned your Priest in a dungeon for being a hindrance… Rumors that raise many doubts about your humanity."

. . . .

I had stopped moving entirely. Sena looked at me suspiciously.

"They aren't true, are they?"

"Not at all."

Riiing.

Sena's earlier cold demeanor returned.

"Your party is your business; I won't say anything. But do you know what the rest of the town calls you? *Trash*-zuma, *Cad*-zuma…"

"Th-that's awful! Who are these people? Who calls me that?"

Then again, I had a pretty good guess. A *lot* of pretty good guesses, in fact.

Sena sighed at me.

"Good lord. I'll ask one more time for the record. You are not connected in any way with the Demon King's army, are you? No other interactions with his generals or…"

"Of course not! Do I look—?"

Riiing.

I'd been about to say: *…that important to you?*

But that was when I realized I'd made a terrible mistake.

With the sound of the magic bell echoing off the walls of the interrogation room, I remembered another of the Demon King's generals: Wiz.

5

"Hey, there ain't enough food here! I need more protein! Who cooked this? Waitress!"

The punk fumed and yelled next to me as I sat crushed under the weight of my mistake.

Guess he figured beggars could be choosers. Maybe I should be like him and just stop caring.

...Okay. Maybe not *quite* like him.

"C'mon, Kazuma, don't get so down. I've had more trials than I could count on two hands. Hell, we make our living beating things up. You're not a real adventurer till you've enjoyed the hospitality of the police once or twice! We've both got our trials tomorrow. So let's have a nice meal and get our rest. I'll treat you to something good. You make enough of a racket around here, and the staff'll bring you all kinds of stuff just to shut you up."

With that, Dust resumed hollering.

The police finally did give him something to shut him up—a beating. He quieted down after that, and given what awaited us the next day, we tried to get some sleep.

Midnight. I woke to the same distant rumble of an explosion as I had the night before.

I sat up with a start, and then, of course, I heard Aqua whispering to me.

"Kazuma! Hey, Kazuma! Wake up!"

I slipped over to the wall below the window.

"Are you here again?" I asked. "What happened yesterday? Was everyone all right?"

"Megumin and Darkness both made it home without being spotted, but somehow they immediately fingered Megumin as the perp behind the explosion. But don't worry! Those two didn't want to, but I forced them to wear masks tonight. No one'll figure it out."

I was pretty sure the problem had less to do with facial identification and more with the number of people in town who could use Explosion.

"But what about you?" Aqua said. "I waited forever last night, but you never escaped! Snow piled up on my head and the police kept asking what I was doing there! It was awful!"

"My cell doesn't have a regular lock. It's a combination lock. And anyway, I don't have a Lockpick skill, so what was I supposed to do with some wire?"

Aqua went quiet for a while.

"...Stupid police," she said. "Who knew they would be so completely prepared against a jailbreak?"

"It's just a combo lock. But seriously, do you have a plan? If we don't do something tonight, I'll be on trial tomorrow."

Aqua gave a confident little chuckle.

Where did she get that confidence? Certainly not from reality.

"I admit we took the wrong tack yesterday. I've got a couple of hacksaws here. I'll toss one down to you."

Hacksaws?

"...Surely you don't mean to saw through those bars on the window and get me out that way?"

"You're a quick one. But we have to do it by sunup. That doesn't give us much time, so get sawing!"

And she shoved a saw between the bars.

She was right. With two of us working at it, it would go much faster. The only problem was...

"I can't reach the window from this side."

The window was so far above my head I couldn't reach it even if I jumped—presumably to prevent me from escaping through it.

"Don't worry, I'm not an idiot. I knew this would be an issue, so I have a step stool here. Use that to get up and cut the bars. One person working alone wouldn't manage it in time, but with the two of us together, I think it should be all right."

Good idea.

"So, uh, how were you planning to get the step stool or whatever in here? Will it fit through the bars?"

It seemed like the obvious question to me, but Aqua went quiet again.

"...Hang on a second."

I heard her going off somewhere.

At length...

"No, you don't understand! I've come to bring Kazuma something he desperately needs!"

"I've never heard of a prisoner getting something like this. What are you doing here at this hour anyway?"

I heard Aqua in the distance. Apparently she'd thought she could sneak it in as a drop-off for me.

Maybe I could learn something from her idiotic optimism.

Listening to Aqua argue in the background, strangely, I found my anxiety about the coming trial fade away.

I tossed the saw out the window to get rid of the evidence, then snuggled up with my blanket and went to sleep.

6

Trials in this world were simple affairs. The prosecutor presented evidence, the counsel for the defense rebutted, and if the judge wasn't convinced, you were declared guilty as charged.

Having said that, "defense attorney" was not an actual job here. It was left up to friends or acquaintances of the accused to mount a legal defense.

The building resembled courts in Japan, with the accused (in handcuffs) and his "lawyer" standing in the center of the room, surrounded at a distance by the judge, the prosecutor, and the plaintiff.

And at the moment...

"You needn't worry so much. We are here for you!"

Megumin tried to reassure me as I stood there tense with worry.

Yep.

Who stood beside me as defense, but my three party members.

How did this happen?

As I fretted, Sena stared at me from the prosecutor's seat.

"It's all right. Leave it to me. The Crimson Magic Clan excels in Intelligence. I will tear apart that prosecutor's arguments so hard she will weep!"

To my right: Megumin, counsel for the defense, talking up her game.

"Stay calm. If worse comes to worst, I'll do something. In this case, at least, you've done nothing wrong."

That was Darkness, standing to my left.

Talk about friends! Talk about people who come through for you! But...

"You can just count on me! They're practically bound to believe whatever I say, as a member of the clergy! Case closed!"

Yeah. She was going to be the problem. I called her over and whispered, "Aqua, listen. There's just one thing I really need from you this time, and that's for you to be quiet. Just sit there until the trial's over. I promise I'll get you speckled crab or whatever you want."

"Don't be silly! If you get hard labor or *death*, how will I receive my payment? Don't worry. I know more about lawyering than anyone in this courtroom. You liked video games, right? You remember *Ace Defense Counsel* and *Manganronpa*? I played all those games."

"You're right, that tells me all I need to know. Seriously, keep your mouth shut."

Aqua made a face and turned away.

Curse this goddeeeeeeess!

A middle-aged man I assumed to be the judge banged his gavel.

"Order! The trial of the defendant, Kazuma Satou, on charges of sedition will now begin. The plaintiff is Alderp Barnes Alexei!"

A rotund man stood as the judge called the name.

He was tall and large, with shaggy hair, except where a receding hairline revealed a glistening forehead.

He must be the lord everyone kept talking about.

Lord Alderp looked me up and down, then cast a lascivious gaze at my three companions.

He seemed to eat up Aqua and Megumin with his eyes, then moved on to Darkness...

...whereupon he froze, an expression of shock on his face.

"Hey, that fat, old guy is *super* staring at us," Aqua said. "I don't like the vibe I get from him one bit. Mind if I go over and poke him in the eye?"

"Stoppit, don't cause any more trouble… But doesn't he seem kind of fixated on Darkness?"

"Yeah! *Super* fixated. He's got kind of the same look you get when she walks around the house in clothes that barely cover her."

"H-hey, I never do that! …Mostly! Seriously, when did I ever look at Darkness like—?"

As I protested, I glanced at Darkness—she was staring right back at Lord So-and-So.

"What's up, Darkness? Does it bug you that he's looking at you?"

"Hmm? Oh, no… Never mind. I'll tell you later."

There was something off about her response, but there was no time to worry about it, as the gavel came down again.

"Order! No private conversations on court time. Now, Prosecutor, please step forward. If anyone lies, we'll know it by the ringing of this magic bell. All are advised to consider their words in light of that fact."

The judge emphasized his point with another bang of his gavel. At the same moment, Sena stood up.

"I will begin by reading the charges. At the time of an attack by Mobile Fortress Destroyer, the defendant, Kazuma Satou, along with other adventurers, bested said fortress. On that occasion, the defendant gave orders to teleport a piece of Coronatite moments before it exploded. The Coronatite was teleported to the mansion of the victim, Lord Alderp, whereupon it detonated. The victim's mansion was destroyed, and Lord Alderp has been forced to obtain lodging in a room at the town's inn since then."

The entire time Sena was reading, the victim in question was focused single-mindedly on Darkness.

"The use of Random Teleport to transport monsters, poisons, hazardous materials, or explosives is prohibited by law. The defendant has violated this law, and his act is aggravated by the fact that in doing so, he endangered the life of a lord, posing a very real threat to the stability of the government. Hence, prosecution seeks a judgment of sedition!"

"Objection!"

The shout came the instant Sena finished speaking.

Next to me, Aqua had stepped forward, her arm out and her voice raised.

"The defense will have its chance to speak. If you have something to say, ask the permission of the Court before you talk... As I presume this is your first trial, I'll overlook your outburst this once. Now, counsel, you may speak."

The judge nodded, but Aqua merely shook her head with a satisfied expression.

"I just wanted to shout 'Objection!' That's all."

"Counsel will speak only when she has something to say!"

That idiot! It was all I could do not to smack her.

Aqua, having angered the judge practically before we'd begun, calmly settled back next to me, appearing genuinely pleased.

The episode had thrown off Sena a bit, and she didn't seem to have quite collected herself as she got back on track.

"...Ahem, that's all from the prosecution. In short, prosecution, uh, seeks a judgment of sedition against defendant Kazuma Satou."

She sat back down as she concluded.

"Very well," the judge said. "The defendant and his counsel may now speak. Your statement, please!"

"...and that's the story of how I brought down the Demon King's general, Beldia, not to mention Destroyer. Would someone who's sacrificed so much for this country actively plan to overthrow it? Hardly! If anything, you could probably stand to be a little more lavish in your praise of me!"

I stood in the middle of the hall, making an impassioned plea in my own defense.

How awesome I'd been fighting Beldia.

How exemplary my command had been in the battle against Destroyer.

It didn't bother me that the judge repeatedly cast a doubtful eye at his magic lie-detecting bell. My descriptions might have been a bit over-the-top, but nothing I said was untrue.

"Th-that will be enough. I think the Court is well acquainted with the defendant's arguments. Now, Prosecutor. Please submit your proof that the defendant is guilty of sedition."

The judge nodded wearily at Sena, who motioned to one of the Knights at her side. He headed for the courthouse waiting area as Sena read from a sheet of paper.

"The prosecution will now present proof that the defendant is a terrorist harboring plans of sedition and an agent of the Demon King's army. Bring in the witnesses!"

At her signal, the Knight ushered several people into the room. Most were other adventurers.

Wait a second...

"Ah-ha-ha-ha... They kinda summoned me..."

It was Chris, right down to the scar on her cheek, wincing apologetically.

And Chris was only the start of the parade of witnesses. They'd summoned every single person who knew me.

7

This was bad. Real bad.

"So, Chris, is it true that the defendant used Steal to take your panties right out in public?"

"Well, uh, I guess it's true, but—but that was an accident!"

"We're only interested in the facts of the case. Thank you."

"What?! Hang on! I don't—! It doesn't bother me anymore!"

Chris was hustled from the courtroom as Sena abruptly concluded her questioning.

I eyed the rest of the witnesses. This didn't bode well for me.

There was the Sword Master Mitsurugi, with his two hangers-on. He was from Japan, just like me, but I had taken his magic sword and sold it.

"Mr. Mitsurugi. You claim the defendant stole a magic sword from you and sold it. You further claim that when these two attempted to get the sword back, the defendant threatened them with Stealing their panties in public. Is this correct?"

"Y-yeah, it is, but— I mean, *I* was the one who challenged *him*, and—"

"Yeah, he threatened us! *'I don't discriminate. I'm perfectly happy to beat up a couple of girls'!*"

"She's right! *'We're out in public here. And there's no telling* what *I might Steal…'!*"

Mitsurugi's two groupies, whom I had indeed threatened—just a little—cut him off mid-sentence.

When their eyes met mine, they stuck out their tongues. They really knew how to hold a grudge.

Ngh… Everyone in the courtroom was looking at me, and I didn't think they liked what they saw—including the judge.

No sooner had Mitsurugi been shoved out of the room than Dust was on the stand. Why would they call him as a witness? I didn't remember specifically wronging him.

He was the one who suggested we should trade parties, anyway.

Dust was just giving me a lazy greeting when I heard Sena again.

"This man is the defendant at our next trial. I believe Your Honor already knows him. He's a thug and a frequent guest in our courtrooms."

"Hey, I'm just quietly waiting for my trial when you drag me out here—and this is how you greet me? I oughta grab those big old boobs of yours!"

Dust was never far from his boiling point, and the prosecution's words put him right over the top.

The judge frowned at the outburst. Sena pointed at me.

"Mr. Dust. Prosecution is told you are friends with the defendant, Kazuma Satou. Is this true?"

"You're damn right it is. He's my buddy, my man. We've been out drinking together and everything."

At that, Sena turned toward me.

"Kazuma Satou, is this ill-mannered thug your friend?"

"An acquaintance."

"Hey! Kazuma!" Dust exclaimed, but the bell didn't ring, despite the judge and Sena both watching it intently.

"I—I see. My apologies. I had intended to argue that all your friends were brutes like this, but…"

"It's all right. It's true we know each other."

"Kazuma! Does our friendship mean so little to you?!"

A Knight dragged off the howling thug as Sena turned to the judge.

"Notwithstanding the unsatisfactory nature of our last speaker, I believe these witnesses have sufficiently testified to the defendant's character. Further, the defendant is known to have borne a grudge against the victim. This leads me to conclude that the defendant is only pretending these events were an accident. He didn't use Random Teleport but a regular Teleport spell, and he deliberately sent the Coronatite to the victim's residence—"

She really needed to stop making up accusations willy-nilly.

"You have proved nothing!" Megumin exclaimed. "I admit Kazuma is rather twisted, but I will not stand for you trying to pin these false charges on him! Bring some better proof! You know, I think something odd is going on here. Do you not see how far she is reaching? Does none of this feel wrong to you?!"

"Restrain yourself, counselor! You will ask permission before you speak."

"You want proof? Very well. I have even more evidence that the defendant is a terrorist who was plotting the destruction of the town—and is an agent of the Demon King!"

Sena began to read from a sheet of paper to the furious Megumin.

"First! Though they succeeded in defeating the Demon King's general, Beldia, Kazuma Satou and his party summoned enough water to cover half the town during the battle, resulting in massive flood damage."

Aqua trembled visibly.

"Second! They erected a massive spirit barrier around the town's common graveyard, depriving evil spirits of a place there and causing a spate of hauntings in town."

Aqua had turned around and put her fingers in her ears. I pulled her hands away, forcing her to listen to the prosecution's statement.

"On several successive days, his party used explosion magic near town, altering the local terrain and ecosystems; further, during this time, magic was used near town at night, bothering residents at a very late hour…"

Now Megumin was turned around and covering *her* ears.

Some lawyers they turned out to be!

"Hey, hang on a minute! This can't be right! Nothing you just mentioned has anything to do with me personally. I know they're my party members, but—show me what this has to do with me!"

As if taking my challenge to heart, Sena pressed on.

"In addition, witnesses observed the defendant using Drain Touch, a skill only available to the undead. Mr. Satou, if you are not associated with the Demon King's army, please explain how you know Drain T—Covering your ears won't make this go away!" Sena jabbed a finger at Aqua, Megumin, and me.

I have my rights! Like the right to remain silent!

"Finally, the most damning evidence. During your interrogation at the police station, I asked you if you had had any interactions with any elements of the Demon King's army. You said no—at which point the magic bell signaled a lie. If that's not proof, then what is?!"

Aww, dang. Awww, dang.

I was cornered. There was nothing I could say—and that's when it happened.

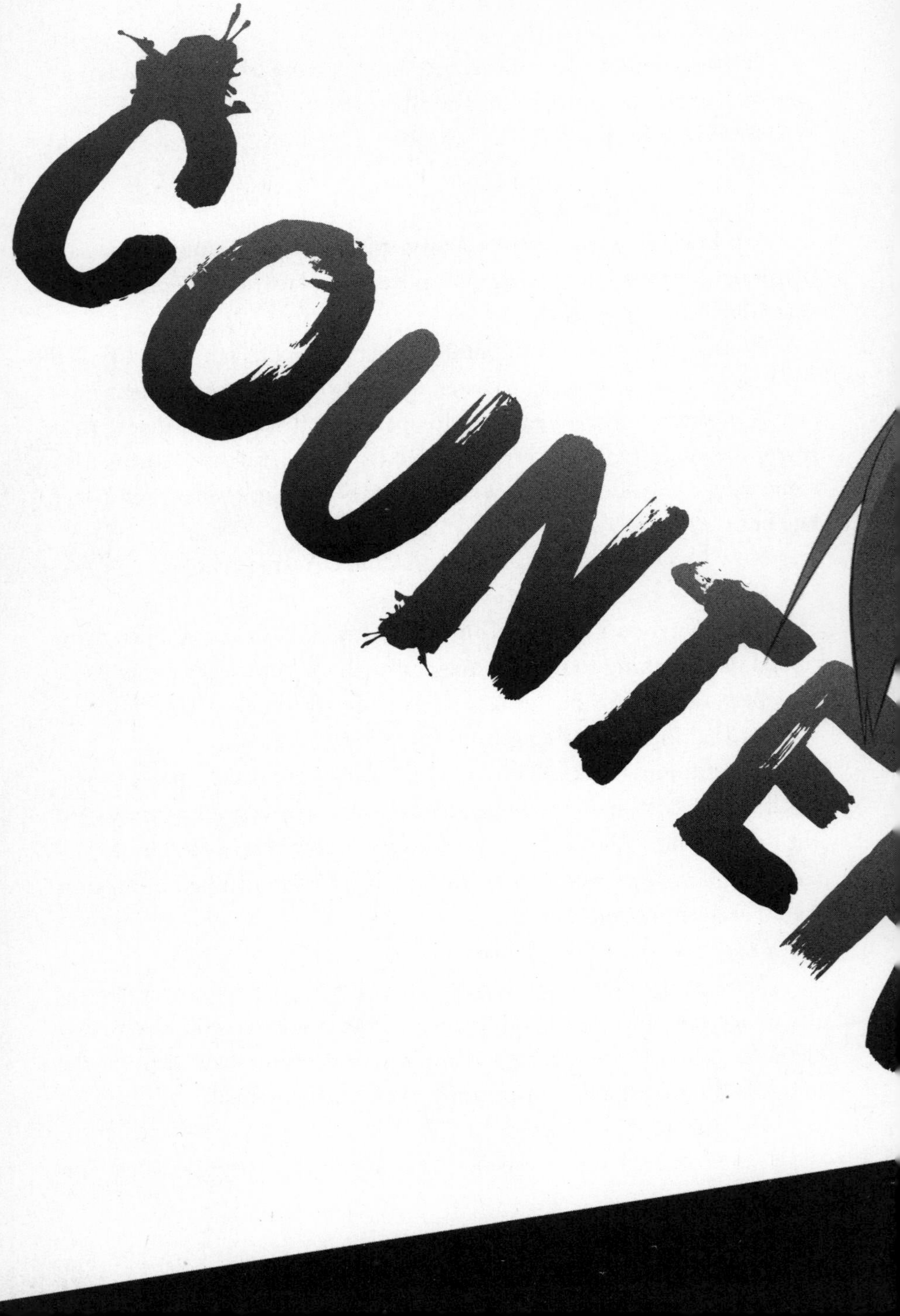
COUNTE

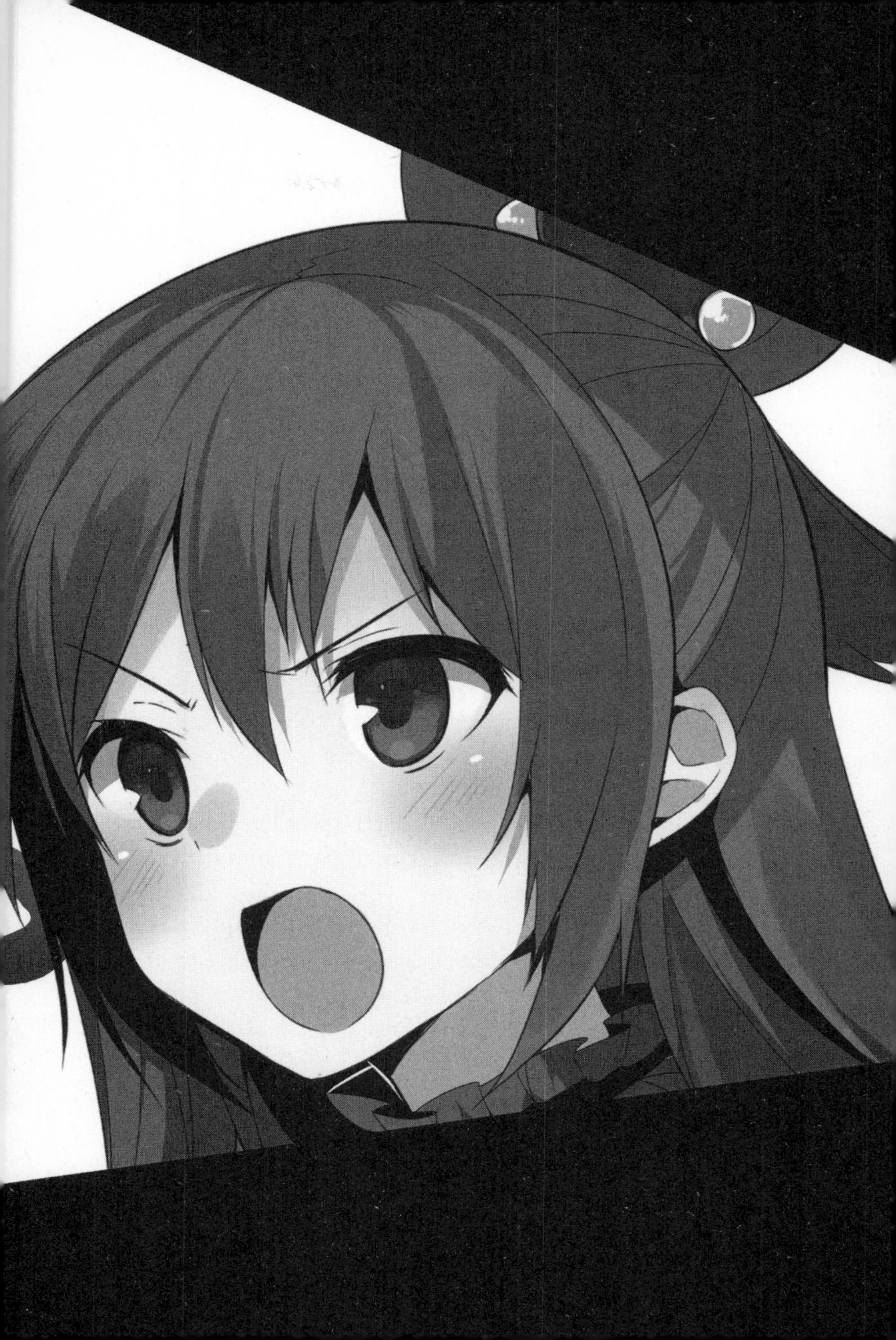

"No, that's wrong!"

The startlingly confident voice belonged to none other than Aqua.

Who would've thought she might be my trump card at a moment like this…!

"You tell 'em, Aqua! Show them the undeniable proof that I'm innocent!"

"Huh? What are you talking about? I don't have undeniable anything. That was just something else I've wanted to say."

"Escort the counselor out of the courtroom!"

"I'm sorry! I really apologize for my lawyer!"

"Owww! Ow-ow-ow-owww!"

I apologized profusely and pinched Aqua right on the head.

You stupid, stinking idiooooot!

A voice tore through our little fight.

"Surely you've seen enough! He must be in league with the Demon King! One of his men! He transported an explosive into my mansion! Kill him! Off with his head!"

The victim, Lord Alderp, who had been silent until that moment, began pointing and shouting at me as I stood there, lost for words.

Okay, old man—this is my chance!

"You're all wrong! I don't work for the Demon King! And I'm not a terrorist! It's true I was upset about the debt, but I would never deliberately send Coronatite to someone's house! Take a good look at your little magic toy, because I'm going to say this nice and clear: I am not the Demon King's man, or agent, or anything!"

The bell didn't make a sound. Alderp, watching it closely, didn't know what to say.

Sena furrowed her brow and bit her lip as she stared at it.

If she could use the bell as proof, well, so could I.

The lordly victim's outburst turned out to be my salvation.

The judge slowly shook his head.

"As we can see, discerning truth and falsehood by magical item is not an exact science. In light of this, I'm afraid I cannot admit the bell's reaction as evidence, nor accept the prosecution's conclusions drawn therefrom. There is simply too little to go on. As such, defendant Kazuma Satou, I judge the suspicions against you unconvincing, and—"

Just as he was about to pronounce his judgment…

"I told you, he's an associate of the enemy. He's the Demon King's man. You must put him to death!"

Alderp, still standing, was now repeating himself.

This time it was Sena who responded.

"No injuries or deaths resulted in the event. I hardly think the death penalty is an appropriate—"

The lord stared hard at Sena.

"—th-thing to deny in this case. Yes?"

…*What?*

"H-hey, hang on! Something's wrong here!"

"He is right—what was that? The prosecutor changed her opinion mid-sentence!"

Under attack from Megumin and me, Sena looked almost pained—even though we were just pointing out what she'd said.

At that moment, Aqua jabbed a finger at the judge, Sena, and then Lord Alderp.

"I felt a wicked power just now! Someone here is using evil power to try to twist the truth!"

Aqua's incredible assertion stunned the courtroom into silence.

Unfortunately, thanks to her earlier outbursts, everyone looked more than a little tired of her.

The collective attention focused on the bell. But when it didn't ring, the air in the room changed noticeably.

This was Aqua, a member of the clergy, an Arch-priest.

The judge's face changed color as he clearly started to think there might be something to her claim.

"Evil power...? You mean to say there is someone committing injustice at our sacred trial?"

"Yes, I do. My eyes are even sharper than that magical dealie-whomper of yours. Nothing can be hidden from me, the goddess of water, who has more than ten million followers in this world! For I am the goddess Aqua!"

Riiing.

The clear sound of the bell could be heard throughout the silent courtroom.

"What?! Wait! I'm not lying!"

"Defendant. You are advised to choose your counselor more carefully."

"I'm sorry, Your Honor. Believe me, I'm as disappointed as you are."

Megumin tried to calm the wailing Aqua after her utter failure to convince anyone she was telling the truth. For some reason, though, Lord Alderp was biting his lip and watching her closely, his face white as a sheet.

"All right, so I exaggerated a bit! The magic bell rang because of the number of followers I gave. It's not ten million. It's more like 9.8 million."

I dearly wanted to point out to the muttering Aqua that she could say a thousand followers and the bell would probably still ring—but this wasn't the time. The judge was about to hand down his verdict.

He cleared his throat.

"Defendant Kazuma Satou. In light of your numerous immoral deeds, to say nothing of your total—indeed, sociopathic—disregard for public safety..."

This was definitely not going in the direction of his earlier verdict.

"...I consider the prosecution's recommendation to be appropriate. I find you guilty—"

What?

"—and sentence you to death."

8

"This is soooo wroooong! Wait—just—wait! You guys are making this trial up as you go along! How about some proof that actually proves something?! You can't sentence a guy to death like this! You must be crazy!"

"The defendant will mind his tongue!"

"Kazuma's right this is wrong—this is all wrong! Sure, he wouldn't shut up about the debt we were saddled with after flooding the town, and sure, he had a grudge against the local lord, and *sure*, I thought he would snap one day, but he doesn't have the guts to teleport Coronatite into someone's house!"

Sheesh! Was she trying to defend me, or get me in even more trouble?

As I struggled to shut Aqua up, Megumin removed her eye patch.

"Very well. If you are so eager to dub Kazuma a terrorist, let me show you what terrorism truly— Oh! What are you doing? Let me go!"

The bailiffs jumped on Megumin as her crimson eyes started to sparkle.

"Heyyy! Really, something is off here! My unclouded eyes can see the oppressive evil in this courtroom! Just hang on—I'll get this place purified in no— Wait! This is good magic! Not bad magic! Let me work!"

"All magic is banned in the courtroom! Otherwise someone might interfere with our magical lie detector."

"You, get those two out of here!" Sena stood up, too, shouting orders for Megumin and Aqua to be taken away.

"Order! Order! ...I said *order*, you cretins!"

The judge finally lost his temper and began shouting and pounding his gavel.

As the bailiffs led Megumin and Aqua out of the courtroom...

"Your Honor. Here."

*　　　*　　　*

Darkness, who hadn't said a word until that moment, pulled something out from her neckline.

It was an expensive-looking pendant, with what appeared to be some kind of crest on it.

I had no idea what it signified, but everyone else in the courtroom seemed to know exactly what it was.

"Th-that's... S-so you're...!"

The judge stood up in surprise and gazed at the pendant, eyes wide.

With the entire courtroom focused on her, Darkness said quietly:

"My sincere apologies, but I will be taking charge of this courtroom. I am not asking you to pretend this never happened. But give me time, and I will demonstrate beyond all doubt that this man is not a servant of the Demon King. Further, I will see you reimbursed for your mansion."

Sena and the judge had both gone stiff as boards, goggling at the crest Darkness held.

Only Lord Alderp, although clearly somewhat cowed, raised any objection.

"That's—! B-but surely we can't— Even at your request—!"

"Alderp. You are the victim here, and I will be in your debt. Name any one thing I can do, and I will do it for you. I am not asking you to withdraw your suit. Only to wait."

His Lordship swallowed heavily as Darkness spoke.

"Anything...? A-a-anything at all...?"

"Yes, anything."

At that, Alderp's eyes glinted, and he ran his gaze over her as if drinking her in.

Then he sat back down.

"Very well. For you, I will do this. Let us postpone this man's sentence."

After the trial, Darkness followed me out of the courthouse. I asked her, "What was that about? Do you actually know that greasy old Alderp guy?"

"...I guess. He's had a certain fixation on me since I was a child. Since his wife died, he's come with proposals of marriage more than once. But my father has always refused him on the grounds that the difference in our ages is too great."

That's...actually pretty creepy. Fixated on her since she was a kid?

"A-are you sure it's okay to say you'll do anything he wants?! He was watching you the way dogs stare at steak! There's no telling what he might ask for!"

"Y-yes...who knows...*what*..."

"C'mon...I'm trying to worry about you here...!"

With Darkness blushing and panting behind me, I went to bail out Aqua and Megumin.

9

Darkness's gambit had landed me with two assignments: one, prove I wasn't an agent of the Demon King. And two, pay for Lord Alderp's manor.

I was at Wiz's shop with Aqua in tow, seeking any possible way to make money.

I had actually planned to go by myself, but Aqua had invited herself along, and I couldn't shake her.

"I know just what you've got in mind, Kazuma! This whole thing started because that stupid undead screwed up. We repossess her store to make up the cost!"

Aqua, who in fact had no idea what I had in mind, stood all but frothing at the door.

"All right, undead, come out! Time for you to say your prayers!" With that ridiculous pronouncement, Aqua kicked in the door of the shop.

"Wh-what's going on?! Are you robbing me? Are you gangsters? ... Eeek! L-Lady Aqua!"

Yes, Aqua, who was evidently scarier than robbers or gangsters.

I walked in a second later to find Wiz cowering under divine assault. I told her how the trial had gone.

"I see... I'm so glad you're all right, though! I'm very sorry, Mr. Kazuma. This is all because I Teleported that rock..."

"It sure is! I'm so glad you understand what's—" I slapped my hand over Aqua's mouth before she could say anything even stupider.

"It's fine. If you hadn't been there, we would've all been done for. I guess that princeling's out a mansion, but no one was hurt. If I can just prove to Sena that I'm not working for the Demon King, that should clear my name. Er...I still have to figure out how to pay for the guy's house, though."

Wiz answered with a small sigh of relief.

"So that's the story. At least you bought yourself some time. But money...? I'd like to help, but my store is in the red, and I don't have any funds... In my days with the Demon King's army, I had a friend who was extremely talented at making money but also a little crazy and hard to understand... If there's anything I can do to help..."

Wiz fretted at the counter.

"Actually, I came here to ask you for something."

"Yeah—to let us send you to the next life!"

I ignored Aqua's incomprehensible blathering and told Wiz what I'd actually come for.

Bluntly speaking, I was already buried in debt and entirely lacking capital. It wouldn't be easy to come by the money I needed to rebuild the lord's manor.

That meant maybe it was time to try something I'd been thinking about for a while now...

This world's technology was far behind Earth's. People who couldn't use Kindle were still lighting fires with flint and tinder.

If I could market some kind of lighter, I was sure it would fly off the shelves. I even had some confidence in my ability to build it. But what store would stock a random lighter I'd happened to come up with out of nowhere?

I had hoped I could display them in some vacant spot in Wiz's shop for a while.

Basically, though, what I said to her was, "I'm going to make a really useful item, and I'd like to display it in your store, if I could."

If it sold, of course I'd share the profits with Wiz. And she didn't have to decide until after she'd seen the item.

"It's all too obvious I'm never going to become rich as an adventurer. Which leaves entrepreneurship… You're kind of the only person I can ask to work with me on this on such short notice."

"What Kazuma's saying is, we're taking over this joint, so hurry up and fork over the dee— Yowch!"

I smacked Aqua on the back of her head with the hilt of my dagger to stem her tide of nonsense. Then I bowed to Wiz.

She smiled sweetly even as she flinched away from Aqua, who was clutching her head and rolling on the floor.

"That sounds just fine to me. In fact, I'd be thrilled to have a wider selection to offer. My store has never been that successful… And anyway, I can't pretend I'm unrelated to the whole manor incident. I don't know what you plan to sell, but I look forward to finding out."

She smiled again, and with her eager agreement to help me out, I couldn't help smiling back.

The moment might've been a little more pleasant without *someone* rolling all over the floor, though.

Then Wiz's expression darkened.

She was obviously trying to decide whether or not to tell me something.

"…? What's up? If there's something on your mind, let me know. I don't want to force this on you. If you've got any ideas…"

Wiz hurriedly waved away my concerns.

"N-no, not at all! I'm very grateful that you want to sell something in my shop! Actually, it's about… It's about Milady Aqua…" She trailed off, clearly hard-pressed.

"…? Her? Oh, you're afraid that if you start stocking my item, she'll be in here all the time. If you're too worried about her, I can try my best to leave her at home."

Aqua was a goddess, after all—much as I hated to admit it. It only made sense that she might make an undead uneasy.

"N-no, that's not... Milady Aqua is welcome here. But every time she comes, she tells my customers that everything in the shop is made by unspeakable, inhumane methods and they'd be better off not buying anything..."

"You. What's she talking about?"

Aqua, still on the floor cradling her head, gave a start.

"W-wait!" Wiz exclaimed. "I-I'm not worried about it! For some reason, sales of holy water to male adventurers have gone way up since then! So I'm not—"

I was glad for her that something was selling well, I guess.

I wonder if it's really okay for a Lich to be selling holy water.

Then again, I wonder if the adventurers of this town are really okay in a number of ways.

"I'm more worried about... Well, milady has a habit of touching everything in the shop, and a lot of my magical herbs and necromancy ingredients end up getting cleansed. Quite a few of my products have become unfit for sale..."

"What's she talking about, you dumbass goddess?"

Apparently this idiot had been coming to Wiz's shop behind my back just to harass her.

I dragged Aqua to her feet, then put one hand on her head and shoved it down in a bow in Wiz's direction.

"I'm so sorry, Wiz! I'll take responsibility for your lost products and take money from this moron to pay you back! H-hey, don't struggle! Come on, apologize!"

"Stop, Kazuma! No way! Why should a goddess bow to a Lich?! Anyway, any liquid I touch is just naturally purified by the divine power that flows out of me! It's not my fault! If you put a plant in the sun, it'll photosynthesize, and if I touch liquid, I purify it! It's just the way the world works!"

No, I'm pretty sure you're going out of your way to touch those items.

Since Aqua was putting all her strength into stiffening her neck so I couldn't force her head down, I bowed mine even deeper instead.

You know, I feel like I've done an awful lot of apologizing for Aqua recently.

"Oh! Please don't do that! It's all right—it's in the past. Just… If possible, maybe don't purify my products in the future… I know I've caused you a lot of trouble lately—asking Lady Aqua to help the souls at the graveyard, asking you to exorcise that haunted house…"

This time it was Wiz who hurriedly bowed her head.

Faced with Wiz's unrelenting earnestness, the person whose lax approach to cemetery duty caused that very haunting averted her eyes.

…Blast you. You and Wiz oughta switch jobs…

Chapter 2 May There Be a Friend for This Crimson Magic Girl!

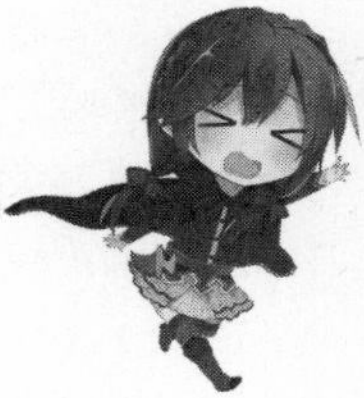

1

"Hey, Kazuma. Where's Darkness? Isn't she home yet?"

Aqua was curled up on the sofa in front of the fireplace, which she'd claimed as her exclusive territory. She sounded almost bored.

It had been several days since the trial. Lord Alderp had summoned Darkness to fulfill her promise…

She had gone out last night and still hadn't yet returned.

The thought of how Alderp had reveled in leering at her, the ugly glint in his eyes—it made my chest tighten.

Then again, this was the person whose instincts and, uh, preferences made her practically throw herself at a general of the Demon King's army. Maybe she actually wanted this.

I didn't have any romantic feelings to speak of for Darkness. It didn't matter to me what she did or who she did it with.

But she'd been away all night to "fulfill a promise." That meant she was at the inn where that lord was staying, and right about now they were…

"Aaaaaaahhhhhh!"

"Yeek! What? What? Don't scare me like that, suddenly grabbing your head and screaming! You're always a little crazy, Kazuma, but today you seem extra weird."

Aqua was cowering at my sudden outburst.

Then in walked Megumin with…something.

She didn't say anything to the two of us about the commotion we'd been making, just silently held the thing in her arms.

You know, I've been wondering about that thing for a while.

"Neeow!"

It was a cat. Megumin was holding a cat.

And she was staring silently at me.

"Are you trying to say you want to keep that thing in the house?"

"…Yes. She is quite tame and will not cause trouble… May I?"

It was the little black cat I saw periodically with Megumin. I had no idea where she usually kept it.

Nestled in Megumin's arms, the cat squinted happily.

"I guess I don't see why not. I don't think anyone in the house is allergic to cats. Hey, she's pretty friendly."

When I reached out my hand to the cat Megumin was holding, the cat laid a paw sweetly on my finger.

It was a pretty rough world out there. And in a party full of problem children, we could all use a little stress relief. A heartwarming addition to the cast would do us all some good.

"Yowch! Why does she only scratch me?! Look at her… That black fur, that rotten attitude. I think I sense an evil aura here!"

Aqua was incensed that the cat had taken a swipe at her when she tried to pet it.

I took the cat from Megumin to protect her from the blue-haired beast. I set her on the carpet, keeping my back to Aqua to shield her.

Come to think of it, we had some fish left over from breakfast.

"Hey, Megumin," Aqua said. "What do you call your evil little magic friend, anyway?"

"Chomusuke."

I took the fish off the table, plate and all.

"…Wait. What did you say her name was?"

"Chomusuke."

I leaned over toward the black cat—I mean, Chomusuke—with the leftover fish in my hand.

Life with such a messed-up owner isn't easy, huh...?

I set the plate down, but Chomusuke didn't eat the fish right away. Instead, she gave it a delicate sniff.

"Hey, Megumin," Aqua said, "isn't that cat a girl? Doesn't she need a more girlie name?"

"No. Her name is Chomusuke."

With the girls babbling behind me, I watched Chomusuke.

Watched her exhale a tiny flame to grill the fish.

......The hell was that just now?

I sat on the carpet hugging my knees as Chomusuke dug in to the leftovers.

"Hey, Aqua," I said quietly. "Do the cats around here...breathe fire?"

I mean, the cabbages fly. Why shouldn't cats breathe fire?

"What in the world are you talking about? Are you feeling all right?"

"Cats do not breathe fire," Megumin added. "Cats go *meow*."

"That's right. And they like fish, and they're very cute."

Thanks. I already knew all that.

"I swear I just saw this thing breathe fire, though. She grilled the fish before she ate it!"

"...Kazuma. I think you need some rest."

"You did go to jail and then endure that trial. It is a lot to deal with."

"I'm telling the truth! I'm not crazy!"

As I pointed at Chomusuke and yelped, Megumin cut back in.

"By the way, what were you two so excited about earlier? Darkness isn't a child anymore—she can stay out all night if she wants. You should both calm down."

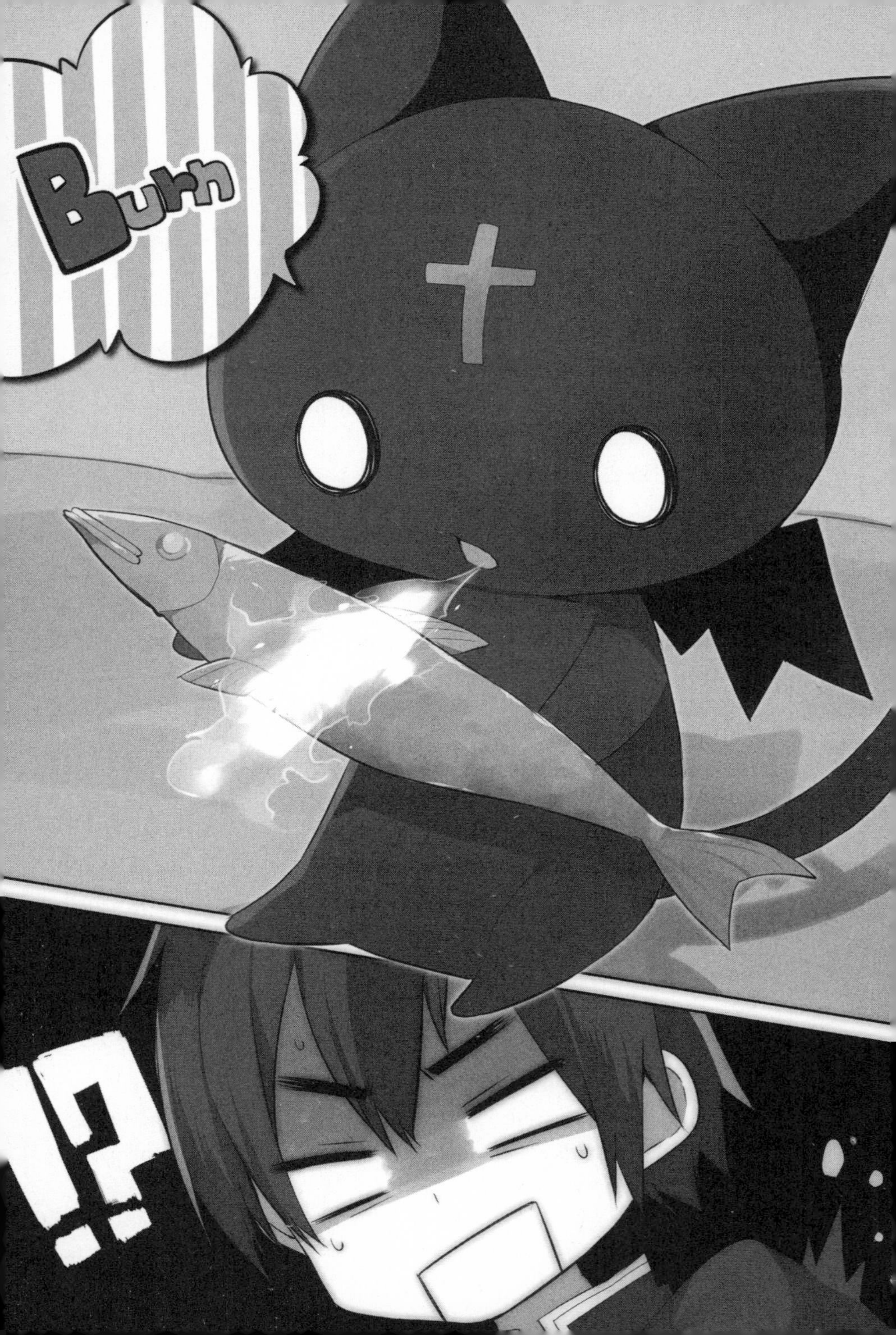
Burn
!?

Clearly, I had failed to convince her.

"You seem pretty laid-back about this. Do you know what could be happening to Darkness right now? I'll bet Lord What's-His-Face is doing something awful to her at this very minute!"

Megumin just snorted.

"With Darkness, not even a lord could… I—I mean, there are certainly lots of unpleasant rumors about him, but Darkness can hold her own as an adventurer. I don't think it would be so easy for him to force himself on her."

This idiot! She didn't get Darkness at all!

"Geez, you're such a kid! You've known Darkness for how long? And you still don't understand that perv! I'm sure she's blushing and saying something like, *Hrk! You can do as you wish with my body, but you can't have my heart! I refuse to give in to you!*"

"?!"

Megumin hugged Chomusuke, who was still nibbling on the fish, apparently grasping the situation for the first time.

"Wh-wh-what do we do? Darkness—Darkness might be in trouble! What do we do, Kazuma?!"

"She's been gone since yesterday, right? A whole night's already passed—we're too late. When Darkness comes back, just be nice to her like you always are, okay, guys?"

"S-sure! That means don't ask what her most recent step on the stairway to adulthood was like."

"Darkness! Ohh, Darkness!"

Aqua clenched her fist in a *You can count on me* gesture while Megumin stood and moaned.

If Darkness hadn't done what she did, they'd probably have executed me by now. No amount of thanks would ever be enough.

Arrrgh, dammit!

Again, I wasn't, like, in love with Darkness or whatever. But still… for some reason, it just made me really angry.

It was kind of like how when one of your female friends gets a boy-friend, it can cause some pretty confusing feelings.

At that moment…

"Kazuma Satou! Kazuma Satou, are you there?!"

There was a shout, then the front door opened.

It was Sena, her face red, her shoulders heaving with ragged breaths as she flung open the door.

"H-hey, I don't have to prove anything yet! Sorry, but I don't have time for you right now. My friend—"

"You don't have time for me?! Cram it! I knew you were an agent of the Demon King all along! I can't believe I let you play us again!"

Setting aside the false accusation, everything about her behavior gave me a bad feeling. Trembling, I asked, "P-played you how…?"

"The frogs! The frogs all over town are supposed to be hibernating for the winter!"

She seemed to be talking about Giant Toads, low-level monsters that were sort of a local nuisance. But I didn't know anything about…

"You cannot just accuse a person of everything, you know," Megu-min said, sounding like she was spoiling for a fight. "You suggest we can control monsters and summon them out of their hibernation? Then show us the proof!"

"According to a Guild employee's report, the frogs appear to have surfaced because something frightened them. Something like the explosion magic that has been used near town repeatedly the last several days and has caused so much trouble for residents."

I grabbed Aqua and Megumin by their collars as they attempted to flee deeper into the house.

"Wait, please hear me out! I only did it because Aqua ordered me to! I am the perpetrator, true, but Aqua is the mastermind!"

"Megumin, you traitor! I remember you being pretty into the idea when I suggested it! *Behold my power* or whatever!"

I kept hold of their collars as things quickly headed south.

"This isn't the time for a stupid argument! We're going to clean up your mess."

2

The whole town was white with snow.

"Nooo! I don't want to be eaten by a frog! Not agaaaaiiin!"

Snow disturbed only by Aqua's tortured shrieking.

"I'm surprised the frogs here don't slow down at all in this cold. They're as quick as ever. Everything around here is just a bit too hardy—including the vegetables," I reflected as I watched a Giant Toad chase Aqua all over the winter wonderland.

"In this merciless world, every living thing struggles at all times to stay alive. We should learn from them. We must get stronger and stronger to survive." Next to me, Megumin looked completely serious.

Even though everything below her shoulders was in the mouth of a Giant Toad.

Perhaps it was her extensive experience in the throats of these frogs that allowed her to remain so calm. She didn't fight back, just let things take their course.

She had already used up her Explosion for the day, taking out a number of the pests.

Notwithstanding the powerless Megumin, the Giant Toad seemed to have had its fill and was completely still. Maybe Megumin's staff was caught in its mouth.

"Hang tight. I'll get you out of there."

I hefted my sword and turned toward the creature that was busy digesting my Wizard.

"It's all right, I can wait till you've taken care of the one chasing Aqua. It's cold out anyway. This toad is nice and cozy."

I had thought Megumin might be normal except for her Explosion mania, but maybe she was worse than I'd realized.

"Y-you seem awfully calm, given that one of your companions is being eaten by a toad and another is being chased around."

Sena sounded a bit miffed. She had come along to keep an eye on us, even as she tried to keep a safe distance.

Well, she could say what she wanted. This was par for the course for us.

Instead of rescuing Megumin, I jabbed my sword into the ground and traded it for my newly purchased bow and arrows.

The golem I'd defeated during our assault on Mobile Fortress Destroyer let me level up twice in one fell swoop. I'd mulled over how to invest the skill points I got and realized that while we had a good, strong tank in Darkness, there was no one in our party who was capable of ranged attacks. We had Megumin, true, but she had only one blast in her, and she was as likely as not to catch Darkness in the area of effect.

That meant it was my time to shine as an Adventurer—a weak class, but able to learn all kinds of skills.

Taking advantage of this unique ability, I had asked Keith, the Archer, to teach me Bow Proficiency and Deadeye.

Bow Proficiency, as the name implied, allowed me to use a bow immediately. And Deadeye increased the range of ranged attacks. It also made you more likely to hit your target the higher your Luck was, so it was perfect for me.

I drew my bow and used Deadeye to take aim at the frog chasing Aqua.

"Kazuma! Quick! Quiiick!" Aqua shouted when she saw me.

You know what? I think I'd rather watch this a while longer.

When she saw I wasn't making any move to shoot, Aqua came dashing toward me, so in fear for my life, I shot the toad in the head.

The bolt brushed Aqua's hair and drove straight into its target.

Aqua, almost in tears, continued straight toward me.

"Okay, Megumin. You next."

"Hey, Kazuma, were you waiting for me to get eaten? Were you?! And didn't I feel that arrow touch my hair? That's my best feature!"

I ignored her verbal deluge and pulled my sword out of the ground.

"Does their fighting style always put them at such risk of their lives? C-could people like this really be in league with the Demon King...?"

Behind us, Sena was taking notes on the fight and muttering something.

I was about to fall on the motionless toad and rescue Megumin when—

"W-wait, please! T-toads—"

Megumin, still sprouting from the frog's mouth, suddenly raised a sound of alarm.

Aqua and I turned around.

"...Ah."

Suddenly we realized there were three new Giant Toads behind us.

My back had been nice and dry right up till then, but now a cold sweat began to trickle down.

Oh man. This made four Giant Toads altogether. We didn't have enough people to be food—I mean, decoys—for all of them.

If I could just get some distance, I could pick them off one by one...!

"Aqua, it's time for a two-pronged strategy. I'm going to put some space between us and try to take one of them out. You go back to being the bait."

"No way! I'm sick of these frogs chasing me! You be the bait this time!"

"You idiot, your attacks aren't strong enough to stop them! If we can take one out, there will only be two left. Then you and Sena can distract them!"

"What?! I'm just your observer; I'm not supposed to get inv— Are you suggesting you would use a bystander like me as a decoy?!"

Somewhere in the middle of Aqua's crying and Sena's shouting, I could hear Megumin.

"Pardon me, but I now seem to be sliding down this frog's gullet bit by bit. If someone could perhaps rescue me..."

"Gaaah, I wish Darkness were here! The frogs can't swallow her and her armor! When the hell is she gonna get back?!"

I locked eyes with the frog swallowing Megumin and raised my sword—!

"Light of Saber!!!"

A clear voice rang out across the snow.

At the same moment, a beam of light shot toward the frog consuming Megumin.

The beam passed through the monster's body. There was a beat, and then it fell clean in half.

I was pulling Megumin clear of its mouth when—

"Energy Ignition!"

The voice came again.

The three frogs closing in on us spontaneously combusted. The blue-white flames engulfed them as if their bodies had caught fire from the inside.

As the aroma of grilled frog drifted by, I contemplated how little I wanted to carry the goop-drenched Megumin on my back. Instead, I used Drain Touch to give her my scant MP.

She managed to stand, albeit with a pronounced wobble.

Her attention rested on a girl in a black robe, maybe a year or two younger than me.

I'd never seen her before, but she was staring at Megumin.

"That was Advanced Magic...! This beginner town has...someone who can use skills like that...?"

With Sena exclaiming behind me, I bowed to the new girl.

"I don't know who you are, but you saved us. Thanks."

She glanced at me and blushed just a little. "I didn't s-save you, all right? I just couldn't let some toad be the one to finish off my rival. What would I do then?" she murmured, looking at the ground.

"Ooh, you know Megumin?" Aqua asked, her enthusiasm restored now that the frogs were gone.

"Yeah, I guess... I mean, we're rivals... Megumin! It's been a while. My training is over and I've come back, just like I said I would. As you can see, I can even use Advanced Magic now! It's time for you to ful-fill the promise we made! After all this time, everything will be settled today!"

She jabbed a finger at Megumin, looking genuinely thrilled.

Man, this was some dramatic twist.

As for the girl being called out...

"I'm sorry... Who are you again?"

"Whaaat?!"

This dispassionate answer from the goop-covered Megumin pro-voked a cry of surprise from the new girl.

I couldn't help noticing the newcomer reminded me of our Arch-wizard somehow.

Her black robe and black mantle looked a lot like the ones Megu-min had on.

She carried a silver wand and wore a dagger at her hip.

A little taller than Megumin, she was maybe a little better propor-tioned overall.

And while she was clearly set on what she wanted, she also appeared to be on the quiet side. Not bad-looking at all.

If she'd been in Japan, I could easily have pictured her as class rep or president of the student council. She had the look of the classic overachiever.

Her hair was tied with ribbons, and she had those distinctive red eyes.

The very same ones as Megumin.

"I-it's me! Your classmate from the academy at the Crimson Magic Village! You were number one and I was number two? And—and I said I was going to go learn how to use Advanced Magic?" The Crimson

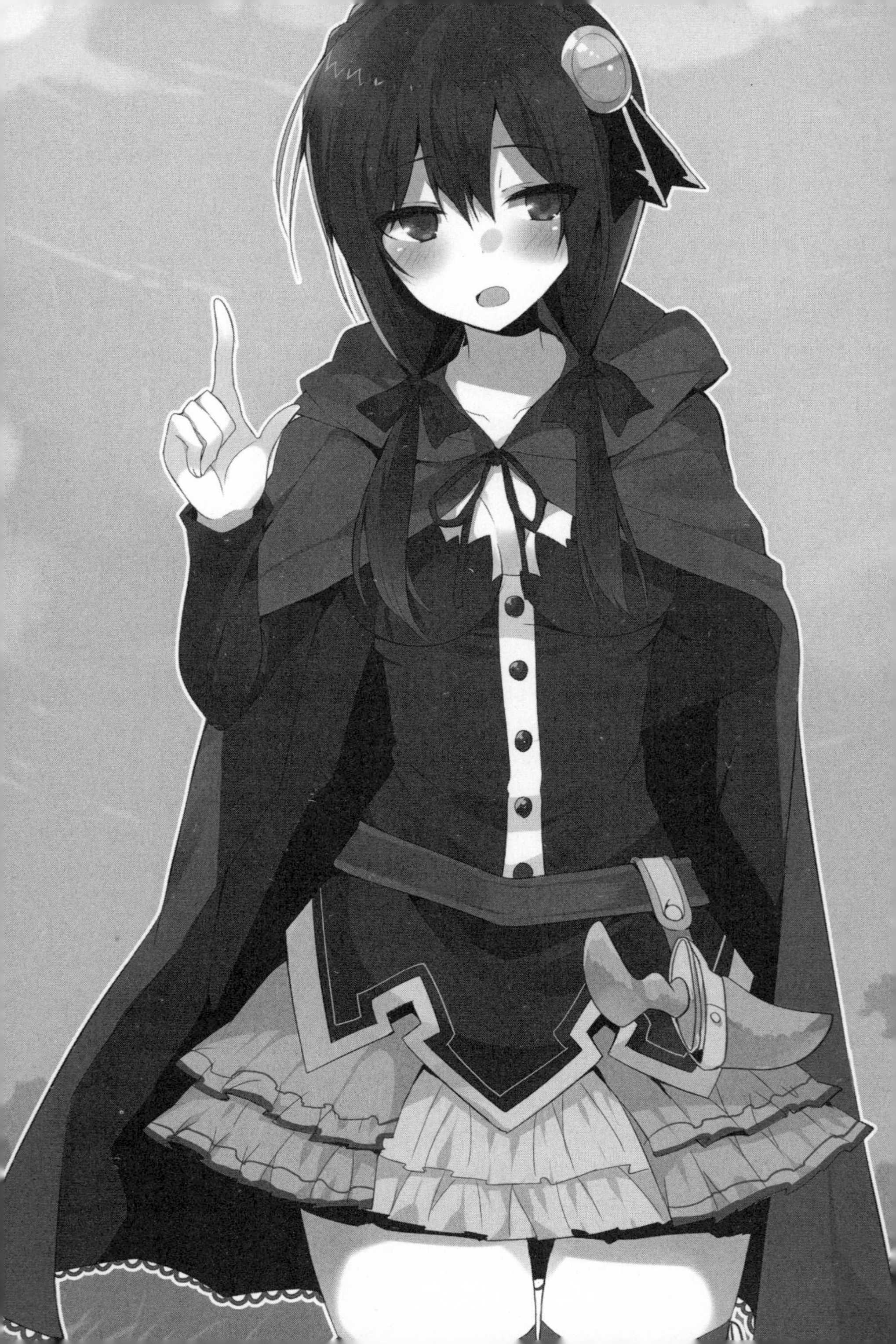

Magic Clan girl pointed to herself, desperately trying to jog Megumin's memory.

Wait, what was that she just said? That sounded big.

"Hang on a second. Did she just say you ranked first at school?"

Megumin only chuckled.

"Why so shocked? When I first met you, did I not tell you that I was first among the spell-casters of the Crimson Magic Clan? It is your fault for not believing me. But now that we have known each other all this time, surely you understand."

"Yeah, that's…a pretty hard story to buy when you're standing there covered in frog spit."

"Wh-what?!"

"Hold it, you two!" The new girl broke into our argument. "Megumin, it's me! Do you really not remember?! How I would always challenge you on tests and everything at school, and you would always say that if there was going to be a duel, there had to be a prize, and make me wager my lunch? I can't count the number of lunches you stole from me that way."

Wow. Megumin did that?

I stared at her, and she glanced away.

"Hey, if you guys are going to be a while, mind if I go ahead to the Guild? I want to get them to take care of these frogs before the meat goes bad." Aqua indicated the cooked monsters.

Frankly, I wasn't thrilled that she was leaving me alone in this situation. But at the moment, we needed every bit of spare change we could get, and it would be better to let Aqua handle things. Anyway, this meant Megumin and I could head straight back home, and she could wash off the amphibian stink that much sooner.

"Hmm. It looks like there's a lot going on. I'll call it a day for now, as well… Kazuma Satou, I admit you looked like an Adventurer today, but I haven't dismissed the possibility that this was all an act to throw me off. I don't trust you yet."

And with that, Sena fixed one final glare on me, then headed to town with Aqua.

3

Left to handle things myself in the snowy field, I turned again to Megumin.

"So, this girl says she knows you, and you...don't know her? She seems pretty familiar with you. You sure you aren't acquainted?"

"I do not, and she has not even told us her name, which is most strange. She must be one of those 'sharks' you told Aqua not to get involved with no matter how badly we needed money. We should avoid her."

She took my hand and tried to lead me away.

Seeing the two of us about to go, the girl said in a panic, "H-hold it right there! F-fine! I hate to do this in front of a stranger, but I'll give you my name! ...I'm Yunyun. An Arch-wizard, wielder of Advanced Magic. And future leader of the Crimson Magic Clan...!"

Blushing furiously as she said all this, Yunyun flung out her mantle with a dramatic *fwap*.

Apparently, there was some rule that Crimson Magic Clan members had to act overly dramatic when they announced themselves.

Observing all this, Megumin said to me, "So, you see? She's Yunyun. Daughter of the current leader of the Crimson Magic Clan and next in line for the succession. Also, my self-proclaimed rival when we were in school."

"I see. I'm Megumin's party member, Kazuma. Nice to meet you, Yunyun."

"S-so you do remember! W-wait, what? Kazu...Mr. Kazuma...? You aren't going to laugh at my name?" Yunyun asked timidly, taken aback.

"So your name's a little odd. That doesn't say anything about you. I even happen to know of someone who's notoriously known as the crazy explosion girl, even though she's already got the weirdest name you ever heard."

"Me? Are you talking about me? I have not heard that nickname! When did I get that nickname?"

A strange but clearly surprised look came over Yunyun's face. "I see. I should have expected it, Megumin. You found some good friends. Nothing less from my rival."

Something seemed to have improved her opinion of me.

"Say, if we're going to chat together, how about we do it somewhere else? You don't just want to stand here, do you?"

At my suggestion, Yunyun's eyes went wide, and she took a step back from Megumin and me.

"Oh yeah! I almost forgot after Megumin tried so hard to pretend she didn't know me! Megumin, I came here to settle things with you! I'm going to be the leader of the Crimson Magic Clan someday. How can I sit confidently on that throne if I can't win against you? And above all—"

Yunyun stood, jabbing a finger in Megumin's direction.

"I've learned Advanced Magic, just like I promised. All I have to do now is beat you and claim the right to call myself first among the spell-casters of the Crimson Magic Clan. Then no one will be able to object when I become leader. No one will be able to say I didn't earn it! Now, Megumin. Duel me!"

The resolve in her eyes was unmistakable.

"I don't wanna. It's cold out and I'm freezing."

Megumin made this sound like a perfectly ordinary response.

"Wha—?" Yunyun stiffened.

"Are you? Let's go home, then. I'll heat the bath. You can go first. Then let's all have a nice meal."

I made to leave with Megumin, but…

"W-w-w-wait a second! How can you do this to me? It's been so long—how can you be so cold? Megumin, duel me! I'm begging you!"

Yunyun was panicked, beseeching.

Finally, Megumin sighed.

"But I'm out of magic for today. I used up all my MP. Do you intend to challenge me by magic anyway? Heh-heh-heh, I think you'll find you're underestimating me. Just now, my power vaporized eight of these foolish frogs in a single blow. Can you match that, Yunyun?"

As Megumin growled this delusionary nonsense, Yunyun looked at me in surprise. She probably wanted some sign whether it was true.

"I guess that's true, more or less."

Though conveniently putting aside her total inability to move afterward.

Yunyun lowered her eyes to the ground and swallowed, a little paler than before.

"You have been away and probably don't know, but...have you heard? How day after day of my magic so frightened the general of the Demon King that he emerged from his castle, and how I then slew him? Or how my Explosion obliterated the invincible Mobile Fortress Destroyer?"

Yunyun's head swiveled back and forth between Megumin and me, looking more and more anxious.

Well, I guess she isn't technically lying.

"It is true that the Demon King's general emerged because of Megumin's magic, and that she struck the final blow on Destroyer."

It's all in how you spin it, as they say.

I wasn't sure Yunyun's face could get any whiter.

"E-e-e-e-even so, I will have a duel! I must...! Even if I have no chance of winning, I will fight you again and again!"

Despite the tears glistening in her eyes and the note of fear in her voice, Yunyun was clearly not going to change her mind.

Megumin heaved another deep sigh.

"...I can see I have no choice. I'll tell you what we'll do. I can't use any more magic today. So how about martial arts? You were always better at that anyway. You seem to be something of an adventurer now yourself. I assume a written test won't be enough for you anymore. We will use no weapons. Victory and defeat will be determined by who gives in first. How does that sound?"

Yunyun wore an expression of open surprise.

"Are you sure? I mean, at school you hardly ever came to martial arts class... Surely you're not trying to make this easy for me? I mean, you would show up as soon as lunch break started and make a big show of walking in front of me so I would challenge you and you could take my lunch..."

"...So you were pretty terrible, huh, Megumin?"

"It was a matter of life and death for me. Because of my home situation, her lunches were my lifeline. If I had challenged her myself, would it not have been little more than extortion?"

Yunyun closed her eyes.

She took a deep breath, then put on a lovely smile.

"Fine. I accept those terms. And someone once told me that a proper duel needs a prize! I'll wager this manatite crystal. It's very pure, a top-class item! Any mage would fall all over themselves to have it!"

Yunyun brought out a small jewel.

Judging by the name, it must be full of MP.

Megumin nodded in satisfaction.

"Very well, I accept! Come at me, then, any way you like!"

Megumin spread her arms threateningly.

Yunyun, for her part, dropped into a low stance and made a fist.

Physically speaking, Yunyun looked like the clear favorite. She was ahead in height and physique, plus she had a well-balanced proportion of muscles on her slim arms and legs. In contrast, Megumin didn't seem likely to be good at hand-to-hand combat by any stretch of the imagination. Honestly, she looked like a completely average girl and a less-than-average Wizard.

Yunyun slid forward, closing up space.

Megumin continued to stand with her hands raised, as if she might give her rival a hug at any time.

"...Hey, Megumin. Hang on a second. Your body looks kind of... shiny. Is that..."

"Yes. This is frog spit!"

Megumin was quick to answer the hesitant question.

Yunyun scrunched up her face, but the other Wizard went right on.

"You saved me earlier. My entire body is covered in frog secretions. But why do you hold back? Come at me! The moment you get near, I shall grab and pin you!"

Having made this announcement, Megumin, her arms still wide, began to creep forward, but for every step she took, Yunyun took one back.

"M-Megumin? Th-this isn't funny... You're joking, right? Th-this is just a strategy to shake my confidence and make me give in. Right? You always used to do that. Y-you can't fool me anymore..."

Yunyun slowly backed away, trying to maintain her bluff. Megumin, red eyes sparkling, slowly edged forward.

She had the look of a kid playing a prank on a close playmate.

"We're friends, aren't we? I believe a friend is one who shares your trials..."

Finally, Yunyun turned and ran.

Megumin gave chase.

"I give!" Yunyun exclaimed. "I give up! I'll give you the manatite— just don't come any closer!"

4

Megumin successfully gooped Yunyun to tears and sent her on her way. We were on the road back home.

"Oh, Kazuma. Here. It will fetch a good price. Use it to help pay off our debt."

She handed me the manatite crystal she had just won.

I recalled Yunyun saying any mage would fall all over themselves to get it.

"Are you sure? You don't want to use it? Not that I know how it works."

To my surprise, Megumin chuckled.

"Manatite crystals are quite helpful. They shoulder some of the MP burden when you use magic. But they are a consumable. A crystal of this size and purity could never power my Explosion. These gems are precious to your average magic user, but a great mage like myself has no use for them."

I see she managed to work in a little pat on the back for herself there...

"Doesn't that worry you? I know I've asked you before, but don't you want to learn some non-explosion mag—"

"No."

"Didn't think so."

Her answer was immediate. I heaved a sigh.

Well, what else was I going to do? This little incident just went to show that even Megumin could step up sometimes.

...Right?

That Yunyun girl had used Advanced Magic. It made for an impressive show and took care of those frogs no problem.

Not only that, but she was pretty and stylish.

Compared to such a striking spell-caster...

"...What? What are you sighing about? ...Crimson Magic Clan members excel not only in magic but in Intelligence. Shall I guess what you are thinking at this moment?"

Megumin regarded me with suspicion when I sighed.

....

"...I was thinking how much prettier you are than that girl."

"Oh, thank you! Such thoughtful praise deserves a hug!"

"N-no, don't! You smell like frog! Keep away!"

When we got back, we discovered Aqua wasn't home yet. Nor was there any sign of Darkness, whom I would have expected by now.

I made a beeline for the bath, deeply conscious of my goopy back.

"Ugh… It stinks… I've never been less happy to get a hug."

"You may wish to be more grateful. There are people who pay money to be hugged by a slimy girl," Megumin said nonchalantly as she followed behind me.

When I started to enter the changing room, Megumin tugged on my sleeve.

"…What do you want?"

"I hate being slimy. Let me go first."

"Well, I don't like it, either, and it's your fault I got this way. Anyway, I have to go first so I can heat the bath. Our tub works by magic, remember? You don't have any MP left, so how would you keep the water warm? I bet the MP I shared with you would barely be enough to make it lukewarm. So just go sit by the fire until I wash up."

I shooed Megumin away, and she shot me a dirty look.

"If I sit by the fire, the goop will dry on my robes, and then I'll never get the smell out. Haven't you ever heard of 'ladies first'? Show some chivalry!"

"Me, I'm for equality of the sexes. You can't crow about how special women are when it's convenient, then turn around and get upset at men. And if you want to be treated like a lady, start by waiting until you're old enough to actually be a lady."

"Hey! Are you treating me like a child?! I'll have you know that we are only three years apart! In ten years we will be twenty-six and twenty-three, and that is not much of a—"

"The future's the future and the past is the past. I live in the present. And at present, you just look like a little kid to me. No ifs, ands, or buts. I'll take my bath now!"

As I spoke, I ducked into the bathing area, lit the water heater with a bit of magic, and peeled off my slime-covered shirt.

"This man bares himself in front of me!"

Megumin drew back a bit, but I wasn't worried about some kid seeing me shirtless.

"You want to see any more, you're going to have to pay. No haggling."

The Wizard bit her lip in frustration, then gave a snort as if she'd thought of something.

With a triumphant smile on her face, she began to taunt me.

"...I understand now. You don't see me as a woman, Kazuma. Well, let's bathe together, then! If I'm nothing more than a child to you, that should be normal enough."

"Yeah, I guess it'd be just as refreshing to be in there together. All right, I'm going in now."

"What?!"

Megumin was the one who'd brought it up, but my nonchalant agreement seemed to catch her by surprise.

"P-pardon me, but is this not the part where you say in embarrassment, *I-idiot, we can't do that!* and then politely allow me to go first?"

"Why should I follow a hackneyed old script like that? Just so you know, unwritten rules don't carry much weight with me. For example—just for example, now. Let's say you fell in love with me, but I was being mobbed by other girls, and you got jealous and decided you were going to try to beat it out of me—you better believe I'd fight right back. When I do something, I do it right. And don't you forget it."

"...I can see I've underestimated you, Kazuma. But I shall not fall in love with you, so there is no need for concern. I'm also not quite sure this is the appropriate time for the expression, 'When I do something, I do it right.' But I shall let that pass."

Perhaps Megumin finally saw she had lost, because she started to leave the changing room...

"What's this? All that taunting and now you're going to leave me in here alone? Sheesh, you really are just all talk. And you wonder why I treat you like a kid."

"All talk?! Me?! What a thing to say! I'll show you! I can get in a little bath! Now stop hiding behind that towel, Kazuma, and get in the tub!"

"Hey, quit it! Stop trying to yank my towel off, you perv! Why are you so strong, anyway? Did Yunyun ever tease you for being like a boy? Have a little decency, will you?"

Once she had dramatically ripped off her robe and covered herself in a towel, Megumin strode boldly into the bathing area.

Huh?

I thought I saw some kind of pattern peeking out from underneath the towel in the vicinity of her butt.

"This water is lukewarm! Give it some more magic! Come on, hurry up and come here!" The Arch-wizard had dipped one hand in the water and was shouting for me.

Maybe it was just my imagination? …Oh well.

5

"Ahhh…"

"Ahhhhh… Maybe a midday bath isn't such a bad idea every once in a while. I feel like I could just drift off to sleep…" I sank up to my shoulders in the huge tub, stretching my arms and legs luxuriously.

The size of the bathtub was the best thing about this house.

"Are you sure we shouldn't have stayed with that Yunyun girl? You guys hadn't seen each other in, like, forever, right?"

"I'm sure we'll meet again. She does consider me her rival, after all."

Megumin, also submerged up to her shoulders, rested her chin on the edge of the tub and closed her eyes, enjoying the water.

"Yunyun, huh? I guess it is kind of a weird name, but she's a cute girl. Plus, she seems to have a lot of sense for being a friend of yours."

"The way you phrase that makes it sound as if you think I do not have sense. She is the same age as me, you know. Do you not see her as a child?"

Chin still resting on the edge of the tub, Megumin opened one eye at me.

So she and Yunyun were the same age... I looked afresh at the girl lounging in the tub with me.

"...Hey. I will have you tell me what you were thinking when you looked at me just now."

"I was thinking everyone grows up at different rates, that's all— Hey, stoppit, don't do your Explosion chant! I know you don't have any MP left, but you're still gonna give me a heart attack!"

I put my chin on the edge of the tub in imitation of Megumin.

"So she's thirteen, huh? I don't go for girls more than two years younger than me, so thirteen-year-olds are out. If she were fourteen, at least that would make her middle school second year and me high school first year. That's almost doable."

I was just sort of talking to myself, but Megumin replied anyway.

"Second year middle school and first year high school? I don't know what you mean, but I will be fourteen next month. Will you stop treating me like a child then?" Her eyes remained blissfully closed as she spoke.

"No way, really? Your birthday is next month? Wait—fourteen? So you're gonna graduate from your jailbait persona?"

"Who are you calling jailbait? And I don't recall ever adopting a persona like that! ...What? What is it? Why do you look so—?"

The girl I'd treated as a sort of ill-behaved younger sister had suddenly started to seem like an ill-behaved younger schoolmate instead.

"Wh-what do I do now? Suddenly this situation seems kind of embarrassing..."

"What do you mean? You changed your mind? Stop it—I'll get embarrassed, too! Anyway, does just one year make that much difference to you? I mean—stop stealing awkward glances at me!"

What was the story here? Why was my heart pounding?

All of a sudden, I realized I'd gotten myself into a pretty tight spot.

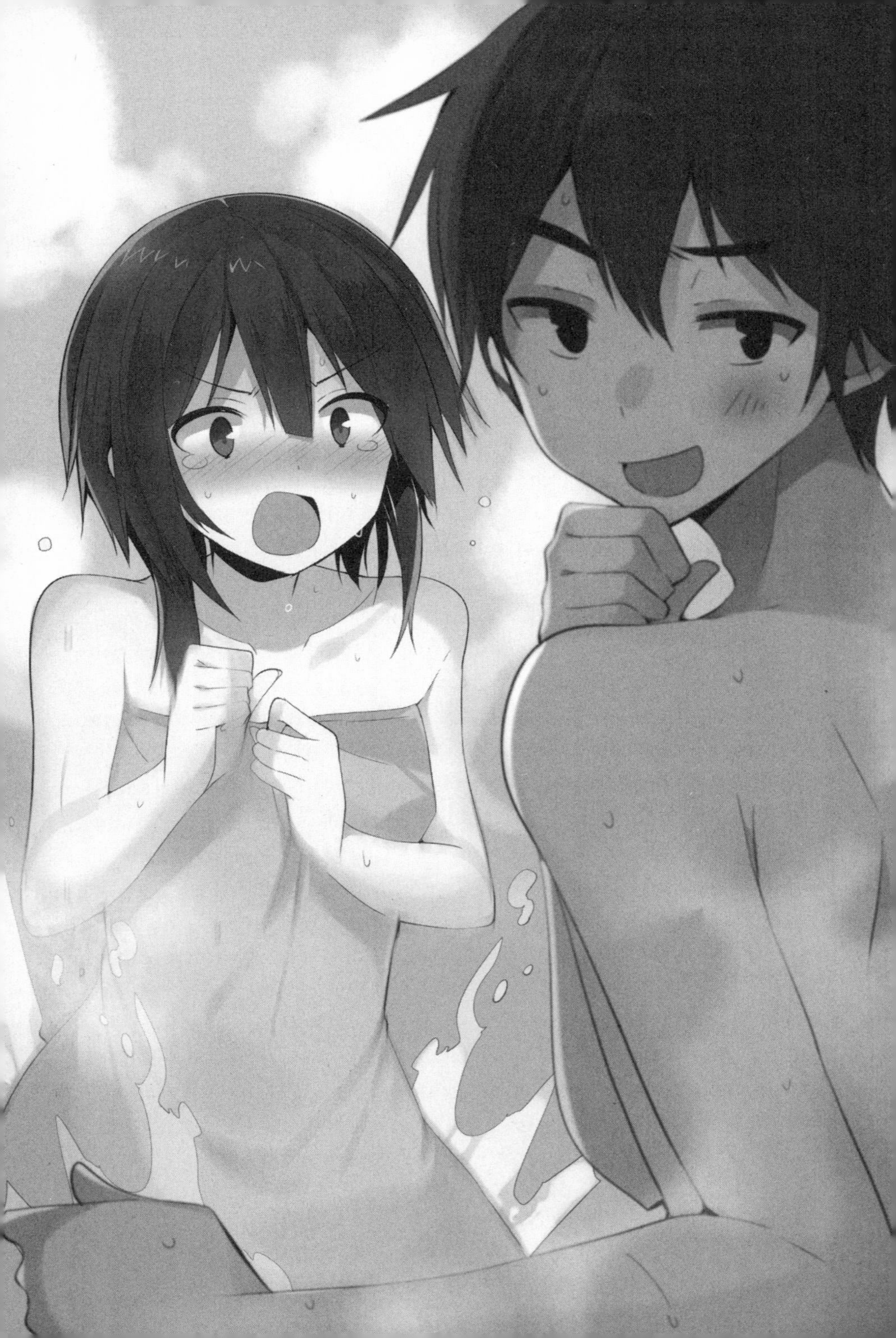

"Hey, why are we in this bath together anyway, Megumin? If you really think about it, isn't this kind of...bad?"

"You're saying that now?! Stop it! Why would you turn all level-headed now?"

Megumin scuttled backward, trying to put as much distance between us as she could. I tried to do the same thing in the other direction.

"I mean—what if someone sees us here? There's no way to play this off as a joke. It's exactly at times like these when someone who can't read these kinds of situations—"

So, naturally, right at that moment...

"I'm hooome!"

...we heard the voice of somebody famous for not being able to read *any* situation.

"You jinxed us, Kazuma!"

"This isn't the time to be pointing fingers! One of us has to hurry and get out of here!"

Megumin and I both jumped up to leave the tub at the same time, then both sank back down in embarrassment.

"Why are you trying to leave with me? Are you trying to see what my wet towel reveals? Are you not worried I will see what yours does?"

"Hey, I'm getting out of here, so you stay in the water. Wait—the key! Please tell me we locked the changing room..."

"N-no, we didn't! And you know this is when Aqua will come straight here. Wh-wh-what do we do? Do something, please!"

Whatever the hell the options even were, obviously the first step was for one of us to get out of the bath.

If Aqua found us here, I was sure she would come up with some slanderous nickname for me—loliNEET or loli-lover or who knows what.

"Kazumaaa! Megumiiin! I'm hooome! Aren't you going to greet me? I brought the money we got for the frogs!"

Her voice was getting closer.

I sprang out of the tub and zipped toward the changing room.

At the sound of my footsteps, Aqua seemed to realize where I was.

"Kazumaaa! …Oh, taking a bath?"

An instant before the changing room door could open, I summoned all the magical power in my body, and with my right arm outstretched, I focused on a spell like I never had before.

"*Freeeeze*!!"

With my entire store of magic behind it, the spell froze the doorknob instantaneously, while I, my MP spent, collapsed to the floor in the wave of exhaustion that followed.

"Kazuma, I left your and Megumin's money on the table, okay? When you're done with your bath, let's go get something to eat!"

Then she walked away, never even trying to open the door.

…Of course she didn't. She knew I was in here. What did I think this was, a manga?

"A-are you all right, Kazuma? Did you use up all your magic? I mean…that was a close one. We almost—"

"I almost got certified with a Lolita complex! That was really a close one… Hey, Megumin. Sorry, but could you dry me off? I can't move, and I don't want to catch a cold…"

I couldn't see Megumin from where I lay prone on the floor. But…

"You say you will be considered a jailbait lover for getting in the bath with me? I shall have you explain this! You make awfully bold demands for someone who can't move a muscle!"

"Hey—hey, stop that! What are you doing, taking my towel off?! Now who's the perv?! Hey— A-Aquaaa! Aquaaa! The jailbait won't leave me alone!"

6

Aqua did burst in to help me, and when the dust settled, I had acquired the nickname of loliNEET.

We ate our second, strangely lonesome dinner without Darkness.

And then, the next morning…

"What, you two are up already?" I asked as I came into the living room.

The night before, we had concluded that going on quests without Darkness was dangerous. So today was going to be free time for all of us.

In the end, Darkness hadn't come home yesterday, either.

I knew she'd said that lord was obsessed with her, but did he actually kidnap her?

Or had something unexpected happened…?

If she didn't come back tonight, I would take matters into my own hands.

I was wandering around town, on the hunt for food after deciding it was too much trouble to make breakfast, when I spotted a certain Crimson Magic Clan girl.

She pattered along by herself, casting a greedy eye at every food stall.

Finally she stopped and gazed at a place selling grilled kebabs.

A moment later, a customer came up, laughed with the clerk, then bought three skewers.

That seemed to help her make up her mind. She made for the stall and bought three, just like the last customer.

…I got the impression she had never ordered street food before and wasn't sure what to do.

I thought about calling out to her, but seeing how she was stuffing her face, I decided to leave her be.

"I've heard there have been some weird monsters around town lately. They're not that strong, but…"

"Oh yeah, I've heard that, too. They look really strange, and if they see a moving object, they latch onto it and then explode. You're talking about those things, right?"

I overheard this conversation between two adventurers while I strolled around town, after getting breakfast from a random shop.

Weird monsters…?

I mean, personally, I find all the monsters around here weird.

But it might be worth keeping in mind anyway.

Such were the thoughts running through my head when I saw that same familiar girl again, this time loitering in front of a shooting-gallery stall.

This wasn't quite like the carnival target-practice places in Japan, though. It featured a real bow and arrows with blunt tips.

Many of the customers enjoying the game were couples. The guy would win a prize and hand it to his girlfriend.

This area must be the place to go for dates around here. And this particular stall seemed to be marketing itself to people sharing a romantic time together. That much was obvious from the prizes.

Maybe the girl was embarrassed to be there alone, because she waited until every one of the couples had left and the stall was deserted before she stepped up to try her hand.

She evidently didn't know much about archery, though, because none of her shots came anywhere near the prize she wanted.

She kept handing money to the stall owner to try again, until finally a couple came up and began shooting, and the girl returned the bow and awkwardly made to leave.

Hmm…

Let's think this through, here. My party includes this girl's rival, so I guess we're not necessarily on the best of terms, but…

"Hey," I said, nearing her.

"…? Oh! Um, Mr. Kazuma, hello…!"

With barely a glance Yunyun's way as she greeted me, I marched straight up to the shooting-gallery owner and handed him some money.

"Deadeye!"

With my sniping skill, I was able to get the prize for Yunyun with one shot.

It was a samurai-like plush toy. As it tumbled off the shelf, I thought it looked somehow like General Winter.

"Here. This is the one you wanted, right?"

I handed it to Yunyun with feigned disinterest.

If I had been in her shoes, I wouldn't be surprised if I fell in love with me on the spot.

Yunyun's cheeks went a pale red, and for a second she didn't seem sure she could accept the toy.

But then a smile spread across her face, and she said joyfully, "Th-thank you very much…!"

"I'm sorry, sir, but the sign clearly says Archers and the Deadeye skill are not allowed. You can keep the prize, but I'll need you to pay double the fee…"

Apologizing and forking over more cash to the shopkeeper, I probably didn't look as cool as I would have liked.

"O-okay then, I've got to go find the rest of my party. See you later."

Partly due to my embarrassment, I raised a hand to wave good-bye to Yunyun…

"What? Oh… Um…"

Yunyun reached out a hand forlornly as if to stop me, but then drew it back and readjusted her arms around the plush figure. She bowed instead.

"Th-thank you again for this General Winter toy!"

So it *was* General Winter.

The trauma of my own death at his hands left me feeling like I'd been shot with an actual arrow, but I decided to try to look pleased.

I parted ways with Yunyun and went back to looking around town.

My party members being as obvious as they were, I figured I'd run into them sooner or later, but…

"Step right up! Who's our next challenger?!"

I turned toward the voice to see a large crowd.

My curiosity led me closer. Everyone else drawn by the voice seemed to be unusually burly.

When I got close enough, I could see…

"All right, me next!"

A beefy muscleman, probably an adventurer himself, stepped out of the crowd. He was in civilian clothes, so I couldn't say exactly what his class was, but he clearly belonged on the front line.

The man took the hammer from the shopkeeper, and…

"YAAAAAAHHHH!"

With a tremendous shout, he brought it crashing down.

The object of his blow was some kind of rock.

The hammer struck it, sending up little sparks. But as for the rock itself…

"Damn. Still no good, huh?"

The man's rueful words were right. The stone didn't have a scratch.

At that, the shop owner raised his voice again:

"Another good man unable to prevail! The prize money is going up to one hundred and twenty-five thousand eris! Ten thousand eris a try! Every time someone fails, another five thousand is added to the pot! Is no one here confident in his strength? Use all the magic you want! Test yourself against Adamantite! Anyone able to break it is qualified to call himself a first-rank adventurer! Who will accept the challenge?"

I see. Boy, they've got everything around here.

Given how I had occasionally thought of starting a business myself, this place had a lot to teach me.

Still, with my skills and strength, I didn't see myself putting a dent in that Adamantite.

Suddenly, as I stared into the distance, I saw her for the third time that day.

"We meet again, Yunyun."

She was by herself as usual, clenching her fists as she intently watched the adventurers slam the hammer into the stone. This time I greeted her openly.

At first I wondered whether, as Megumin's self-proclaimed rival, she might see me as an enemy, too, but judging by how things had gone earlier, she didn't dislike me that much.

When she saw me, she exclaimed happily, "Oh, Mr. Kazuma! Thank you again for getting me that plush toy. Look at this! They claim that rock is Adamantite!"

Maybe they didn't have street games like this in the Crimson Magic Village.

"Yunyun, you can use Advanced Magic, right? Think you could break that stone? They say magic's allowed."

"Me? Against Adamantite? I'm afraid not," Yunyun said. "You would need to blow it up with some extremely powerful magic. Explosion might be a little much, but you'd need some kind of explosive magic, or at least blasting magic, to get the job done." She smiled ruefully.

As we were talking, yet another challenger showed up, failed, and went on his way.

Before I knew it, the prize was more than two hundred thousand.

The crowd got bigger and bigger, and the barker got more and more excited.

"Maybe Adamantite was too much for the adventurers of this town! I came when I heard you had felled Mobile Fortress Destroyer. Are you going to let this stone go unshattered? Come on now, step right up! Have we no challengers?!"

As he heckled us at the top of his lungs, adventurers began giving one another little shoves, urging their peers to try their strength.

Everyone knew it was just a ploy on the barker's part, but they also couldn't stand that no one had managed to break the rock.

As the gathered adventurers exchanged glances, a young woman slipped out in front.

There stood my party member, puffing out her chest importantly. Her usual robe had been replaced with a black dress meant for streetwear.

The look on her face was as satisfied as the day she had brought down Destroyer.

"Your challenger," she declared, "has appeared."

No sooner had Megumin said this than all the other adventurers there, including me, rushed to hold her back.

7

"Hey! Is this any way to treat a young woman who has not even done anything yet?"

I had Megumin pinioned so I could clap my hands over her mouth if she started chanting.

Each arm was in the firm grasp of an adventurer.

"Hey, man, now that this kid's here, you better close up shop! The whole town knows she's crazy for explosions. She won't be able to resist your challenge!"

At my urging, the stall owner began to clean up, his face pallid and drawn.

At the sight of the owner making his escape, Megumin began to struggle.

"Ohh! But I can break that stone! My Explosion will annihilate it!"

"Run, man! Run as fast as you can!"

"Yeeeek!" The owner snatched up his supplies and departed with haste.

Megumin watched him go in disappointment.

When I was sure he was a safe distance away, I let her go.

The crowd began to disperse.

"Geez," I said to Megumin, "I already can't take my eyes off Aqua. Speaking of which, isn't she with you?"

"No. She said she had somewhere she wanted to go, so we split up. With all the money this town has received for annihilating Destroyer, we've been flooded with people hoping to take advantage, right? A little while ago, she had set up next to some street performers and was offering to do a better show for free than the one they were charging for. I believe they were in tears."

Actually, I…kind of feel sorry for them.

I wanted to do something to help, but I also wanted to avoid getting caught up in anything else.

I felt bad, but those performers would just have to manage on their own.

That was when Megumin tugged on my sleeve.

"Since we are here, how about we walk around town together? There are stalls all over. I considered wandering around intimidating shopkeepers."

"A-and here I thought you had more sense than that. Notwithstanding the explosion-crazy thing."

Amid this banter, as the two of us got ready to leave, a small voice came from behind us.

"Um…"

I turned around. Yunyun was watching us forlornly.

"…Wanna come with?"

For a second she looked thrilled—then she glanced at Megumin and seemed a bit stricken.

"I—I came here to beat Megumin, not to get all buddy-buddy with her! Thank you again for your help at that archery stall. I really appreciate it! …But I certainly won't go with you!"

Then, hugging that unsettling plush toy to her chest, she backed away a step.

"You heard her. Let us go, Kazuma."

"S-sure…"

We left Yunyun, who had pointedly turned her back to us.

"……Ahh……"

With a deep, lonely sigh and a slump of her shoulders, she trotted away.

She glanced over her shoulder as if she'd felt a tug on her pigtails…

…and found us, following not far behind and eating a crepe-like thing we'd gotten at a nearby stall.

"U-um…why are you following me?"

"I thought I might be able to witness the familiar sight of your tears when the loneliness finally got to be too much for you."

With that, Yunyun leaped at Megumin.

8

"Yunyun, you were always known for being embarrassed about your name despite being a member of the Crimson Magic Clan. At school you usually ate by yourself. I would parade around in front of you while you ate because you were so happy to challenge me…"

"Now, hold on! I d-don't think…it w-was…that bad… I—I mean, I do feel like we fought every day, but it wasn't because I was lonely. I even had friends."

The three of us headed for the edge of town as we chatted.

Why? Because in the course of our conversation, these two had decided to duel again.

At Yunyun's words, Megumin stopped dead.

"Doth mine ears deceive me? Yunyun…*friends?*"

"Wh-what? Of course I had friends! You knew them, too, Megumin. Funifura and Dodonko and everyone? They'd always be like, *We're friends, right?* and then I would pay for their meals…"

Aww, man. I don't wanna hear any more.

Basically, it sounded like this girl was the one sane person in a village full of crazies, and it hadn't made her popular.

What a tragic backstory…

"And how do you plan for us to duel today? Being able to use only Explosion, I would prefer to avoid a magical contest."

"Good question… Wait, I mean, don't you think it's about time you learned some other magic? I'm sure you've earned some skill points since we were kids."

"I have. Every last one of them I have put into raising the potency of my explosions along with high-speed incantations…"

"You nut! Why are you so obsessed with explosions, anyway?"

Yeah! Preach, sister!

"But this is a problem… How are we ever going to duel…?"

"Whatever you like. I am no longer so childish as to be worried about these games," Megumin said.

Yunyun frowned to hear this detached pronouncement from my jailbait friend.

"Oh, you're not childish, are you? I recall we once had a contest to see who could grow the fastest. If you're not a kid anymore, we could do that again…?"

It was a good try, but Megumin wasn't biting.

"No, that is not what I meant by saying I am not childish. You see, I am so close to Kazuma here that we have already been in the bath together."

"?!"

"H-hey! What's wrong with you, spreading that around?!"

"?!!?!?!"

Yunyun had turned bright red and was working her mouth open and shut.

"……I-I'll give you this one todaaaaay!"

And with that, she ran off crying.

Megumin and I didn't move for a moment. Then the little Wizard took something out and began to write.

When I leaned in for a better look, she seemed to have some kind of notebook.

She wrote down today's date and a white circle of approval.

"Another victory."

"Y-you call this a victory…?"

After the weeping Yunyun had vanished, Megumin and I decided to head back to the house, too.

"Oh, welcome home. Hey, look at these. One of the performers in town said he didn't need them anymore and gave them to me. I guess he's going to go back to his home and take over the family farm or something. I didn't really follow. But it seems to be my lucky day!"

When we got back, Aqua was sitting on the couch in the living room with some juggling rings and an air of self-satisfaction.

Rings she had gotten by shattering a performer's heart.

I was about to tell her not to ruin people's lives, but...

"Darkness still isn't here. I wonder if she'll be back tonight," Megumin murmured despondently, watching Aqua juggle the rings.

But no. She wasn't.

Chapter 3 May There Be a Good Match for This Noble Daughter!

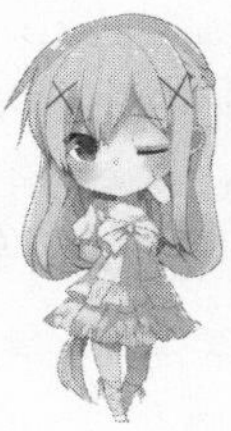

1

"Hey, Aqua. I'm kind of getting tired of saying this all the time—move it. Since Darkness isn't home yet, we still can't go on quests. I'm going to work on the blueprints for the item I want to sell in Wiz's shop, so make some room."

Aqua, as ever, had claimed the couch in front of the fireplace and curled up on it. She regarded me coldly.

"What are you so upset about? You've been so prickly lately with Darkness not coming home… You know, when Megumin used to challenge that Yunyun girl, she always said everything has its price. Meaning, if you want me to give up this spot, you have to give me something I want in return. Like, say…"

She stopped for a moment as if mulling it over. Then she said, "O you who would dwell in the place of the gods… Present me with some classy wine. Only then shall I let this warm light shine upon this wandering NEET…"

Maybe I'll just smack her.

Stupid Megumin, teaching her to say something like that.

"Listen, you worthless goddess. If you can demand a drink first thing in the morning, you can think of a plan. Why am I the only one doing all this work, anyway? I'll figure out a way to cover the bill for Alderp's mansion, so you come up with the money for the flood damage.

Or maybe, if you have one apologetic bone in your body, you can just get out of the way."

"You know, could you stop calling me names? 'Worthless goddess' or 'useless goddess' or whatever? If you keep talking about me like I'm some fallen creature, one day you might really get punished for it. Who knows? Maybe this thing with Lord Alderp is actually payback because you don't have proper respect for the gods. Maybe if *you* had an apologetic bone in *your* body, you'd say, *I'm sorry, my radiant lady Aqua*, and offer me some expensive wine. Go on, go buy it. I'll wai—"

"*Steal!*"

I stuck out my hand toward Aqua and intoned my skill as she spouted nonsense from the sofa.

With a jangling sound, her purse appeared in my hand.

"Hey, what are you doing, you thief? You criminal! I should turn you over to the police! If they found out about this, you'd never prove your innocence! Eeek, criminal! What, you wanted money to buy wine? Of course, I meant buy it with your own mon—"

"*Steal!*"

I intoned my skill again over Aqua's babbling.

One of her socks appeared in my hand.

Aqua stuck out the toes of her now bare foot and wiggled them vigorously at me as if in defiance.

"What are you doing? It's cold. Give me back my sock, you weirdo. If you don't give it back right now, I'll call the police and tell them someone is holding my sock and panting. If you understand—"

"*Steal!*"

What did Aqua even have this for?

In my outstretched palm was some kind of seed.

Her expression turned very uncomfortable.

"H-hey, Kazuma, your cheap prank really isn't very funny. I admit I went a little too far. I see that now. So let's just say sorry to each other and make up, okay?"

"*Steal!*"

Aqua's other sock teleported to my hand. I tossed it on the carpet.

"I'm going to make some money. Give me that feather mantle—your 'divine raiment' or whatever you call it. I'm going to sell it. If you don't want me to just strip it off you, go in the other room and change by yourself... Who am I kidding? You'll never agree to that. I might as well just grab it."

I made sure she could see me flexing my fingers. Aqua scrunched up her face.

"What are you talking about? This feather mantle is my very identity as a goddess—we can't possibly sell it! That's the most idiotic thing any idiot has ever suggested in the history of idiocy, and it's not funny!"

"*Steal*!"

"Ahhh, Kazumaaa! My dear Kazuma! I was wrong to act all high and mighty! I was wrong! So stop! Please stop!"

Several minutes later...

"Aww...*hic...sniff...hrrrgh*..."

Aqua sat on the couch, her knees in her chest and her face in her knees, sobbing.

She was wearing...

Well, other than the two socks she was missing, the same outfit she normally wore.

"D-damn. Why would my Luck fail me at a time like this? What do you do with all this junk anyway?"

At my feet was a mountain of worthless items.

Seeds, cups, glass beads... Did she use them all for party tricks? It looked like some kid had turned their pockets out on the carpet.

Damn. Thanks to Aqua and all the crap she was carrying, I'd used up way more magic than I'd meant to.

"At it so early again? What is going on?" Megumin came in dressed as if for a quest and spotted me standing in front of the weeping Aqua.

"*Hic*... Kazuma... He said he would sell...sell my clothes to pay our debt! He tried to...to take them from me!"

"H-hey, shut up already! You want people to get the wrong idea?!

I-I'm sorry. I apologize, too, so—don't look at me like that, Megumin! I was just going to sell her equipment!"

So Aqua was crying and Megumin was eyeing me with contempt. Just another morning.

"Th-this is bad! Kazuma, it's awful!"

The peaceful atmosphere shattered when a beautiful young woman came dashing in.

She wore an expensive-looking white dress that formed the very picture of purity and white high heels, and her long, lovely golden hair had been woven into a braid that hung over one shoulder. She looked like a runaway daughter from some noble's household.

For all the purity of her clothing, though, she couldn't hide the eroticism of her body.

But I'd never seen her before. How did she know my name?

"...Who are you?"

"Hrr—! Hrk! Kazuma! This isn't the time for games! I appreciate your attempt at play, but save it for later, please!"

The no-good nonsense spouting from this beautiful woman as her cheeks turned red made everything clear.

"Geez, Darkness, is that you? We were so worried—you're finally back!"

My words distracted Aqua from her sniveling long enough to exclaim, "Waaaah! Darkness! Kazumaaa! Kazuma, he—he tried to strip me! He was going to sell my most prized possession—!"

"I told you not to put it that way! What are people going to think?!"

As Aqua and I argued, Megumin turned to our Crusader and said, "Welcome home, Darkness. I won't ask what happened. Please, start with a nice bath. Relax your body and mind."

"A...a bath? What in the world are you talking about, Megumin? For that matter, what is *Aqua* talking about? That unique kind of play sounds rather interesting..."

Darkness stood there in her dress, stealing glances at Aqua and me and muttering.

"You're probably tired," I said. "Just take it easy for today. You're finally back; that's enough for us. Take a warm bath and have a good cry."

"Will someone *please* tell me what is going on? Why do you all think I need to cry? Why do I have to take a bath? …What is it, Aqua? Why are you pulling on my sleeve?"

Aqua's tears had dried up, and she was tugging at the white dress as if trying to figure out what it was made of.

"No doubt this is some high-class clothing. Definitely the sort of thing a lord would give as compensation."

"Darkness," I said earnestly, "you really did a good job this time. Putting yourself through all that to save me…"

"Idiot! I don't know what any of you are thinking! Lord Alderp didn't do anything untoward to me, and this is *my* dress. What, did you think I wasn't able to come home because Lord Alderp was having his way with me all this time?!"

"Well, sure we did. We figured you'd be in pretty dire straits right about now. But wait… If that dress didn't come from him, where'd you get something so expensive? You said it's yours. Do you do princess cosplay? Are you trying to pioneer some new genre?"

"I am not! Th-this isn't cosplay! I am sorry to have worried you. That lord doesn't have the guts to do anything indecent to me. But that's not important now. Look at this!"

Darkness thrust a sort of photo album at me.

Well, not so much an album…

"What's this? Huh? Who's the hot dude? Ooh, I hate guys like him!"

I unconsciously reached out toward the breezy-looking young guy and… *Riiip…*

"Huh?! What are you doing?! That's a matchmaking picture! If you do that, I won't be able to refuse the meeting!"

Huh?!

"What? I'm sorry! My hand just kind of moved on its own… Wait, *matchmaking picture*?!"

I gaped at her, dumbfounded, still holding the pieces.

"Yes! That underhanded Alderp! I said I would do any one thing he asked, but that was because I knew my father would never stand for him requesting anything inappropriate," she said with a groan.

"H-hang on, take a step back. Who is this guy? Anyway, I'd say being forced to marry someone you don't want to is pretty inappropriate. What's the connection between Lord Alderp and the guy in this photo? And if you hate him so much, why not just have your dad refuse? Here, I'll fix this tear. Aqua, sorry, but could you bring me a little bit of rice?"

"Sure thing."

After Aqua pattered off, I urged the tearful Darkness to sit on the sofa, hoping to calm her down.

"That's a photo of Alderp's son. That old dog, he knew he could never get away with asking to marry me himself. But my father has a pretty high opinion of his son. He's probably more in favor of this marriage than anyone else. Although I don't understand why Lord Alderp would want to marry his son to me…"

As she spoke, Darkness lowered herself onto the couch and looked at the chaotic tabletop.

Aqua came back with the rice and sat next to Darkness, then took it upon herself to begin repairing the picture. In another corner of the table from where Aqua was working were the blueprints for the item I had devised for Wiz's shop. Darkness picked them up and said with interest, "What's this? What a strange thing you've drawn. What's it supposed to be?"

Megumin, putting on her boots in the foyer, responded, "We came up with some schemes to make money in the time you were out, Darkness. That's a useful device Kazuma designed. He plans to stock it in Wiz's store."

"Oh? You always did have good Luck, didn't you, Kazuma? You'd probably do well in business."

"Yeah, good Luck. I've been having some serious doubts about that lately. If my Luck's so good, shouldn't I have more helpful party members? Should I be under a mountain of debt and getting involved in every stupid fight that comes along? Shouldn't I have a better life?"

All three of them gave a start.

"I-I'm being married off because I covered for you! And not because I want you to be indebted to me, but because I believe in party members helping each other! I know I'm a lot of trouble most of the time, but it's just as natural for me to help you like this!"

A single bead of sweat ran down Darkness's cheek as she made her case.

"A-and I am going to meet Yunyun now! And actually—yes! It is to brainstorm ways to clear your name, Kazuma!"

This came from Megumin in the foyer, not quite able to look at us. So that was why she'd been getting ready to go out.

"Welp, it looks like you two have Kazuma covered, so maybe I'll go clean the toilet or something! I don't know why, I just feel like it needs it. Don't get up—I'll handle it!"

And so our toilet goddess left off repairing the photo and practically ran out of the room to go clean the john.

As everyone seemed about to go their separate ways, Darkness waved her hand frantically to stop us and, nearly in tears, said, "Wh-what am I going to do? I was... I was out all that time because I was trying to find some way to stop this match, but it's proceeding further and further along. Actually, I came here because...because the actual meeting is this afternoon. I'm out of time. I'm really sorry, but could one of you come with me and help talk to my father?"

2

"...So let me see if I understand this correctly. Your father has always wanted you to quit the dangerous work of adventuring, so he has tried to arrange matches given the slightest chance. But you, Darkness, do not yet want to get married, and have refused all such proposals." Megumin summarized as she stood in the foyer with her boots on.

At the table, Aqua had resumed trying to repair the picture. As the one who had damaged it, I had meant to fix it myself, but she seemed to be having fun and, more importantly, to be doing a great job. So I decided to let her do what she liked.

She sure had a lot of really random talents...

"...Ngh, that's right. Honestly, I'm happy living the way we are now. If we keep adventuring like this, then one day I might become more widely known, and then an evil Wizard or an agent of the Demon King might notice me, and then he might take me helplessly prisoner and subject me to terrible torments. He'd dream up something awful, I'm sure. He'd slap me in chains and manacles, make me most unlike a lady...! N-nooo! Stooooop!"

"Maybe you really should get married and settle down." I took a step back from Darkness, who was red-faced and sweaty from her own fantasy.

Twirling her staff, Megumin said with some bemusement, "I see. Normally these meetings are your father's suggestion, so you can turn them down. But this time, you've said you will do anything Lord Alderp asks, and he is a local ruler, so you cannot refuse. But why should he take such a circuitous route to get you? And why marry you to his son? A person of his station could get away with taking you as a concubine by force, if he really wanted to."

Darkness looked at the ground. She put her hands together in front of her chest and twiddled her thumbs for a moment before replying:

"My... My real name is Lalatina Ford Dustiness. I'm the daughter of a...a fairly substantial noble house."

"*What?!*" we all exclaimed.

Our collective surprise caused a painful cloud to flit over Darkness's face. For a second, she looked terribly lonely.

I guessed we weren't the first to have that reaction upon hearing her true name.

"Dustiness...! You mean the Dustinesses who are supposed to

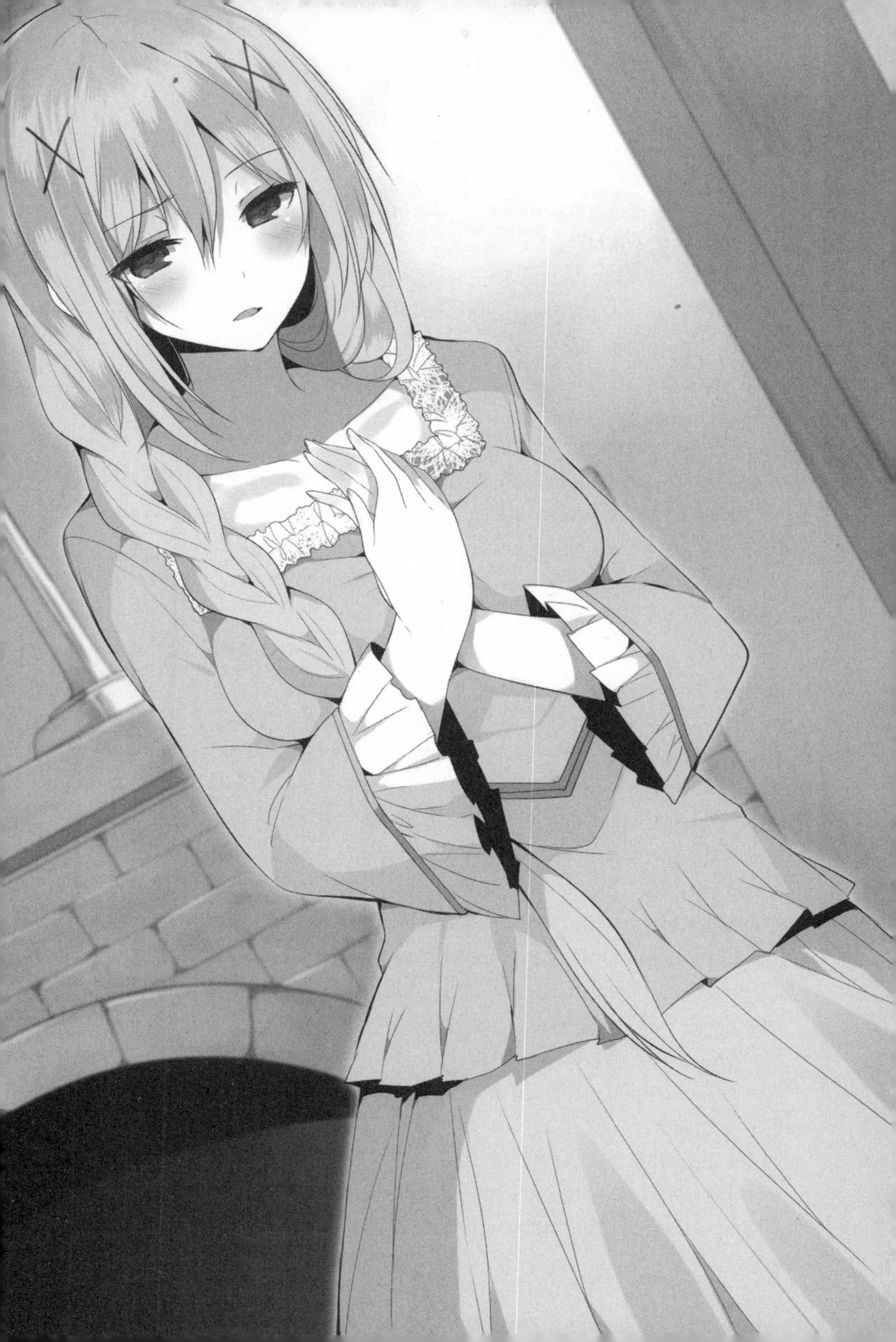

practically run the country?! They're not 'substantial,' they're huge! They're based in our town?!"

Darkness responded quietly to Megumin's surprised yelp:

"...Yes."

Aqua was next.

"What?! You mean if your family adopted me, I could spend all day, every day in the lap of luxury?!"

Darkness, clearly not expecting this turn of the imagination, said hesitantly, "Y-yes... I mean, wait. My family isn't looking for an adopted daughter right now."

I, however, immediately latched on to the most important thing.

"Darkness... You're normally all *Mm* and *I concur* and serious Knight stuff. And all this time you've had an adorable name like Lalatina?!"

"D-don't call me that...!" Lalatina shouted, her face red and her eyes brimming with tears.

Megumin finally unfroze from her shock and sat down on the carpet near the foyer.

"Whew. Well, I am certainly surprised. But Darkness is Darkness. To me, that means an extremely tough Crusader and a valuable friend. Nothing more, nothing less."

The words seemed to cheer Darkness a little bit.

"......Right. We'll come through this together," she said, then gave a relieved smile.

Aqua looked at the two of them beaming, then pointed to herself.

"Hey, can I share a shocking revelation, too? I mean, I know you didn't believe me last time, but...I'm really an actual goddess!"

"Are you?" they replied. "Good for you!"

"Please believe meee!"

Sniffling, Aqua returned to trying to repair the damaged matchmaking picture.

I thought to myself as I watched the three of them.

All of a sudden, a lot of things made a lot more sense.

This explained why Darkness seemed to know less about this world than I did, even though I had come from Japan. And it explained why she'd shown up today in such a weird costume.

Maybe Lord Alderp's attempt to marry Darkness to his son was some kind of strategic move. If he couldn't have her himself, at least he could have her in the same house.

If we didn't do something, our beloved Crusader was going to be somebody's bride.

Our...beloved...hmm? Hmmm?

"So we have to take this and make a case to persuade your father, right? Here. What do you think? Good as new!"

My train of thought was interrupted by Aqua, who handed me the matchmaking photograph with a self-satisfied look. She had repaired it so carefully you would never have known it was ever damaged.

Hang on. Darkness was going to be a bride.

In other words, the Crusader who was totally unable to hit her target was going to leave our party.

And didn't they always say weddings were a joyful occasion?

It wasn't as if we were kicking anyone out of our party, even if she was kind of useless.

I didn't dislike Darkness, after all. Sure, she could be pretty strange, but she wasn't a bad person.

But who knew what the future held for our party? Was it really fair to restrict the daughter of a noble family to a life of adventuring with us?

No, it certainly wasn't.

If Darkness got married, it would be a load off her parents' minds as well. And truth be told, I often worried for her myself.

What would happen on the off chance we actually made it to the Demon King's castle? We'd just get in trouble, and then she would be sure to happily say something like, *Forget about me! Run!*

No doubt she would be imagining what kinds of things would happen to her when she was captured and joyfully saying, "Ki...kill me..."

In other words, this was a great idea! Everyone could be happy.

"Right... We just give this back, make up some reason I can't

accept, and apologize. Then all we have to do is persuade my father…
And for that, I'd really like one of you to come along…"

Darkness, looking at the picture in my hand, seemed to be a little
bit more at ease.

"I've got it!"

"Whaaaaat?!" the girls cried as I tore the picture clean in half.

3

"All right. I promised to meet Yunyun, so I'm going out. Kazuma, I can
only say your plan gives me a very, very bad premonition, and I hope
you're sure about it. I'm trusting Darkness to you."

Megumin glanced anxiously over her shoulder several times, then
left reluctantly.

Frankly, I was just as happy that Megumin had somewhere to be.
Between her, Aqua, and Darkness, she was the one I was most worried
about leaving here alone.

"Sniiiiff… After I… After I worked so hard to put it back together…"
On the couch, Aqua blubbered over the ruined matchmaking photo she
had so recently repaired.

As I watched Megumin go, I could feel an intense gaze drilling into
my back.

It was Darkness, glaring at me silently with tears in her eyes.

And Aqua doing the same, also with tears in her eyes.

I—I admit, I'm a bit scared…

"C-calm down, you two. This is going to work out in the end."

Darkness didn't seem persuaded by my pained excuse.

"…And just how is that?"

I gave her and Aqua the rundown.

That is, I explained why she ought to go along with this one meeting if she wanted to continue adventuring.

This was a meeting with the son of a lord. If Darkness refused it,
her father would only come up with another match soon enough.

What was she going to do, just keep turning him down? Eventually, he would run out of patience and try to force her into something.

So why not take him up on this meeting and make sure things went wrong?

Not wrong enough to embarrass Darkness's family, of course—just enough that the other party would decide he wasn't interested.

Maybe that would make Darkness's dad a little more careful about who he tried to introduce to his daughter.

After all, if too many of them turned her down, it would be a disgrace to his household.

Aqua and I would attend the meeting, too, in the guise of servants. We would help make sure the guy walked away with zero interest in Darkness.

The prospective bachelor came from the house of a lord nobody liked much. Screwing things up here would presumably be less hard on the Dustiness family name than if her suitor were from a more well-respected household.

I finished explaining all this to the girls.

"Th-that's it, Kazuma! Let's do it! If your plan works, I won't have to knock my father around every time he comes up with some match for me!"

Man, I…I kind of feel sorry for him.

"I get it, that's a good idea! I figured your whole plan would be like, *If one troublesome person gets married off, we'll have room for a new party member and our lives will be that much easier!*"

I was shaken after hearing Aqua's words.

"O-of course not. We can't just let a great Crusader like Darkness go, can we? …Stoppit, you two, don't look at me like that… I'm serious, for the most part…!"

4

The Dustiness household.

Their residence was situated right on the town's main street, a testament to their status as a major noble family.

"I-is it true, Lalatina?! Will you really consider this offer of marriage?!"

Lalatina's—that is to say, Darkness's—father grasped her hands and exclaimed joyfully.

We were in the mansion her family kept in this town. We had come to let her father know that Darkness was willing to meet Alderp's son.

"It is true, Father. Your Lalatina has come to see that it may be best to entertain this prospect."

Aqua and I turned our faces down to hear her speak that way.

"H-hey, Kazuma, did you hear that? She calls him Father—capital *F*!"

"I-idiot... I'm more surprised to hear her call herself 'your Lalatina'..."

Our shoulders shook as we tried to hold back our laughter at the way this young rich woman, "Lalatina," talked. She blushed and glared at me.

Her father seemed dubious about our behavior.

"Lalatina, who are these people?"

Darkness raised a hand toward Aqua and me.

"These two are my most esteemed fellow adventurers. I have considered requesting them to accompany me to the meeting as my temporary butler and maid."

Her father frowned, unsure.

"Hmm. But..."

This was bad.

I took a confident step forward, put one hand in front of my chest, and stood up as straight as I could.

"A pleasure to meet you, sir. My name is Kazuma Satou. I'm an Adventurer, and I owe a great deal to Miss Lalatina, who has been with me constantly. If this match should indeed be safely made, sir, I fully expect that the difference in our stations shall prevent me from seeing Miss Lalatina again. I understand it is a most unusual request, but in light of this, I dearly wish to be by her side at this meeting to see that this man is someone I can truly trust with my most precious companion."

I delivered this entire speech without stumbling once, then gave a deep bow of my head.

I'm pretty darn cool, if I do say so myself.

I had the feeling that if I could safely send a fancy noblewoman off to marriage, I could do just about anything.

Darkness and Aqua gaped at me as if they had seen a leopard change its spots.

A servant showed us into a parlor.

"Please wait here a moment. We will select appropriate garments for you."

He sat us down on a couch, then prepared tea, after which he urged us to be at our leisure and left the room.

The parlor unmistakably belonged to a noble house. It seemed modest, but enough money had been spent on it to ensure it had the appropriate gravitas for such an important family.

We sat politely for a few minutes, but quickly tired of that.

I paced restlessly back and forth through the room, picking up one article after another and examining them. I didn't know how to appraise them, but I'm sure they were all expensive.

This painting, for example. At a glance you might mistake it for a child's scribbles, but I'm sure it was very modern.

I gazed at the image, rubbing my chin and muttering "Hmm" in a way that looked very much like I knew something about art.

"Kazuma, you like those scribbles that much?"

Aqua, who knew nothing about art, apparently felt she could criticize this show of appreciation.

"Well, what can I expect from the hoi polloi? This is called 'avant-garde art,' and for those who know how to assess it, it's truly spectacular. I'm sure this is the work of someone very famous."

I did my best to pretend I knew what I was talking about, while Aqua lounged on the couch and sipped tea.

"Well, I know something about art," she said, "and that just looks like scribbles to me."

I shrugged dramatically at hopeless Aqua. "I guess this just goes to show that the ability to create art and the ability to appreciate it are two separate things. Take this part, for example. It may look nonsensical, but clearly..."

As I began to lecture by the seat of my pants, Darkness walked in the room.

"Sorry to keep you two waiting... Kazuma, that's a picture of my father I drew when I was a kid. Dad loved it and hung it up there so he could brag about it to visitors, but personally I think it's embarrassing, so please don't examine it too closely... Wh-what are you doing?! Don't pull on my braid!"

I tugged on Darkness's hair to let off some of my humiliation as Aqua smirked at me. In the middle of it all, a maid walked in carrying outfits for a maid and a butler.

The maid bowed to me, the outfits still in her hands.

"Master Kazuma, this is your butler's uniform. I believe it should fit you, but please try it on to be sure."

I took a set of clothes from the maid and was led into the next room, where I changed.

Perfect fit.

"Looks good to me."

At that, the maid bowed and withdrew to a corner of the room.

Having convinced Darkness's father to take me on as a "temporary butler," and now really looking the part, I came out to where Darkness was waiting.

Aqua was already there in her maid outfit.

They say clothes make the man—or in this case, the woman. The uniform suited her surprisingly well.

"Hey, Aqua, that actually looks good on you. You'd fit right in with the staff here."

"Speak for yourself, Kazuma—you just scream 'apprentice butler.' I can picture it now: the more experienced butlers hazing you, you crying in some hidden corner of this mansion. Not bad, not bad at all!"

"What an interesting little scenario you have there. It's so interesting, in fact, that if we weren't in a noble's house right now, I'd make you pay for it... Oh well. Are you ready, *Miss Lalatina*?"

"S-stop calling me that! In public, at least…at least call me Young Lady."

Darkness's name seemed to embarrass her quite a bit.

Apparently the meeting was to be held at this house. And unfortunately, Darkness's dad had already made a certain request of me.

A very inconvenient request.

He had asked me to help make sure his daughter didn't act inappropriately toward the young man.

And he'd said something else I was having trouble with.

He'd told me that if the match went well, there would be a reward.

So not only had he asked me to look after his interests, but he'd thrown in a reward to sweeten the deal.

It couldn't help but motivate me.

I had planned on getting in the way as well as I could if Lord Alderp's son turned out to be no good, but now I was starting to think that maybe it would be possible to forgive some minor flaws.

"Come on, you two, this way. Are you ready? Do you both understand what to do? I'm counting on you." Darkness, visibly anxious, gave us final instructions, and then we turned toward the foyer where we were to meet our guest.

As she strode forward, flanked by Dustiness maids, Darkness was nothing so much as the precious daughter of a noble house.

As we made our way to the foyer, Aqua, walking behind me, eyed a number of the objects we passed.

"Hey, that looks pretty fancy…" She stared at a vase with a handle like she'd never seen one before.

Well, she'd seen through the drawing earlier. Maybe she did know what was valuable.

I began to take an interest in the vase that caught her attention. I picked it up casually, but it was surprisingly heavy.

"Fancy, huh? How much do you figure it's worth?"

"H-hey, don't go touching everything. That's my father's favorite vase…"

Darkness reached out for the handles on either side of the vase I'd picked up.

"My unclouded appraising eye can tell that this vase is worth…"

Ping!

""*Huh?!*""

With a ringing sound and a soft exclamation from both Darkness and me, a single handle was left in Darkness's hand.

"My appraising eye can tell this vase is junk now."

"Wh-wh-what do we do?! That was my father's vase!" She held the grip in her hand, fretting.

"St-stay calm! Your dad's not here right now. There are two possibilities. One, we tell him after the other guy gets here. He can't get angry with you in front of a guest. Two! We make some quick repairs with rice or something, then move it somewhere where it'll just fall on the floor when your dad picks it up."

"I—I see; that's brilliant! Good thinking, Kazuma, you're sharp! If we tell him about it in front of our guest, he'll just wait till the guy goes home to get angry. Let's do some temporary repairs and put it where it'll be easy to knock over—I'll tell the servants to be sure not to touch it!"

A Dustiness maid who had overheard our conversation said, "Pardon me, young sir, but…please do not teach the young lady such inappropriate things…"

5

Servants formed a neat line just outside the foyer, while Darkness and her father stood square in the middle of it.

Aqua and I were on either side of Darkness. It occurred to me to wonder where her mother was, but I couldn't spare too much thought for it right then.

"I can't tell you how happy I am that you've accepted this meeting. When Alderp came to me, I wondered what he could possibly want, but when I heard him out, I told him you wouldn't refuse. Alderp himself notwithstanding, his son, the young master Balter, is truly a good man. He will make you happy, Lalatina!"

Darkness's father smiled broadly at her.

But Darkness replied unequivocally.

"I find that most uncongenial, Father. Your Lalatina said only that she would consider the proposal. Heh-heh-heh… And after consideration, I have determined that it is too soon for me to be a bride. At this point in time nothing can be done—I have accepted this meeting, but I never said I would marry him! I shall make a mockery of this arranged match. A mockery! Ha-ha-ha-ha!"

Darkness had apparently decided there was no more need for games.

Her father regarded us seriously, his face growing pale.

"D-don't tell me… You two helped plan this all along…?!"

He eyed me with something like fear.

This was trouble. The blood had rushed to Darkness's head, and she was in danger of forgetting to stop before she hurt the family name.

She probably figured we were in too deep to pull back now.

Well, if she was done playing games, so was I.

"…Young Lady, please refrain from such unbecoming pronouncements."

At my words, Darkness and her father both looked at me in shock.

Aqua, who seemed to have taken a liking to the maid's outfit, happily flicked at the hem of her skirt, totally oblivious to what was going on.

Darkness, however, grasped all too well what was happening and scrunched up her face. Her father, on the other hand, beheld me with tears in his eyes as a savior from heaven.

"Kazuma, y-you fiend! You traitor!"

"It is hardly a betrayal, Young Lady. I am a butler, however temporarily, of the Dustiness household. Your happiness is my abiding wish."

"Oh-ho…," responded her father with admiration. "Y-young Kazuma—that's your name, isn't it? Even if this meeting doesn't result in a match, I'll— If only you can help Lalatina not to do anything ill-mannered—you will be rewarded generously! So p-please…!"

Before he could finish his thought, I gave a deep bow.

"Leave everything to me, sir. My every strength and effort shall be directed to the young lady's—"

Then it happened.

The door to the foyer opened with a click, and there was the young man from the picture, accompanied by an entourage of his own.

Darkness, seeking to seize the initiative, folded her arms, glared at the guy, and burst out:

"So you're the one I'm supposed to meet, huh! I'm Lalatina Ford Dustiness! You may call me Lady Dustiness."

"Oh, Young Lady! I'm afraid a mosquito has landed on the back of your head!"

And with that, I gave Darkness a firm smack.

6

Shortly after I had reined in Darkness…

On the pretext that I wanted to make sure the mosquito hadn't bitten her, I bought us some time by hustling Darkness away into the next room, leaving the guy with only her father to talk to.

"Geez, what's the big idea?! Weren't you supposed to be helping me?!"

Darkness grabbed me by the collar and dragged me out into the hallway.

Next to us, Aqua, who still hadn't fully grasped the situation, appeared to have grown enamored with the texture of Darkness's braid and poked at it contentedly.

Time for me to take the stand for a cross-examination.

"Now, now, calm yourself, Young Lady. You're forgetting one important thing."

"Don't call me Young Lady when we're alone! …And what important thing?"

Darkness seemed slightly mollified and ready to listen.

"You're losing sight of the fact that you don't want to do anything to damage your family name. If the Dustinesses get a bad reputation, it'll hurt you more than anyone, right?"

Darkness furrowed her brow.

"How will it hurt me? The worse my reputation gets, the fewer proposals I'll receive, and then I can just go adventuring like I want. The worst thing that can possibly happen is my father disinherits me, and I'm ready for that. With no home to inherit, I'll have to fight valiantly to survive—maybe it'll even become necessary to take the truly crazy quests! And eventually one will be so insane that I can't handle it, and some agent of the Demon King will capture me, tie me down, and...!
......That's the life I want to lead."

The young lady had expressed her ridiculous hopes for the future, but she wasn't finished.

"That guy's not even my type. My father has never brought me a decent prospect."

I looked askance at her then. I thought he seemed like a pretty good catch.

"Are you sure he's as bad as all that? Your dad made it sound like he was pretty great. I mean, I only have his looks to go on, but..."

She answered, "His name is Balter Barnes Alexei. He's a cool young man who seems to be made of better stuff than his father, and he's well regarded among the populace, too."

This brought a reaction from Aqua.

"Balter of the Alexei household has a good reputation in Axel, too. He often gives to the less fortunate. I've benefited from his generosity a number of times."

Wh-why, you...!

Darkness looked put out.

"No means no! My father should be giving to the poor! Not some noble family that just wants to marry us!"

"O-oh, so you mean... I get it. He puts up this great front, but actually he's involved in all kinds of shady stuff? S-sorry, I didn't realize..."

I should've known I was too quick to embrace that kid. I kind of regretted it. But Darkness went on:

"No! He's actually supposed to be a really good guy. He never gets angry, doesn't berate his servants when they make mistakes, just tries to figure out why the problem happened—it's so...so *weird*!"

...? He sounds pretty nice.

"He's also a really hard worker—he studies every day because the more he knows, the more he can help people. He's smart, and so good with a sword he was the youngest person ever to be knighted. There isn't a single bad rumor about him—he's like the picture of the perfect man. He speaks out against his father's poor leadership and is trying to change things."

....

"Hey," Aqua said, puzzled. "Everything you've said so far makes him sound like a pretty great catch, Darkness. So what don't you like about him?"

"What don't I like about him?! Everything! Anything! First of all, nobles are supposed to act like nobles! Have a permanent condescending smirk on their faces! Yet he looks at me with those clear, honest eyes—what's *that* about? Can't he, you know...look at me with a nasty drinking-me-in expression like Kazuma does when I'm hanging around the house lightly dressed?"

"Wh-wh-what? I d-d-do not look at you like that!"

Darkness ignored my questionable protests and went on.

"And he doesn't get angry when his people make mistakes? Ridiculous! When a maid screws up, you do whatever you want to her and call it punishment—it's practically a sign of good breeding among the elite! He doesn't understand anything! His servants probably mess up on purpose because they *want* him to yell at them! If you call yourself a noble, you should at least have the resourcefulness to have a tryst with every single maid in the house!"

"I'm pretty sure you're the only one who thinks any of that."

Darkness completely ignored my interjection—her fist was clenched as if to say she could hardly take it anymore. Her torrential argument continued unabated.

"That guy could probably take on the world by himself—he's the exact opposite of my type! I don't care if he's thin as a rail or big as a boulder, he just shouldn't look so striking. I want him to be totally devoted to me—but he should be weak-willed enough that if a pretty young thing passes by, he can't help leering at her. And he's got to be kind of pervy, in the mood at every hour of the day—that's a must. It sure wouldn't hurt if he was in a bit of debt! And he should never work, just drink all day—but he'd blame society for his problems. Then he'd throw an empty bottle at me and shout, 'Hey, Darkness! Go use that worthless body of yours to scrounge us up some cash!' ...Nnggh..."

Her explanation ended as she began to quiver and blush too hard to go on.

Damn! There's no hope for this girl—I'm already too late.

Aqua and I stood there, despair looming over us, when suddenly—

"...Enough!" Darkness announced. "I'll ruin this meeting myself! If you want to try to stop me, Kazuma, just be ready for the consequences!" Then she left the room, her fury obvious.

Aqua and I stood there by ourselves for a moment, silent.

Finally Aqua said in a barbed tone, "Kazuma, just what are you playing at?"

"You saw her father's face," I said. "That's a man who's genuinely worried about his daughter's future. And you heard what she said about the guy's reputation. In other words, this isn't a political marriage—it's a dad who really wants his daughter to be happy."

"So what?" Aqua said hotly. "He still doesn't have the right to make life decisions for her just because—"

But I didn't let her finish.

"Darkness is nobility. I think it's pretty common for nobles not to be able to make their own marriages. If you're born an aristocrat, you get to grow up in the lap of luxury, receive the best education...not that you could tell by looking at Darkness. But in return for living off tax money, you don't get as much freedom as the common people. Every status in life has its pros and cons. Commoners have freedom but no money. Nobles have money but no freedom. To grow up with everything—and then to want to determine the course of your own life, too? That's just selfish. If anything, I'm impressed she got away with living her own life for as long as she did. And then she gets to marry a guy with no flaws! I'll bet no one would be very amused to hear she objected to that."

But no matter how long I talked at her, Aqua didn't seem convinced.

"...But! Doesn't it still just seem like too much...?!"

"Well, that's not the only reason..."

Aqua stood stock-still at that.

"...What?"

I crouched in toward her, my face serious.

"Aqua. Our goal is to defeat the Demon King and make it back to Earth, right? And what does Darkness really want?"

Aqua leaned in, too, looking slightly confused, as if she wasn't sure I was asking her honestly.

"Um... I don't...? T-to skip marriage and just go adventuring with us...?"

When she tried to give a safe answer, I found myself shouting:

"Wrong! I'm not asking about what she wants on the surface! You know what I'm talking about—say it! Don't be embarrassed; just say it! I want to see the expression on your face when you have to put it into words!"

"She wants super-strong monsters to overpower her and do all kinds of pervy stuff to her! ...K-Kazuma, I think this counts as sexual harassment already..."

She was on the verge of tears, but I pushed on.

"No, it doesn't! Look, you may be a real idiot yourself, but she's an *absolute* idiot who's way beyond help! Her dream is to be abducted and tortured by monsters? Moron! Try telling her dad that! If you've got the guts! *Sorry, sir, but your beloved daughter has big dreams of being assaulted by monsters! Please put off the wedding so she can go make her dreams come true!* You go tell him that!"

"I'm sorry! I can't! I can't tell him!" No sooner had she apologized than Aqua said hesitantly, "B-but does that mean you think marrying that guy is the right thing to do? I mean, Darkness seems to have her own type and all…"

"Dumbass. So she doesn't get to marry her type. Boo-hoo. You heard how she described her 'type.' Just imagine if she actually found her ideal man and brought him home. Listen up. We're going to push ahead with this Balter guy. He looks like a good person, so we're going to take the hit on this one. Darkness is sure to try something, so we have to keep a short leash on her. It sounds like Balter's way nicer than his dad. So even if they get married, he'd probably let her go on an adventure every once in a while. So Dad's happy, I'm happy, Darkness stops going on all those dangerous adventures, and best of all, we get rid of one of our three problem party members."

I thrust my fist in the air and straightened up.

"Anyway, you can't make a living as an adventurer your whole life! It's such a grim occupation—if you have a chance to get out, you should take it! Heck, I'm constantly thinking about quitting! Let's not mince words. Darkness is an idiot. If it were just that she wanted to be an adventurer, sure! That'd be great! I'd even cheer her on! But no, again, she's an *idiot*. It may not be exactly right to stick your nose into another person's family business, but our goal is to get Darkness safely married off! And if we can't manage that, Plan B is to leave the Dustiness name in good enough condition that she can be married out of the party at any time!"

"Hey, wait a second! You never actually answered my question!"

7

"Very sorry to keep you waiting, sirs and lady."

"Very sorry."

Aqua and I came in as Balter and Darkness's dad were having a chat. We stood next to Darkness, who shot glances at both of us.

"I can see your point of view, Kazuma," Aqua said. "I really wish Darkness could marry a person she loves and be happy, but things are going to get out of hand here."

"I'm so glad you understand. Now, you do whatever you want. I'll be trying to make sure that guy is in love with Darkness by the end of this meeting!"

I couldn't tell if Darkness was able to hear what the two of us were whispering, but she hissed in my ear, "Stop right now, and I won't blame you for any of this. Otherwise, when this is all over, I'll make you wish you were dead."

Yikes.

But at the moment, I was immune to intimidation.

After all, right now I could hide behind an ally even more powerful than Darkness.

That's right...

"Sir, I hope you will not consider me too forward, but perhaps the moment has come to begin the meeting of the young lady and Lord Balter. Our young lady has been most eager."

Darkness ground her teeth at me in a silent demand to not say another word.

Her father, of course, didn't notice but happily agreed with me. In his own fatherly way, he didn't seem particularly perturbed that I'd smacked his daughter upside the head to shut her up just a few minutes before. In fact, he seemed kind of relieved.

Now I knew I had his blessing and that I could get away with a certain amount of tomfoolery.

"Very well. Lord Balter, Lalatina," Darkness's dad said. "Come with me. Let's go to the parlor."

Darkness suddenly stumbled.

"Oh, the heel of my shoe seems to have broken. Lord Balter, would you lend me your hand...?" And she stretched out her hand toward Balter.

Her tone, at least, was perfectly polite, perhaps in an effort to avoid another smack from me. But alarms were going off in my head. She had to be planning something.

I quickly held out a hand and said, "At your service, Young Lady. However much you may fancy young Lord Balter, surely you mustn't ask him to support you before you are even engaged. My apologies, milord. Our young lady has been in a most unusual humor toda— Oowowowow you're gonna break it—shall break— Young Lady! Cut it— Please st-stop these p-pranks…"

Tears brimming in my eyes, I shook out the hand Darkness had grabbed as hard as she could.

C-curse her…! Maybe that was what she'd planned to do to Balter if I hadn't intervened…

"Wh-what's wrong? Are you all right?" Balter asked me with concern as I pressed on my hand and wiped the tears from my eyes.

What a sweet guy! Please, please take this crazy lady off my hands!

"Heh-heh-heh. Nothing at all, milord. Shall we go?"

As I watched Darkness stride off with Balter, Aqua discreetly leaned in and cast Heal on my hand.

Darkness's father put his palms together apologetically and dipped his head.

"Now then, let me introduce myself properly. I am Balter Barnes Alexei, eldest son of the Alexei family and assisting in my father's governance."

Darkness and Balter were seated across from each other at a white table in the parlor.

Balter was quite the charmer.

He was about a head taller than me and so well built, you could tell it even through his clothes—he probably trained every day.

And he gazed at my charge with a calm smile on his face.

Aqua and I stood unnaturally close to Darkness.

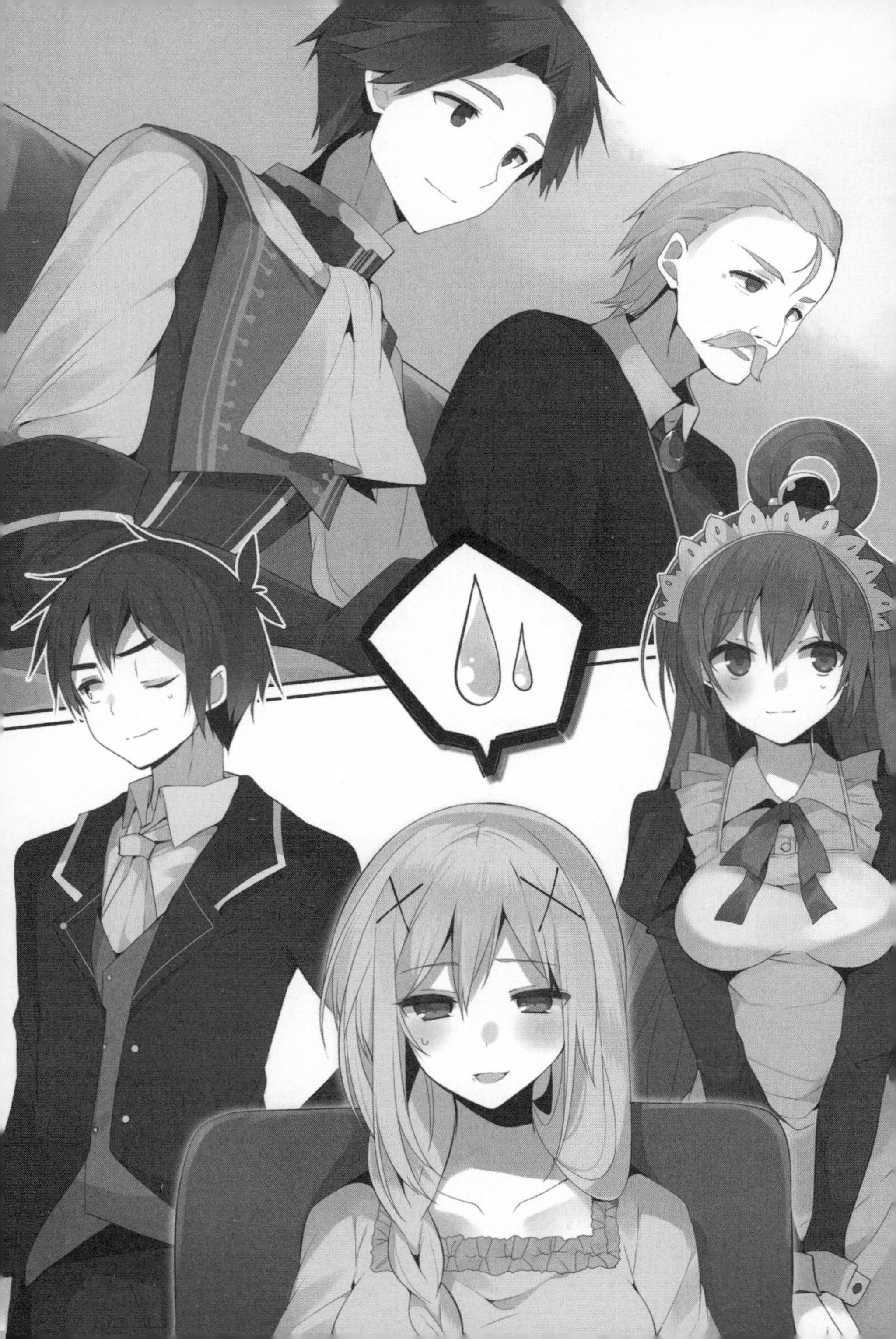

Balter seemed to take note of this, but as Darkness's father didn't say anything, he could hardly bring it up.

"I am Lalatina Ford Dustiness. I will forego a lengthy introduction of my family, which I presume even the son of a playboy lord knows wel— Eeyowch!"

As she veered into an insult, Darkness was suddenly facedown on the table, blushing and quivering slightly.

"Wh-what's wrong?" Balter asked in concern.

"N-nothing... I simply couldn't stand to look at the young lord's face anym— Hrrgh!"

Down again, this time red up to her ears.

"Young Lady Darkness has been feeling ill to her stomach since this morning. Oh, Darkness! If you have a stomachache, you shouldn't overexert yourself!"

"What? Th-that's not—"

Darkness, embarrassed, tried to deny Aqua's improvised remark.

I nudged Aqua, whose bit of ad-libbing caused more problems than it solved, and said, "Our young lady has been in a tizzy of excitement since this morning in anticipation of meeting Lord Balter. Observe our young lady's countenance! She is quite crimson with modesty!"

"I-indeed, my face is red... How e-embarrassing..."

I leaned a little harder on my foot and whispered so only Darkness could hear—as I crushed her foot under the table: "Okay, *Young Lady*? Any more shenanigans and I'll stomp even harder."

I wasn't completely sure Darkness had heard me, but with strained breath, she muttered, "...Y-you'll pay for this..."

Ah, our young lady. Ever civil.

By that point, her dad seemed to have grasped what was going on underneath the table. He'd figured it out quickly enough to suggest he was familiar with his daughter's quirks.

I wanted to give him a piece of my mind for letting his daughter grow up like this, but now wasn't the time.

Her dad picked up the flow, changing the subject to Balter to help cover for what was happening with Darkness and me.

"Lord Balter, I've heard your mansion was recently destroyed. Have you any place to live? I'm sure we have space for you here—in a separate room from my daughter, of course."

His tone was joking, and Balter played right along.

"Ha-ha-ha! No, sir, I'm sure I could barely restrain myself even being in the same house with someone as lovely as Lalatina..."

Darkness's face remained red, and she still trembled gently, but otherwise the talk went smoothly after that.

8

Darkness's father said he was probably just getting in the young people's way, and he excused himself.

As he walked out, he patted me on the shoulder and whispered, "I'm counting on you."

Now Darkness and Balter were taking a walk in the garden of the Dustiness mansion, with Aqua and me in tow. And what a garden!

The sprawling grounds boasted a huge lake, and even though it was winter, colorful flowers bloomed everywhere—maybe they'd been bred for it, or maybe they were just that high quality.

Aqua watched the fish in the lake, then gave a whistle and a clap.

At first I wondered what she was doing. Then I noticed the fish had flocked to her.

...Actually, that's pretty neat. I'll have to have her teach me how to do it later.

"Milady Lalatina, do you have any hobbies?"

While we stood there, quite taken by the lake, Balter asked the kind of inane question usually required for a get-together like this.

"Oh, I've always been rather fond of goblin hunti— Grrrg!"

I jabbed an elbow into Darkness's ribs as she began to run her mouth.

Balter responded with a crooked smile and a cock of the head. I had, after all, been staying abnormally close to Darkness all day.

"...You two seem like quite good friends."

I frowned. *Aww, crud.*

Darn! What was I going to do if I'd gone too far and was about to hurt Darkness's reputation instead of helping it?

After all, how could two prospective partners meet each other with a butler an elbow length away all the time?

Darkness saw me grasping for the words to smooth this over and gave me a vicious smirk.

Oh no. What's she...?

"My butler, Kazuma, and I are indeed very close. We're together every day. We eat together, we bathe together, and of course at night we—we— Hrrr...!"

One ridiculous thing after another came out of her mouth until, suddenly, her face turned red and she swallowed her words.

Geez, doesn't she have any shame?

"My young lady does love to joke. She has an adorable way of saying things that are personally embarrassing. Isn't it sweet? Miss Lalatina? What's wrong, my dear Lalatina? Lalatina, your face is so red..."

"Hrr... J-Just...you...wait..."

Darkness grit her teeth and held back tears at hearing her cute little name so many times in a row.

All right. That ought to keep her in line for a few minutes.

Balter gave us a bittersweet smile and said, "You two are as close as you say. It's enough to make a man jealous."

"Oh, you jest, sir. We are merely a lady and her butler having a jape..."

At that, Darkness gasped a little and took a quick step away from me.

What's this?

"This has gone on long enough! When are you going to drop this stupid act?!"

And before I could stop her, Darkness ripped the hem clean off her dress.

Her thighs were clearly visible; there was no way to avoid her *ero*-ness. Or the perv-ness of the way she had shortened her skirt so it was easy to move in, with a slit down the side.

Balter quickly averted his eyes, and Darkness yelled, "You—Balter! Your class is Knight, so you know how to use a sword, don't you? My class is Crusader, and you're coming with me to the training grounds! Then I'm going to find out what you're really made of. Now, come on!"

I had no hope of stopping Darkness. This crazy fit had come on too suddenly.

"Look at this man, Balter. At this Kazuma, who has gazed lasciviously upon my noble self for all this time!"

I w-w-wasn't looking!

I just glanced out of curiosity...

9

"The duel goes until one of us cries uncle. If you can make me cry, *Hold, enough!*—if you can wring the words *I can't take any more!* from my lips—then I will marry you or go anywhere you wish!"

Darkness had brought us all to the training grounds.

In the middle of the field, she tossed a wooden training sword to Balter. He caught it, then gave it an exploratory swing with a troubled expression.

"Ahem... Milady Lalatina, I am a Knight. A training implement this may be, but I cannot raise a sword against a woman."

Darkness appeared profoundly displeased at this.

"You soft-headed lout. You see Kazuma over there? He prides himself as a proponent of equality between the sexes, and he's told women he's more than willing to drop-kick them. You could learn a thing or two from him."

Balter did look at me, but somehow, I didn't want him to.

He exhaled as though he'd made up his mind.

"...Very well. To be honest, I came here fully intending to refuse the match my father was trying to force upon me... But when I saw you, I had a change of heart. You are unlike the other run-of-the-mill noble girls. Nothing less, I suppose, from the only daughter of the 'kingdom's confidant.' You were unaffected yet charmingly shy about your own words. You were so willing to speak your mind and so willing to treat your servants as if they were your peers, not your inferiors. I admit my interest was piqued... En garde, then, Milady Lalatina!"

The only thing more sudden than his declaration of infatuation was the way he leaped at Darkness!

His stroke was swift; it knocked Darkness's sword clear out of her hands, and then his wooden blade rested at her shoulder.

Balter gave a small sigh. He must have thought that meant the duel was over.

But Darkness picked up her weapon as if nothing had happened.

"All right. Next. Have at you!"

About thirty minutes later...

"S-surely this is enough! Surely you can see who has the advantage? Why will you not concede?"

Balter had been the better fighter in every bout, yet he was the one who seemed to be at his wit's end.

In terms of sheer skill, Balter was clearly superior. Darkness's blade had never so much as grazed him, but his had delivered more than a few sound blows to her. Some of them were starting to bruise already.

But despite her ragged breathing, the light hadn't gone out of Darkness's eyes. Drenched in sweat, her cheeks glowing, she shouted, "What's wrong? No need to hold back—give me all you've got! Let me witness a truly dominating strength!"

Faced with such a woman, he cast his sword aside and raised both hands in a gesture of surrender.

"...I give, Milady Lalatina. I have lost. I may have outdone you in swordsmanship but not in strength of spirit. I cannot strike you again... You are a very strong person."

Balter gave Darkness a starstruck sort of look, then smiled.

Darkness, for her part, slumped her shoulders dejectedly. "...What, it's over? Pathetic. Go train some more, and come back when you can fight."

Balter positively laughed at that—a joyous, unrestrained laugh.

Then he said, so softly I wasn't sure Darkness could hear him, "...I really have fallen for you..."

Just a little murmur.

Someone who didn't know any better might have taken it for a nice story. How Darkness outlasted Balter and was able to show how resolute she was.

But I knew what was going through her head, and the scene couldn't move me the same way...

Balter probably took Darkness's harsh breathing and ruddy cheeks as the signs of a Crusader straining to endure pain.

Aqua went up to Darkness, who was still panting, and healed her wounds.

I heaved a deep sigh. My companion picked up the sword Balter had thrown away.

"All right, Kazuma, come at me. Show Balter your mercilessness and total disregard for human decency!"

I was just sitting in a corner of the training ground with no idea what she was going on about, but she gave me the sword.

All right, what *is going on here?*

No way. She had that fire in her eyes from the fight with Balter—no way was I going up against that.

"I, too, would like to see the fighting style of one whom Milady Lalatina trusts so deeply," Balter said.

He just couldn't keep his mouth shut, could he?

"Ooh!" Aqua, done healing Darkness's wounds, seemed eager to see how this would play out.

Geez, what's the deal?

"Okay, fine. I get it. Guess the matchmaking's scuttled anyway. And you aren't the type to spread nasty rumors about the 'young lady.'" I dropped my pretense toward Balter, talking to him like a normal person, and stood with a grunt.

"Excellent, Kazuma! I've always wanted to try sparring with you! The complete lack of moral grounding that makes you willing to Steal a girl's underwear the first time you fight her—the cruel cleverness that allows you to attack your opponent's weakness! Now—come at me with everything you've got!"

Balter looked at me as Darkness spoke, but I really, really didn't want him to.

I had no intention of going toe-to-toe with such a hot-and-heavy opponent on such a cold day.

I stuck out my free hand.

"*Create Water!*"

Liquid appeared over Darkness's head.

"Wha—?!"

I cocked my head at Balter's surprised reaction.

"Something wrong...?"

Balter replied a bit stumblingly, "N-no, it's just... Typically, one doesn't use magic in a duel of swords..."

Oh, I get it.

...Wait a second...

Aqua was looking at Darkness and murmuring, "You've done it again, Kazuma. You've proved no one is a more talented sexual harasser than you. You've actually done it."

I followed her gaze and looked at Darkness. She was drenched—turning her undergarments transparent. Combined with her torn skirt, it... Let's just say I was very grateful. Very grateful.

Balter found himself completely unable to look at Darkness. Instead, he stared intensely at the ground.

"Heh... Heh-heh! Behold, Balter! I thought I was in a sword battle—and now here I am in this humiliating state! This is what you can learn from this man!"

Darkness stood there dripping and apparently eager to invite a misunderstanding.

"I—I didn't mean to...! Aww, damn it!"

She'd wanted me to come at her with everything I had, and...well, I did.

I'd used magic once already—no point in not using it again!

"*Freeze!*"

"?!?!?!"

Suddenly Darkness was turning blue and hugging herself.

"Y-you devil! To get me soaking wet in the middle of winter...and then use *ice* magic...!"

"Well, they don't call him Cad-zuma and Trash-zuma for nothing!"

Geez, enough from the peanut gallery!

"Heh—ah-ha-ha-ha-ha-ha-ha-haaa! Yes! This mercilessness! This is it—!"

And before she'd even finished speaking, Darkness leaped at me!

10

This was bad. And at this rate, it was only going to get worse.

Darkness raised her wooden blade tauntingly at me as I stood there looking stricken.

To be fair, I could dodge the attack easily—no matter how frenzied she was, she always launched herself in a straight line, sometimes at the wrong distance or even in the wrong direction.

"What's wrong, Kazuma?! Starting to sweat?!"

As she jumped at me, I could see Darkness trembling from the cold, but her fervor was causing her to sweat. She seemed to be enjoying herself.

I had landed several blows, but she had never so much as yelped.

"That's the way, Darkness! Kazuma's a beanpole! No way he can keep up a fight very long!"

Darn it, I said enough *from the peanut gallery!*

"Heh-heh, you're not moving so well anymore. I think it's about time to end this!"

Darkness, egged on by Aqua's shouting, smiled dauntlessly, threw away her sword—she couldn't hit anything with it anyway—and flew at me barehanded.

Aww, crap! I've got zero chance in a hand-to-hand fight!

"That's it! Grab him! Wring his neck! When you get your hands on him, there's no way that scrawny Kazuma can stand up to you!"

Dammit, why is she cheering for Darkness?! We'll see whose neck gets wrung when this is all over!

As I mentally cursed Aqua, Darkness came at me with her arms open wide as if for a big hug.

I threw away my sword, too, and prepared to clasp my hands with hers as we pitted our strength against each other.

"You think you can beat me in a contest of brawn? You fool!" Darkness exclaimed, and gleefully joined hands with me. "I don't know what you're thinking, but a mere Adventurer is no match for a mighty Crusaderrraaaghhh!" Her revelry turned to a scream.

Now she tried to break away from me, but I held fast to her hand.

"What, not so confident anymore? Come on, Darkness, say something! Bwa-ha-ha! Surely you didn't think I would face you head-to-head? You know me better than thaaaaahh!"

Now it was my turn for triumph to become a scream as she grabbed my hand as hard as she could. She wore a mad grin, and her eyes burned.

"Heh... Heh-heh-heh-heh! S-so this is D-Drain Touch...! But I can break your arm before you can drain my health...!"

"J-j-j-juuust see i-i-i-i-if you caaan! Eeeeyowowowow!"

There we were: me trying to absorb her HP with Drain Touch, her trying to shatter my limb through brute force.

Neither of us asked any quarter; neither gave any.

I was starting to bend under Darkness's sheer power, but I could see her face crumpling as well.

Geez! I was draining as hard as I could, but I couldn't seem to find the end of her HP...!

"H-hey, Darkness! W-wanna make a little wager? You challenged me b-because I p-pissed you off, right? W-well, the loser has to d-do any one th-thing the winner asks...!"

I spoke through gritted teeth. Darkness leaned in to get every bit of advantage out of her strength.

"A w-wager—?! Heh... Heh-heh...! Y-you're just trying to b-buy time with chatter... We can wager or d-do whatever you want... If I win, you'll h-have to apologize with your f-forehead in the dirt...!"

There's my chance!

"Promise? Y-you're sure...?!"

"Y-yeah, that's it! And you b-better get ready—give up now! Or I really will break your arm!"

She was throwing her entire body weight into the effort, but my tone suggested I had already won:

"S-sure? Totally s-sure? You prom—promise...?! When I win, you won't get off with a weepy little apology...!"

It sure didn't look like I had any chance. I gave Darkness an unexpected grin.

It must have taken her by surprise, because she relaxed ever so slightly.

"...? What do you mean? What will you ask if I lose?"

"Something that'll leave you bright red and weeping with humiliation...! Bwa-ha-ha! You've already promised! All right, it's on! I can already see you begging for my forgiveness after I win...! *Please*, I'll make you say! *Please forgive me!*"

Darkness trembled slightly at that. And the twisting on my arm lightened just a little.

"Hrk…! Wh-what is it you'll make me do? T-tell me! Out with it!"

"Bwaaa-ha-ha-ha-haaa! Something far, far worse than you're picturing right now, I guarantee!"

"Wha—?! St-stop it…! Hrk… I-I'm trying to resist, but I'm still being drained…! At this rate…!"

Drain Touch affects only vitality, but I could feel Darkness's strength waning until she dropped to one knee.

"*Haaah… Haah…* Wh-what will you make me do…?! *Haaah… Haah…* At—at this rate, I won't be able…to go on…"

Darkness was red and breathing hard. A single bead of sweat ran from the nape of her neck to her collarbone.

"First I'll keep on draining until you lose consciousness. You can savor the anticipation of what will happen when you wake up…!"

"Ahh! Wh-why, you…! Hrrgh… I've lost this bout… But no matter what humiliations you inflict on me, you won't…have my…heart…! Will it…will it be…something awful?!"

Psst.
The next two pages reflect the original Japanese orientation, so read backward!

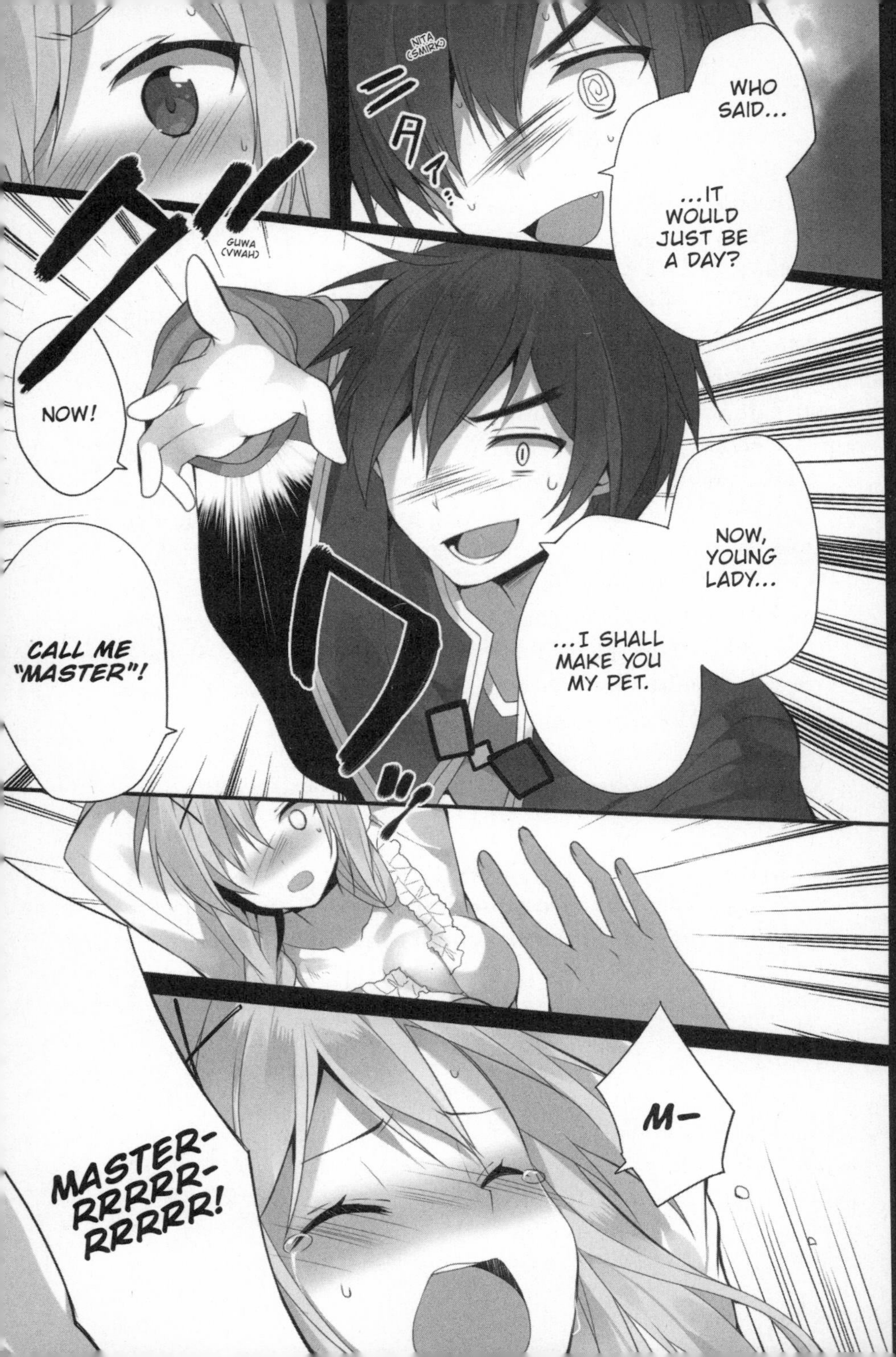

WHO SAID...
...IT WOULD JUST BE A DAY?
NITA (SMIRK)
GUWA (VWAH)
NOW, YOUNG LADY...
...I SHALL MAKE YOU MY PET.
NOW!
CALL ME "MASTER"!
M-
MASTER-RRRRR-RRRRR!

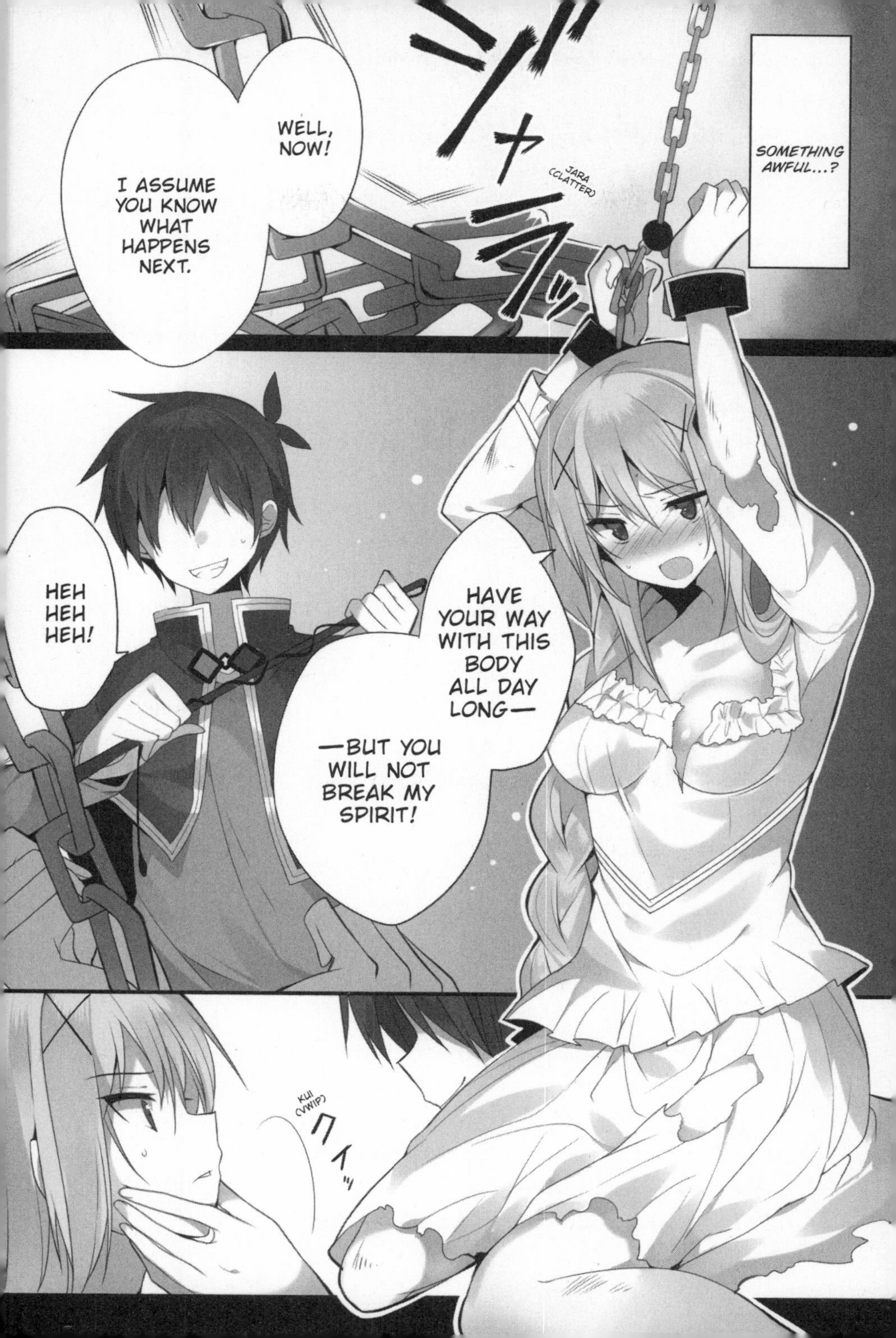
SOMETHING AWFUL...?
JARA (CLATTER)
WELL, NOW!
I ASSUME YOU KNOW WHAT HAPPENS NEXT.
HAVE YOUR WAY WITH THIS BODY ALL DAY LONG—
—BUT YOU WILL NOT BREAK MY SPIRIT!
HEH HEH HEH!
KUI (VWIP)

Both her hands in mine, her face upturned with anticipation, Darkness collapsed into a sitting position on the earth of the training ground.

Balter said in a shocked voice, "You didn't simply win—when you knew victory was yours, you forced her to wager! How merciless! Not for nothing do they call you Cad-zuma!"

"H-hey!"

Aqua went over to where Darkness was slumped on the ground and began to administer first aid.

And then...

"I heard you all were at the training grounds, so I brought drinks for—"

With the best worst timing, Darkness's dad walked up.

The tray of drinks he was carrying fell from his hands and clattered to the ground.

Servants rushed up to find out what was the matter, then their jaws hung open.

All of them gaped at Darkness—bruises all over, skirt torn, absolutely drenched, leaving nothing to the imagination and completely unladylike, while Aqua tended to her.

As everyone else looked at Darkness, Balter and I instinctively exchanged a glance.

Aqua pointed at us. "It's their fault!"

"Very well. Put them both to death."

"No, sir, this is a misunderstanding!" Balter and I yelled in unison.

11

Between us, Balter and I desperately explained the situation, and somehow we managed to come out unscathed.

Balter knew now who Aqua and I really were—though to be fair, he seemed to have suspected all along that I wasn't a butler.

Darkness—the reason we were in this mess—was still asleep, thanks to the beating she'd taken from my skills.

Conducted to the parlor, we watched over her. She had been changed into the tight black skirt and shirt she usually wore for adventuring.

Finally her father spoke, looking at his daughter.

"She never was much of a people person...even with those who were close to her. Young Kazuma, you are a member of her party, aren't you? She didn't talk overmuch of herself, did she?"

I cocked my head at him.

I wonder.

Now that I thought about it, I realized I didn't actually know a whole lot about Darkness.

I mean, she never talked that much, and when she did, she was usually spouting some no-good nonsense.

"Even after my daughter became a Crusader, she was often alone. She spent every day at the church of Our Lady Eris, praying that she might find companions to adventure with. She told me joyfully once that on her way home from church one day, she finally made a friend, a companion—a Thief girl..."

I knew Eris was a goddess you could count on! Ah, my lady, what fine work you do...

"She lost her mother at a young age... I never took another wife and have had to raise her myself. She's had only a man, and a doting one at that, to bring her up. Perhaps I did her a disservice in that way," he said, looking solemn. He seemed to be talking about Darkness's... tendencies.

Was he implying that she liked being chained because she'd had too much freedom growing up? *Sorry, Dad. I think she's just always been this way.*

"Miss Lalatina outdoes any man I've met and is, I believe, a truly wonderful woman. If young Kazuma were not in the picture, I would indeed wish to take her as my wife!"

Aaaand there went Balter. What the hell was he talking about? Darkness was just a friend.

I won't lie—there were plenty of things about her that made me pretty horny, but that didn't mean anything. True, I'd never want her to end up with someone like Lord Alderp, who was just going to use her, but I would be perfectly supportive of a match with a decent guy who appreciated her.

"I'm sorry," I said, "but I'm not quite sure I follow."

"Come now," Balter replied in a *You don't need to hide it* tone. "You are clearly more able than I to make Miss Lalatina happy. I saw how implicitly you trust each other. Are you two not very much in love?"

"Okay, let's step outside. Lord's son or not, I've gotta set you straight about a few things."

"Kazuma, stop! If you have to beat him up, do it when I'm not around! I don't wanna get executed, too!"

Aqua tried to hold me back as I went to Drain Touch the daylights out of Balter.

"Baaah-ha-ha-ha-ha!"

Darkness's dad suddenly let out a huge guffaw.

What now? There have been way too many twists and turns already today. I don't think I can take any more.

"All right then! Sir Balter. If my daughter ends up too old to marry, will you take her?"

The spontaneous offer caught Balter off guard.

"O-of course, I would be most pleased, but—"

He seemed to be looking at me, but Dad cut him off:

"And young Kazuma."

"Huh?! I mean—yes, sir?"

I was every bit as startled as Balter.

"I ask that you look after my daughter. Try to make sure she doesn't do anything *too* stupid. Please."

Wait—what exactly was he saying?

Surely he meant as her friend and fellow adventurer, right?

I mean, of course I would. It would be exactly what I'd been doing all along.

*   *   *

"...nn...? Hmm......? The parlor? ...Ahh... I see..."

Darkness sat up.

At the same moment, the memories of what had happened before she lost consciousness seemed to rush back.

"C-could it all be over now? What indecent things did you do to me while I was asleep?!"

"Nothing! I haven't done anything to you! Stop saying things everyone's gonna take the wrong way! Everything got a little tense after you conked out."

At that, Darkness scanned the room, then smirked at me.

...What? What was she thinking?

I recalled what Darkness had said before the meet-up started.

When this is all over, I'm gonna make you wish you were dead.

No—I was safe now. No matter what she said next, there would be no problem.

Just stay calm. I'm super-cool today.

Just stay calm and deal with whatever...

"Father. Sir Balter. Please pretend this matchmaking meeting never happened. There is something I have been keeping from you until now... But I am carrying Kazuma's child."

"What the hell?! I'm a virgin; you can't play that card! How are you carrying my child when we've never done anything? You're a virgin, too! Are you Mary? I oughta whack you right in the stomach!"

Darkness's outrageous announcement and my reaction drew a strange smile from Balter.

"I see—so you've been pregnant with young Kazuma's child all this time. In that case, I suppose there's nothing to be done—I concede my pursuit of you."

Then he stood up.

Curse you, Darkness...

She'd been asleep. She didn't know she didn't have to come up with some ridiculous way out of this anymore.

Konosuba: God's Blessing on This Wonderful World! You're Being Summoned, Darkness

"I'll tell my father that it was I who refused the match. I believe that will be more convenient for all of us."

...Geez. What a class act.

Are you sure *you don't want Darkness...?*

Darkness was giving me a *Gotcha!* look. I heaved a sigh. Fine. I could adventure with her a little longer...

That was when Darkness and I realized that two other people in the room were wearing odd expressions.

"A grandchild... My first grandchild... Sh-sh-sh-shall I have my first lovely grandchild...?!"

"Whaaaaaaaat?! Kazuma, when did you and Darkness get to be—y'know—that close?! I've gotta tell everybody! Everyone in town's gotta know!"

Dad was weeping from joy, and Aqua was completely taken in. It took about a half hour of persuading to convince them both that it wasn't true.

12

"Good gods. If I'd known things would turn out this way, I would've just outright refused the meeting in the first place!"

"You're telling me! I admit I'm really lucky you covered for me against Lord What's-His-Face. But look. In the future, don't pull another self-sacrifice stunt like that. Everyone was worried sick waiting for you to come back!" I said.

"So Kazuma tries to foist Darkness on that guy Balter, and now he wants to pretend like it was no big deal! Shows you what kind of a man he is!" Aqua exclaimed.

"Yeah! Worried sick, indeed!" Darkness said. "Just now you were trying to get rid of someone you didn't like...! And Aqua, I'm pretty sure you were looking to get me married off, too."

Aqua and I just plugged our ears and pretended not to hear her.

Darkness sighed deeply—but then something seemed to occur to her.

"You know what, Kazuma? You did win our duel earlier. So what demand do you plan to make of me? What could be worse than my most awful imaginings…?!"

As she spoke, her cheeks got redder, and she watched me with anticipation.

Huh. I guess we did agree to something like that.

Hoo boy. What should I make her do?

Wait a second…this could be the perfect chance.

…Wait a second again.

"A-Aqua, you're…you're really close…"

"…I'm just curious what you're going to make Darkness do. What kind of awful thing do you have in mind? Hey, I know you're angry with Darkness for making you worry like that, but don't make it *too* awful, okay…?"

So Darkness watched me with anticipation, Aqua with trepidation.

"I-I'll take my time deciding after we get settled in the house…"

And with that lame attempt to buy myself time, I opened the door…

"*Sob… Sniff!* Th-this is too muuuuch! Megumin! It's too muuuch!"

"Stop crying! Kazuma and the others will be back soon!. If they showed up now, they would surely think I was the bad guy h— Oh."

Yunyun, a crying mess, was in our foyer.

I locked eyes with Megumin, who was trying to comfort her, and quietly closed the door again.

But it immediately burst back open.

"Please pretend you did not see that! I can offer a full explanation!"

"Don't worry. We already knew you were a bully anyway," I said, as though I'd figured it all out.

"I'm not! In fact, in school I used to—! But that's neither here nor there! This is not the time to be fretting over Yunyun…!"

As the words tumbled from her mouth, Megumin waved her staff frantically.

"It's all right! I'm f-f-f-ine! She's right—this isn't the time to be fretting about me…! Wah—waaaaah!"

"Ahh! Goodness, what a troublemaker…! Excuse me—please leave the two of us alone for a moment!"

Then Megumin shut the door again. We could hear Yunyun and her talking indistinctly inside.

At length, the door opened a third time, and Yunyun came out, blowing her nose.

"S-sorry for the fuss…"

And with a little bow, she hurried on her way.

Uh…huh.

We all looked at one another, then at the mournfully departing Yunyun.

We went inside again, to find Megumin slumped exhaustedly on the carpet.

But she jumped up when she saw my face.

"Kazuma, this is bad! Most terrible!"

"Yeah, I kinda figured that out from the way you two were acting."

"No! Forget about Yunyun for a minute! That is something like a family dispute, and you needn't concern yourself with it. I'll explain everything sometime when we have a moment!"

Actually, I'm extremely interested in what happened, but okay.

Megumin, however, seemed like she was more concerned with something else.

"I am more concerned with something else! It's bad—that prosecutor? Sena or whatever her name was? She's coming here right now! And apparently she's set on arresting you this time!"

As she spoke, she was breathless and pale.

Chapter 4
May This Masked Knight Submit!

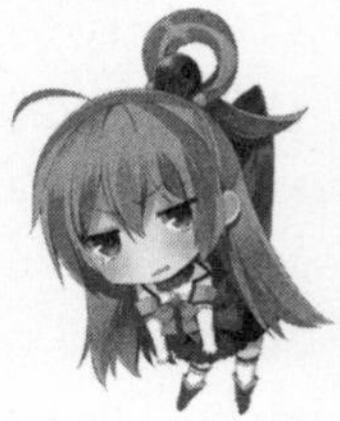

1

"Kazuma Satou! Are you there, Kazuma Satoooooou?!"

Just as Megumin had warned me, Sena came storming up to the house in a towering rage.

"Wh-what? More frogs? Or is this some other problem you want to blame me for?"

I had to admit she was a bit intimidating.

"It's the dungeon! What have you done to Khiel's Dungeon?! All kinds of strange monsters are showing up!" she bellowed, her face bright red.

Strange monsters? I guess I'd been hearing some rumors around town…

"Hold on, that has nothing to do with us. Yeah, I dove that dungeon, but you can't blame me for everything that goes on just 'cause I happened to be within a hundred yards!"

Everyone else nodded in agreement.

Well, good. Maybe that means they haven't done anything to cause this while I wasn't looking.

Sena, however, glowered at me, clearly unconvinced.

"Say what you like. Reports indicate you were the last one to go into that dungeon. Judging by what else has happened so far, I have to suspect you're behind this."

"T-talk about crazy! Anyway, for once I have no idea what you could possibly be talking about. Right, everybody? Right? We're in the clear this time?"

Everyone nodded assiduously.

Sena appeared awfully dubious, but for a moment she backed off.

"But that would leave me in a predicament. I was so sure you had a hand in it... Instead, we'll have to hire someone to investigate..." She looked pointedly at us as she spoke. *Whatever shall I do?* her glance seemed to say. *If only some person would conveniently volunteer...*

"Hmm. Surely the esteemed prosecutor wouldn't be seeking help from the people she was just accusing? Anyway, we are somewhat busy trying to clear our own names." Megumin seemed to know exactly what Sena was thinking and beat her to the punch.

The prosecutor bit her lip, but she didn't respond to Megumin; instead, she turned to me.

"I'm afraid we just don't have the time, so we'll need to refuse," I said as clearly as possible. Sena sighed, and her shoulders slumped.

"If you're really not involved in this case, I suppose I can't force you. But if you change your mind, I would truly appreciate your help. I'll be going to the Adventurers Guild next."

Then she turned and left.

I really didn't like her type.

Way too serious—and possessed of a good sense all too rare in this town.

"Hrm," Darkness said. "I admit I'm curious about the monsters in that dungeon... But we have work to do. First, we need to clear Kazuma's name. Then, we need to pay back Lord Alderp for his mansion. So far, I can't see that we've made any progress on either front."

She was right.

"Hey, Darkness. Can I ask you...?"

"I'm not lending you any money. I feel I've well and truly done my part already. And frankly, I think I'd enjoy watching you squirm a little more."

She looked at me, and a smile came over her face.

Hmph! So she was holding a grudge about the meeting…

…Strange monsters, huh?

"I'm gonna ask again, just for the record. None of you knows anything about this, right? We're really okay this time?"

They all acted slightly annoyed that I kept asking.

"If it does not involve explosion magic, then I assure you, I have no idea."

"Me neither. Though I'd like to point out that, unlike these two, I'm not known for causing problems everywhere I go."

"What?! …I admit Darkness has never been behind any very big problems. But she has not helped very much, either—including in the fight with Destroyer!"

"Huh?! Megumin, you—!"

I let the two of them argue as I returned to the matter at hand.

"How about you? Any idea?" I asked Aqua with a twinge of concern.

"Of course not," she said. "Geez! When are you ever going to learn to trust me?"

I breathed a sigh of relief.

"I…I thought not. You haven't caused that many problems, I guess. This trial's just got me doubting everything…"

I apologized to Aqua. I'd been wrong to assume everything was her fault.

"You sure were! Just trust me for once. If anything, you should be thanking me that more monsters *don't* show up in that dungeon! You remember the room that Lich lived in? I really put everything I had into the magic circle I used when I performed the rite. I bet it's still there right now, keeping evil things from going into that room!"

…I abandoned my apology and grabbed Aqua by the shoulders.

"Wh-what did you just say?!"

"Huh? Why so panicked? It's just like I said. I worked really hard on that magic circle, and it's probably still there, keeping monsters awa—"

I didn't let her finish.

"You idiiiiot!"

I could only cradle my head in my hands and shout.

2

We walked along a snow-covered path, making for the dungeon.

"...*Sniff*... It's not my fault... I swear it isn't...!"

There was Aqua, still sniffling away.

She walked behind me, and Megumin and Darkness followed behind her.

I turned toward her. "Why is it that every single time you do something helpful, you end up doing something totally unnecessary and obnoxious at the same time? Do you have some kind of sickness where you need to balance out the pros and cons of everything you do?"

Though in this case, she still hadn't managed to balance out the cons.

"Now, just a minute! This time it is absolutely not my fault! Please, you have to believe me! I mean, all I did was put up a magic circle of purification in the boss room! That's not enough to spawn a horde of monsters! This is totally different from our ghost problem!"

Aqua grabbed my shoulders as I made to keep walking, and she shook them violently.

"Hey, stop that! I can't walk! Look, I don't care if you did this or not! Sena's going to investigate that dungeon, and she's going to find the magic circle you left there! That's the problem!"

The magic circle deep in the dungeon. Somehow I just knew I was going to pay for not having destroyed that evidence.

We did have a device with us for cleaning up magic circles, but if possible I wanted to settle things without needing to enter the dungeon.

Finally, all of us, the blubbering Aqua notwithstanding, arrived at the entrance with no further trouble.

"...Huh. Those are some weird monsters, all right."

From a safe distance, we observed the creatures pouring out of the dungeon's opening one after another.

They wore little masks, stood about knee-high, and walked on two legs—in a word, they looked like masked dolls.

"I wonder what these strange things could be. I have never seen nor heard of anything like them," Megumin said curiously, watching the dolls with interest.

"At a glance, they don't look like they could do much in a fight," Darkness said disappointedly, her heavy armor clanking.

"Something about their masks just doesn't agree with me. I wonder why. They just make me kind of sick somehow…" As she spoke, Aqua picked up a nearby rock.

At that moment…

"Mr. Satou…! Why are you here? Have you decided to help me investigate these monsters?"

I turned toward the voice to see Sena, accompanied by a crowd of adventurers.

Sena herself wore no armor, just light outerwear, but she carried a tag with a strange symbol drawn on it.

Damn. She was already here.

Well, all right. Nothing for it but to talk to her.

"When we really thought about it, we realized these monsters weren't totally unconnected to us. And anyway, we have to protect the people of the town who are threatened by them. That's an adventurer's duty."

"I've never wanted a magic lie-detecting bell more in my life… But all right. I am grateful for your assistance." Sena bowed her head deeply.

Now what? My sense that I was a good person had come under serious attack.

This woman didn't hate me. She was just very serious about her job and was pursuing her doubts about me with maybe just a bit too much enthusiasm.

"In any case, Mr. Satou, please come this way. We don't know exactly where the monsters are coming from yet, but it seems most likely that someone is summoning them. If that's the case, then please take down the one responsible and put this on the summoning circle." She handed me the tag she was carrying.

"What's this...?"

"It's a tag with powerful sealing magic. With it, any magic circle, no matter how powerful, will immediately be rendered useless. It is possible for a summoning circle to continue to call forth monsters even after the spell-caster has been defeated, so please take it with you."

I got it. Pretty convenient. But not necessary.

"That's all right, we don't need it. Don't worry, I've got a plan. One that doesn't involve walking straight into a dungeon that's currently spewing monsters... Megumin! You ready?"

"Very much so. You can count on me."

Megumin popped out in front, her staff at the ready.

Sena looked alarmed. "Wh-what's this? What are you going to do?! You can't possibly...!"

"Ah, figured it out? Right, we just block the dungeon entrance with Explosion, and..."

"Y-you can't! Please find out what's causing this! These monsters clearly are not natural. And the sheer number suggests a powerful force behind them. You might close off the dungeon, but if the summoner can use Teleport, they'll simply escape. Consider what they're capable of. Please find them and eliminate them."

Oh man. This is starting to look dangerous again.

This was no good. I hadn't come here to actually go dungeon crawling.

And once we were inside, we wouldn't be able to use Megumin's Explosion...

As I fretted, Aqua prepared to throw her rock at the masked monsters.

I got that she didn't like them, but I didn't think they were that bad.

Until that moment, the creatures had shown no hostility toward us, but as soon as Aqua lifted the rock, one charged her at a mad dash.

"Hey, wha—?! Wh-what's going—? Ahh!"

And then, instead of attacking, it clung to Aqua's knees.

"What's this? I think it likes me. That mask is a little gross, but this is kind of endearing… Hey. Hey, Kazuma. What's going on? This doll is getting warm. I've got a bad feeling about this!"

Aqua lurched in my direction as she shouted, but I had a hunch what would happen and backpedaled as quickly as I could.

Then…

There was the sound of a massive blast as the doll holding on to Aqua simply vanished.

All that was left was a goddess with clothes torn and singed from the explosion.

"As you've discovered, these creatures grab on to anything that moves and detonate themselves. Even the Adventurers Guild is at a loss as to how to deal with them."

"I see. That's no good, is it?"

"How can you both be so calm?! You could worry about me a little bit! Where's the sympathy?!"

Aqua, on the verge of tears, came bustling up to where Sena and I were maturely assessing the situation.

She seemed in pretty good shape to me.

"We're really in a bind here," Sena said. "These monsters don't appear to have any attacks besides self-destructing, but…if you damage one even a little, it blows up. If you don't cause any damage, it tries to find a moment when to grab hold and blow up. It seems our only choice is to take them out one at a time, from a distance."

As she spoke, Sena looked at Aqua, who had curled into a ball while Megumin comforted her.

Aqua clearly wasn't well, but she had her "divine" feather mantle wrapped around her. Without that for protection, she probably would've come out a lot worse for wear.

Another life-threatening monster, huh…?

Maybe we could forge ahead, throwing stones as we went?

There were so many of them out here, though. I could only imagine how many must be hiding inside the dungeon. There was no way we could deal with every last one of them…

The problem was, we still had no idea what they wanted.

Who was letting these monsters out, and what in the world for?

As we stood there worrying about all this, Darkness approached one of the dolls and then, without warning, wordlessly gave it a smack.

"Wha…?! What the hell are you—?!"

Everyone around me started to panic, as did I. The assaulted doll simply grabbed on to Darkness.

Then, just like the one that had grabbed Aqua, it went *boom* in a big way.

And as the smoke cleared…

"Mm. This will do. This'll do just fine."

There was Darkness, perfectly in one piece despite the blast.

For the first time, Sena and the other adventurers got a taste of her toughness firsthand.

"I'll take point to clear the way. Kazuma, follow me."

Darkness's words were more suited for a guy in shining armor.

I guess we weren't going to be Ambushing our way into the dungeon like we did last time.

We—all the other adventurers and I—were going to mount a frontal assault.

I felt Megumin tug on my sleeve.

"Kazuma, Kazuma. I won't be any use to you inside that dungeon, so may I stand guard out here? I will make sure I'm ready to cast a spell on the dungeon entrance at any time—if you encounter a huge monster, please simply come running out."

True, there was probably someone inside summoning these creatures. And true, they were probably plenty strong. Maybe it wouldn't be such a bad idea to have Megumin waiting here as our ace in the hole in case some killer beast tried to run us down.

"Sounds great," Aqua said, brushing soot off her sleeves. "I'll be right out here with her! Don't worry; I'll put some buffs on you before you go in so—"

"Wait a second! You're coming with us! Unlike Megumin, your abilities work perfectly well in that dungeon!"

"Waaaaah! I'm sick of dungeons! You'll just try to leave me in there again! And what if undead mob us again? Waaaah!"

She plugged her ears and sat on the ground, repeating, *I won't I won't I won't.*

I guess my almost abandoning her down there before really traumatized her.

I considered it for a moment and ended up leaving Aqua outside, too. There was just too much chance of drawing the undead with her around. We had a bunch of other adventurers with us this time. Even if we did happen to run into a ghost or some other incorporeal enemy, surely someone would figure out a way to deal with it.

"Looks like we're the only ones from our party heading in there, Darkness."

"Mm. Alone with you in a dark dungeon… Somehow I can't help thinking you're more dangerous than the monsters."

"Hmm, maybe I need to leave you in there, see if I can traumatize you like I did with Aqua."

While we bantered, the other adventurers seemed to have settled in to their groups.

Some of the adventurers would stay aboveground to act as Sena's bodyguards and clear out the monster-dolls up there. About twenty other men and women would join Darkness and me in heading underground.

The plan was for Darkness to carve a trail up front, while the others and I followed behind…

*　　*　　*

The light from the lantern I held played across the dim dungeon corridor.

Darkness didn't have a lantern, just in case she got blown up—she carried only her great sword. I walked a few steps behind her, holding the light up so she could see ahead.

The rest of the adventurers shuffled along after me.

The dungeon was as dark and dank as ever, but it was hard to feel scared with this many people around.

Although, our goals and theirs were different.

They all wanted to find out where the monsters were coming from, but we wanted to get rid of the magic circle in the Lich's room—destroying the incriminating evidence.

So it was actually really inconvenient to have everyone else right behind us.

But even so...

"Heh-heh-heh-heh-heh. Ha-ha-ha-ha-ha-ha-ha! Look, Kazuma! Look at me hit them! Even my blade can strike these things!"

Ahead of me, Darkness swung her sword gleefully, slicing through the dolls, which made no move to avoid her attacks.

Naturally, they responded by self-destructing, but Darkness seemed perfectly happy with this, even as her face and armor became covered in soot.

I didn't realize her total failure to hit anything in the past had been bothering her. If it was that big a deal, she should've just swallowed her pride and taken the Great Sword skill or something.

Apparently elated to be fulfilling her role at last now that she could land some hits, Darkness cut a path for us, rolling through the dungeon like a proper tank.

Despite the repeated explosions, the dungeon did justice to its reputation as the creation of a famous Wizard turned Lich—there was no sign of anything crumbling.

"Heyyyy! Hang on a minute—slow down!" one of the other adventurers called from behind us.

I turned around and saw that Darkness's inexorable advance had left the rest of the group some way behind us.

And more and more of those monsters were pouring in from the dungeon's side tunnels.

"Wai— Oh no! One's got me! Someone, get this thing off me!"

"Yipes, stay back! Don't bring it this way!"

The blasts from the critters were pretty powerful. But even without Darkness's toughness or Aqua's celestial gown, I figured they wouldn't kill an adventurer in full armor.

So, sorry guys, but—!

"That's it, Darkness! Straight ahead! Onward, brave Crusader!"

"You've got it! Oh, I've never been so exhilarated! This is the first time I've ever felt like a real Crusader!"

She seemed to be having too much fun to notice what was happening behind us.

At this rate we could bust right into the deepest part of this dungeon and then be on our way!

3

Getting to the innermost part of the dungeon was almost too easy. Before long, we had almost reached our objective.

If memory served, the Lich's room should be right at the end of this hallway.

"…What's this? Whatever that is, it's got to be the leader of those monsters."

In front of Darkness and me, a shadow sat cross-legged outside the Lich's room, kneading dirt into dolls.

It wore a black tuxedo—a strange sight in a dungeon—and shaped the dolls without removing its white gloves. It had a mask with exactly the same design as the dolls it created.

The mask, which didn't cover its mouth, gave off a sinister impression.

The creature couldn't possibly have missed us standing there with our lantern, but it paid us no attention at all, perhaps too caught up in creating.

The mask hid its face, but its body suggested it was a man.

Just as I was trying to decide what to do, Darkness strode boldly up to the figure.

"...Hey, you. What are you doing there? I see you making that doll. That means you're the one behind this monster scare, right?"

Then Darkness raised her great sword and took up a fighting stance, facing the masked man.

He raised his head as if he had only just now realized someone was there.

Upon closer inspection, I realized how tall he was.

He didn't seem to have any weapons, but he was no small fry, either.

The eyes on his mask glowed red, and his mouth twisted into a sneer.

"...Oh-ho. How good of you to make it this far. Welcome to my dungeon, adventurers! Indeed, I am he who lies at the root of all evil! A general of the Demon King, the Duke of Hell who commands Devils! I am the Great Devil, the one who sees all in this world—Vanir!"

I wasn't expecting a boss *this* big!

In the darkness of the dungeon, I started to back away. Darkness kept her sword at the ready, but even she was intimidated by the thought of challenging a general of the Demon King.

This was bad. I had absolutely not counted on Darkness and me facing one of the generals alone.

On reflection, maybe we'd had a few hints.

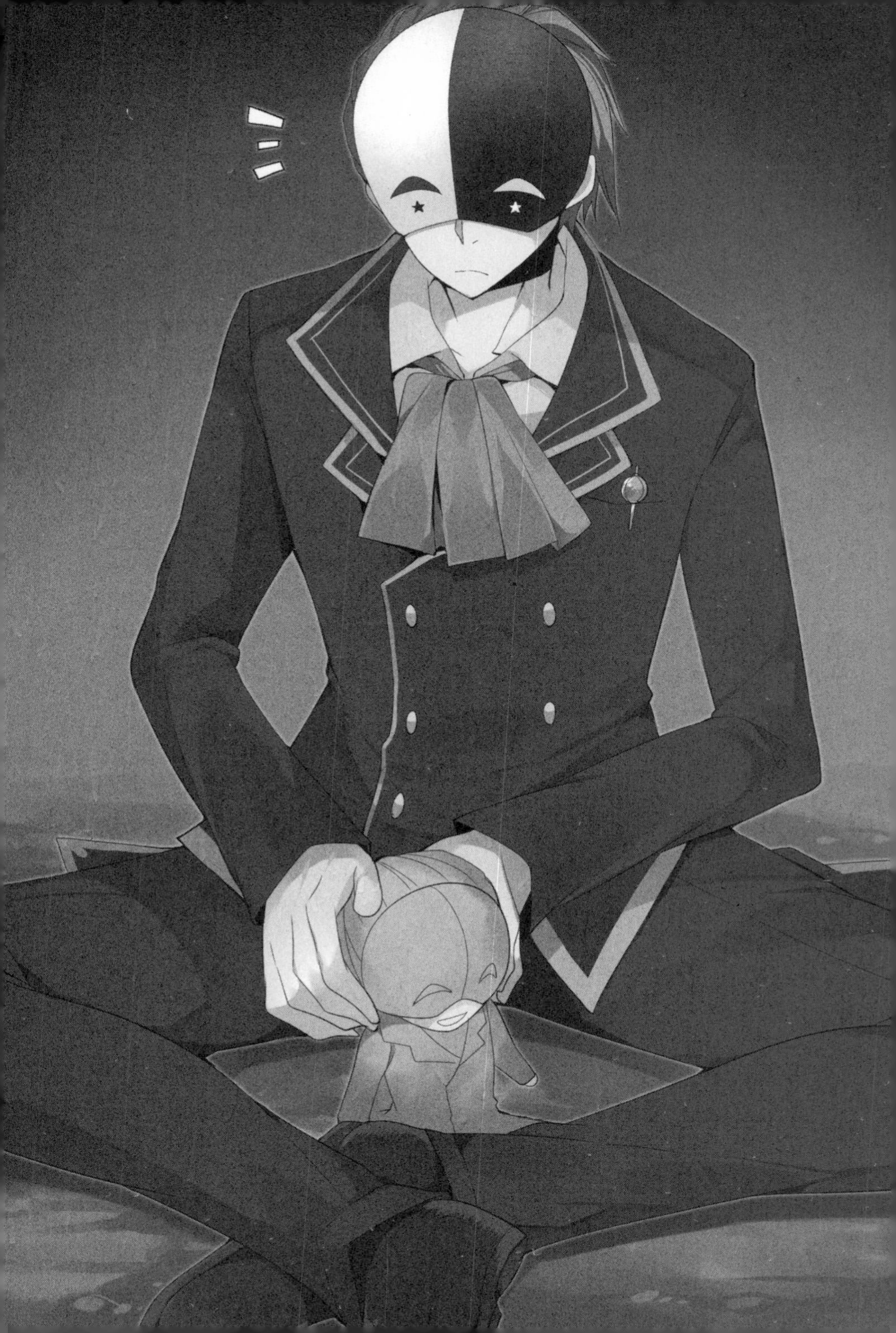

Like the frogs that came out from underground as if they were flee-ing from something—maybe it wasn't Explosion that had scared them.

When Beldia had been around, the weaker monsters had all made themselves scarce then, too.

"Darkness. H-hey, Darkness! This is too much for the two of us. We've got to get out of here!"

"What are you saying?! How can a servant of the goddess Eris flee before a Devil and general of the Demon King? I will end him here and now, even if it costs my own life!"

Why does she have to be so stubborn?!

Vanir answered Darkness's declaration with amusement. "Oh-ho. End me, you say? Me, sometimes rumored to be more powerful than even the Demon King? But... You, girl, the one who was worried that boy over there might notice her too-well-sculpted abdominal muscles when he saw her naked in the bath that one time... I don't know what you are chattering about, but I have heard that chewing on a little bone helps when you are angry. Part of my mask is made of the bones of a magical dragon. Would you like me to break off a piece for you?"

"T-t-too-well-sculpted—! D-don't insult me, you dirty puppet of the Demon King! Kazuma! Everything he says is a lie! My abs aren't even that built, and I definitely didn't worry about your seeing them!"

"C-calm down, Darkness—get your head on straight, and we'll go from there."

I held Darkness back—she had started to swing her sword around wildly in an attempt at an attack.

Vanir paid no mind to the enraged Crusader but just sat there on the ground.

"Oh, calm yourself. I did not come here to fight with you two. I've come to investigate something, as requested by our dear King. And I have business with someone in Axel Town—a certain shopkeeper. One who supposedly has the exceptional ability to get poorer every time she does anything."

At that, Darkness and I exchanged a glance.

4

Beside me, Darkness stood with her sword at the ready, prepared to attack at any time. I, however, sat down on the dungeon floor to hear what Vanir had to say.

"First of all, though I call myself a general of the Demon King, I am a rather lackadaisical one. At His Majesty's request, I merely help maintain the magical barrier around his castle. I am what might be more widely known as a Devil. Among Devils, the most prized delicacy is the negative emotions you humans give off, which you find so unpleasant. You are the source of what we most love to eat, so it would be sheer folly for us to destroy or harm you. Indeed, we dance for joy each time a human is born."

"Is… Is that right…? But doesn't a little crisis help fuel that animosity? I mean, if we're living in peace, we don't produce that much ill will, do we?"

Vanir didn't seem hostile at the moment, but if he was a general of the Demon King, he would be too much for the two of us to handle alone. Right now, it would be better to talk than to fight.

He claimed to be just helping maintain the spirit barrier around the Demon King's castle, though. Wasn't that what Wiz was supposedly doing?

Still sitting cross-legged on the ground, Vanir nimbly fashioned a mask for a doll as he spoke.

"Well, what we consider negative emotions encompasses a wide range. And every Devil has personal tastes. Some enjoy humans' terror and despair. Others like to disguise themselves as impossibly beautiful women and make men fall in love with them—then savor the bitter tears when they reveal themselves."

"I'm starting to think it would make good sense to get rid of you." I regarded the obnoxious masked monster with some suspicion.

Apparently the Demon King had tasked him with investigating the humans who had defeated Beldia.

"I had been passing my time taunting His Majesty's minions and feasting on the resulting ill will. But His Majesty came to me wanting to know if I might make myself useful, instead of simply bullying his subordinates all the time. I accepted his request to investigate around here, thinking it would give me a chance to visit an old friend in town. But as I was passing through, I noticed this dungeon had no master and simply decided to set up shop here."

I wanted to ask him what happened to investigating, or meeting his friend. I wanted to tell him that there were limits even to being easily distracted. But if that actually put him back on task, well, it would be the worse for us.

After all, *we* were the ones who had defeated Beldia.

I wanted to just leave this guy where he was and go home, but there was one thing I couldn't overlook.

"You said it wouldn't make sense for you to hurt humans, but what's with these dolls, then? They come marching out of this dungeon and cause all sorts of trouble for the townspeople."

"...Hmm? I have been using these toys to clear out the monsters. If they are beginning to wander outside the dungeon's confines, it must mean there are no more monsters within. In that case, I will cease production of my Vanir dolls and move on to my next plan."

"...Your next plan? What exactly is it you're playing at?"

Vanir took the doll he had just made and turned it back to earth.

"*Playing at* is a strong phrase, young man who paced his room like a bear in a cave, sick with worry just because your armored friend didn't come back for a few days. As a Devil, I have a grand dream. And I have come to this land to bring it to fruition."

"Hey, quit it. I know you said you're all-seeing, but why do you talk about that stuff like you were right there? ...A-and you, stop squirming."

Next to me, Darkness seemed downcast, her cheeks flushing just a bit as she shot glances at me.

Sure, I'd been worried about her, but I hadn't paced around my room...much.

"I assume Devils don't yearn for anything we would consider good. Perhaps you could tell us what this 'dream' is?"

Darkness leveled a dangerous glare at Vanir, who made an *Mm* deep in his throat.

"Understand that I have existed for countless eons. For some time now, I have been conceiving a most extraordinary way to meet my end. I shall feast on the greatest acrimony of all and then go gloriously into the night... I have nursed this aspiration for so long that I can no longer remember when I first imagined it. But how could I obtain the tremendous rancor I seek? I had an idea..."

I swallowed hard at the smirk that came over his face.

"First, I needed a dungeon. Then, I would station my Devil minions in every room of it and fill it with the most terrible traps! The most renowned adventurers would come to challenge it! Again and again they would try themselves in my dungeon, until at last one of them reached the innermost sanctum!"

He had begun to gesticulate wildly and speak with real passion, perhaps inspired by his own excitement.

"And in this deepest place, I myself would of course be waiting. Then I would say to them, *How good of you to make it this far. Now, strike me down, and claim for yourself vast riches...!* And then the final battle would begin! After a mighty struggle, the adventurers would best me at last. As I crumpled to the earth, a tightly sealed treasure chest would appear behind me. And as my consciousness slipped away, the adventurers would work it open...!"

Darkness and I both found ourselves swallowing now, but we kept silent.

"......Within would be a scrap of paper with a note that says, *Sorry, please play again*. Seeing the empty look on their faces as they read it—that is how I wish to meet my end."

"Aww, spare 'em that. It's just too heartbreaking."

"Listen, Kazuma. I think we'd better get rid of this guy now."

Vanir chuckled at the two of us and said, "My friend runs a shop in this area. It was my intention to work there to earn money, and then with those resources and my friend's power build the great labyrinth I dreamed of. But then I passed by this place and noticed it had no master. I thought perhaps it would do for my needs, and I settled here."

"That's a pretty dumb reason for sitting in a dungeon. But what do I care? I know what you're doing here now. And it sounds like you'll stop making those dolls, so I don't really have any beef with you. My friend and I just have some business with the magic circle in the room behind you. In fact, we came here to get rid of it."

"Wha…?! Kazuma, this Devil is more important than any magic circle! Are you going to just walk right by a general of the Demon King?! An enemy of all mankind is sitting right in front of you!"

She wasn't necessarily wrong, but what did she think the two of us alone could do to him?

I stood up, intending to dispel the magic circle and get out of there.

"…A magic circle? Oh-ho. You are going to dispel this magic circle, which even I struggled with? How kind of you. I don't know what troublesome meddler set it up, but I've been totally unable to go in that room thanks to that despicable design, and it's been quite frustrating. If you can indeed remove it, I shall present you with a special handmade Vanir doll that cackles in the middle of the night."

"Th-thanks but no thanks. Actually, that circle's a problem for us, too. Once we get rid of it, we'll be heading home. You can do whatever you want then."

I nonchalantly explained that we would be getting rid of the circle and heading back, but Vanir asked:

"In what way is that circle disadvantageous to you? Just a moment, let me take a look at your past…"

He sounded very interested, and also treated looking at my past like it was no big deal for him.

…*Hey, wait a…!*

"………Bwa-ha-ha!"

*   *   *

Vanir seemed to have found something before I could stop him. He cackled in a dry voice.

Darkness moved in front of me as if to cover me from this strange new turn.

"Bwa-ha-ha-ha! Bwa-ha-ha-ha-ha-ha-ha-ha! Bwaaaa-ha-ha-ha-ha-ha-ha-ha-ha! If irony were as delicious as animosity, I would be feasting! It was your Priest friend who created that troublesome circle! To set up magic even I cannot penetrate—this Priest must be immensely..."

This was bad. I didn't quite get what was going on, but apparently he was really into it now!

Vanir stood lazily, his eyes glowing red through his mask. It wasn't the red of the Crimson Magic Clan. The color was definitely devilish—a hue that played upon an ancient human fear. The color of blood.

"Oh-ho... I see, I can see it! Up above! I can see that Priest indolently drinking tea at the entrance to this very dungeon!"

Was that true? If that was true, I wanted to head back up there and ask Aqua just whose fault it was that we were going through all this. And maybe give her a smack for good measure.

Vanir glared through his mask.

"Now, young woman who lost a bet with that man and has been most fretful wondering what awful thing he will do to her, waiting anxiously for it, hoping for it—and young man, who is nervous with having to decide what he will do to this young woman after all this is over. I ask you to step aside! Don't look so worried; you know I shall never kill a human. And I shan't. I shall not kill any...*humans*. But I shall exact my revenge for this bothersome magic circle!"

"I'm not fretting—and I'm not anxious—and I'm not hoping! Stop making stuff up! J-j-just stop saying anything at all!"

"Y-yeah, she's right! I'm not nervous, either! T-totally not!"

We somehow managed to endure the mind games of someone who could see right through us. Vanir made to take a step forward.

A Devil who sees all had just made a point of saying he wouldn't kill any *humans*.

Did that mean he'd already realized Aqua's true identity...?!

Darkness held her sword out toward Vanir as he began to close the distance between us.

"If you mean Aqua harm, then I will never stand down. As a Crusader in the service of Our Lady Eris, I shall not let you pass!"

"I see your head is even harder than your abdomen, girl. If I wanted to, I could bury you both without a second thought. But I have no desire to kill you humans. Not least because I have no way of knowing which of you might one day help me obtain the greatest bitterness. Scurry home and get on with that 'awful thing' you're both so excited for. I, the all-seeing Devil, promise you: If you leave now, all will go just as you wish. No one shall bother or interrupt you."

Wh-why, this guy...!

"Don't listen to him, Darkness! He's a Devil! He's trying to mislead us!"

"Wh-who's being misled?! There's a time and place for these things, Kazuma!"

Wait, what? I'm this tempted by him and she...isn't?

Some all-seeing Devil. Here I'd assumed *Young woman who has been most fretful with wondering, waiting anxiously, hoping*...was all actually true.

But when I stole a glance at Darkness, I saw her cheeks were slightly flushed, and the trembling tip of her sword betrayed a hint of inner conflict.

"Bwa-ha-ha-ha-ha-ha! Ahh, sweet cowards. Not uninterested in each other as man and woman but unable to cross that line as members of the same party. Now, out of my way! Once I've gone, you shall be quite able to enter your precious magic-circle room. You can spend as much time there as you like—and then go home!"

What a Devil! Had we ever run into an enemy who'd set such a devious trap for us?

"Kazuma, don't be taken in! How could we go on living under the same roof if we were in such a weird relationship?! Stay focused!"

"Huh? R-right, stay focused, me! This is Darkness we're talking about! Nice to look at and definitely my type, but you know what she's like inside! Don't get confused by some passing lust!"

"H-hey, you'll pay for that later…!"

Man, this girl is so complicated.

"Ho-ho! Not going to be led astray by my temptations, are we? Well, well, what to do now? Many of my abilities are so powerful as to be practically cheating. For example, consider my Vanir Death Ray. It is a death ray, so if it hit you humans, you would die. Even if it didn't hit you, you would die. There's also my Vanir Eye Beam. That skill, however, has the drawback of burning my own eyes if I use it, so I have yet to try…"

"Th-that's enough! I feel like I might go crazy talking to you! I won't let you reach Aqua and the others! If you want her that bad, you'll have to go through me!"

Darkness seized the initiative and leaped at Vanir.

5

Vanir laughed joyfully as he dodged one of Darkness's attacks after another.

"Bwa-ha-ha-ha-ha-ha-ha! Your strikes are as inaccurate as they are spirited, girl! …Hmm? Where did your friend go? The one who seems to be all talk and no action?"

His head turned this way and that, trying to see where I had disappeared off to.

…Sorry I couldn't do something flashier. I'm trying to make do with beginner skills, here!

"What are you looking at?! I'm right in front of you!" Darkness exclaimed.

"Where did that underhanded little boy get to? I have an inkling he is far more dangerous than any muddleheaded Crusader. I still sense him, but where...?"

While Darkness kept Vanir busy, I had set my lantern on the ground and was using Ambush to sneak around behind him.

Underhanded—well, what did he expect? Who would be stupid enough to fight one of the Demon King's generals head-on?

"Keep your eyes on me when we're fighting, alreadyyyy!" Darkness took a sweeping sideways swing at Vanir.

Vanir, in turn, took a big leap backward—his rear directly facing me.

I stopped using Ambush and threw all my weight into a kick squarely at Vanir's spine.

"Gurgh?! You knave! When did you—?! H-hrk...?!"

He stumbled forward, returning into the path of Darkness's blade.

Darkness may have been clumsy, but she had strength in spades. Her sword cleaved straight through him. His left arm went spinning through the air; his torso sported a gaping, critical wound. He fell to his knees...

"Impossible! To think that I...! I underestimated you...! Who knew that such worthy opponents as you lay concealed in this beginner town? Hrr... Impossible...that I should...be destroyed...here..."

With that, Vanir's body, tuxedo and all, crumbled to dust, leaving only his mask.

The lantern, which had been knocked on its side, dimly illuminated the scene. The only sound was Darkness's ragged breath.

"No way... Did I really just...defeat a general of the Demon King?"

Darkness couldn't seem to believe it herself. She stood with her sword in hand, still shaking from the thrill of battle.

"Usually, if you say *Did I really do it?* or whatever at a time like this, it means you haven't really done it. But Vanir seemed pretty surprised to be cut in half, too. Maybe for once we actually accomplished something."

"All as I expected," a voice said suddenly, as if in reply. It seemed to be coming from the mask lolling on the ground.

The dust of the dungeon floor began to rise up in the shape of a body. Soon that body was clad in a tuxedo, in the exact state it had been a few minutes earlier.

"Did you perhaps imagine you had defeated me? I'm sorry to tell you that you didn't even damage me! Bwa-ha-ha-ha-ha-ha! Bwaaa-ha-ha-ha-ha-ha-ha-ha! Ahhh, your ill will! Exquisite!"

Aww, man! I'm gonna kill this guy!

"What, your body is actually made only of dust? The Demon King's generals just keep getting crazier and crazier!"

"Ohhh… I thought we beat him… I thought one of my attacks finally hit and beat a general of the Demon King… I thought maybe I'd finally made up for not doing much during the fight with Destroyer…"

Darkness's sword trembled as she muttered dejectedly. Vanir, however, laughed merrily.

"Bwa-ha-ha-ha! This is a false body made by my magic—the mask is my true form! Strike my body however you will—it will only return to dust! And then I will feed on the abundant magic in the earth, petals shall dance, and butterflies shall fly…"

"You're not making any sense! Talking to you gives me a headache! Dammit. Darkness, what do we do? Time for a tactical retreat?"

"Never! He has mocked me, to my shame as a Knight! I must repay him…!"

It happened as Darkness made this forceful declaration.

"Mm, I see, I see. I haven't much time to entertain myself with you. But I have a special ability for moments just like this! Observe: I shall not harm anyone, but I shall have all your enmity!"

Vanir took his mask in his right hand.

"Hey, Darkness! I don't like where this is going! Get away from him!"

"You're too late! Tough-bodied Crusader! I will borrow that sinew of yours!" Vanir bellowed, and then he thrust the mask at Darkness…!

6

"Darkness…? H-hey, Darkness! Answer me!"

Darkness had taken the mask full in the face, and now she stood there wearing it, gazing at the ground, her sword hanging limply. She wasn't moving.

I didn't like this at all.

Judging by Vanir's words and the way Darkness looked right now, I could only assume he had possessed her.

Vanir's former body had crumbled into dust when he launched the mask.

Darkness swayed slightly, mask and all, then raised her head…

"Bwa-ha-ha-ha-ha-ha! Bwaaaa-ha-ha-ha-ha-ha! Now hear me, you impudent rogue! By my power— (**What should I do, Kazuma? He's taken over my body!**) What now, you insect? Can you bring yourself to attack this—? (**I don't care! Attack us! Attack us now! This is the best possible situation!**)"

A practically incomprehensible stream of words came from Darkness's mouth.

"…What are you two talking about?"

"What in blazes? What is this (**beautiful!**) girl? …Stop interrupting! What is going on? Such a resolute spirit she has… (**It's like I'm the model Crusader!**) You are growing most tiresome!"

Gosh. You'd think this would be a real crisis, but Darkness seemed to have things pretty under control.

In fact, she kind of seemed to be enjoying it.

"How can this girl be so strong as to resist my control? (**Aww, go on…**) But the longer you resist me, the more piercing the pain of the struggle shall become! (**Wh-what?!**) Bwa-ha-ha-ha-ha! Let us see just how long you can endure! …What's this? You show no animosity. In fact, you might be feeling something I like very little… Joy…?"

Since Vanir and Darkness didn't appear to be going anywhere, I decided to take this opportunity to do what I'd come here for in the first place. I walked into the Lich's room and used the magic-cleaning equipment to make short work of the magic circle.

Even as I worked, I could hear:

"**(I... I shall not bend to this pain...!)** Your determination is admirable! But to attempt to endure further is to invite the destruction of your very spirit...! ...Don't tell me you're enjoying this...?!"

Vanir sounded downright confused.

I finished cleaning the magic circle and went back to where the two of them were still battling for control of Darkness's body.

"All right, Darkness, all done! Now we just need to get back to the surface. Then we can collect Aqua and beat our retreat!"

I had been walking toward Darkness as I spoke, but I found her great sword pointed at me.

"Not another step, boy. **(Don't worry, Kazuma! Leave me here and go on ahead!)** Surely you don't think things will go so easi— **(Ahh, I've always wanted to say that!)** This girl you do not dislike, surely you don't wish to see her harmed? **(?!)** If she continues to resist my power... **(K-Kazuma! Did I hear correctly what this self-proclaimed all-seeing Devil just said?)** Now, if you wish to prevent this, then explain to her that— **(I'm really happy. I'm happy, but—our social standing is too different. And we are members of the same party...)** *Will you shut up?!*"

"Both of you, shut up! Seriously, could you *please* take turns talking? I have no idea what either of you is saying!"

Vanir and I were both bellowing, but the top of my lungs was higher than the top of his.

"Hrr... It seems this body was a mistake. **(Hey, that's a rude thing to say about someone's body!)** Again I implore you to be quiet! I'm leaving, already, so just keep silent!"

It seemed Vanir couldn't control Darkness's iron will and had decided to leave.

I was pretty impressed—our resident perv had outlasted a general of the Demon King.

Vanir's shoulders slumped wearily, and he raised a hand to take off his mask.

Then something occurred to me.

If Vanir got his power back, wouldn't that be a bad thing?

After all, as long as he had that mask, he could just make himself a new body any time he was in trouble. Plus he'd boasted about having those nasty rays or beams or whatever. I wondered if he could use those skills while he was in Darkness's body.

If Vanir got serious, Darkness and I wouldn't be able to stop him from heading to the surface.

But what if we kept him trapped in Darkness's body?

He would be in the body of a human he wasn't used to, and he would have Darkness making his life miserable.

…So we keep him bottled up in Darkness, take *her* to the surface, and have Aqua do something about it.

That was it. He wanted to meet Aqua, and we would make sure he did.

I approached Vanir as he went to take off his mask. I took the sealing tag Sena had given me and slapped it right on his face.

"What's the matter, boy? …? What's this? …I can't touch it… Why, you— What is this tag? When I try to touch my mask, my fingers are repelled. **(Hmm, it sparkles right in front of my eyes, and it's kind of annoying… Wait a minute, Kazuma. Isn't this…?)**"

The two of them struggled valiantly to remove the tag, but the person it was placed on couldn't break the seal.

"It's that tag Sena gave me. Okay, Darkness. We're taking you and that seal up top. Just keep Vanir inside until we get to Aqua. She'll purify him right out of you!"

"(Wha—?!)"

Their mutual exclamations were in perfect harmony.

7

Enough of the dolls had been cleared out of the dungeon that they didn't get in our way.

"Boy! This girl is in constant agony from her attempts to resist me! The pain will surely shatter her! So you had best hurry up and remove this seal, for otherwise… **(You heard him, Kazuma! I'm in dire straits here… Ahhh, I've never felt something so intense—he really is a general of the Demon King! I don't think I can…stand it much longer…!)**"

Maybe it was the pain that caused sweat to run down Darkness's neck and her breathing to get heavy.

Apparently she was winning the battle for control of her body, at least for the moment.

On our way out, we ran into the other adventurers who had come in with us. They goggled at the masked Darkness, but we didn't have time for them.

"Just a little farther, Darkness! Hang in there! As soon as we get back up, the hard part will be over!"

"Hnnn… How did I succumb…to this bizarre twist…? **(Don't worry about me!)**"

……

"What did you just say?" Vanir and I found ourselves asking at the same time.

I admit I had some doubts about bringing the general to the surface.

But just think about the body we were keeping him in. Darkness wasn't just a little clumsy. If she took five swings at a hay bale, one of them would miss. Sometimes I wanted to ask how she could have made it this far with such poor aim.

But with her as our opponent, the adventurers on the surface would almost certainly be enough to restrain her if there was any trouble.

152 Konosuba: God's Blessing on This Wonderful World! You're Being Summoned, Darkness

"Great job, Darkness! Aqua can handle the rest. You just let the other adventurers hold you back, and—"

I was interrupted as sunlight met my eyes.

"...Bwa-ha-ha-ha-ha! Bwaaa-ha-ha-ha-ha-ha-ha! Just whom are you talking to?"

He didn't sound like he was struggling with Darkness anymore.

No way...

"My takeover is complete! You've underestimated me, boy! I was holding back until this moment. I knew your friends would let their guard down if I approached them in this guise. Just wait until I'm face-to-face with that Priest of yours! I'll get her before she can say hello!"

As he shouted all this, Vanir leaped up the stairs, moving faster than me despite being clad in full armor.

Oh man! This was *not* good at all!

He was after Aqua. And no one was likely to try to stop Darkness, even if she was wearing a weird mask.

"Darkness, open your eyes! I know you've got more in you! Are you going to let some Devil beat you?"

"Bwa-ha-ha-ha-ha-ha! It's futile, boy! Whatever this girl may 'have,' after a certain level of agony she— **(N-noooo!)** H-hey, hey you! Enough with the strange interjections!"

Damn—I guess our perv couldn't hold out anymore.

Vanir had full control of Darkness now.

"Now for a joyous reunion! Everyone will be so happy to see their companions emerge from the dungeon unscathed! And then, my obnoxious age-old enemy, you will discover I possess your friend! And what will you do then?!"

Shouting, he bounded up out of the dungeon...

"*Sacred Exorcism!*"

"(Ahhhhhhh!)"

...and was immediately enveloped by a white flame from Aqua, who had been waiting at the entrance.

8

Vanir was fried as he came out of the dungeon. He collapsed to one knee.

"D-Darkness!"

Still in Darkness's body, of course.

I rushed out of the dungeon and ran over to see if she was okay. But her body didn't show a single scorch.

"B... Bwa-ha-ha... Bwa-ha-ha-ha-ha-ha... Bwaaaaa-ha-ha-ha-ha-ha-ha-ha-ha!"

In fact, for having taken a direct hit from Aqua's magic, Vanir seemed pretty perky, too.

"Hey, watch it, Aqua! What do you think you're doing, slamming Darkness with magic like that?! You're gonna give me a heart attack!"

Aqua seemed totally unfazed by my scolding.

"What are you talking about? That magic has no effect on humans. I sensed an evil presence, so I just thought I'd try it..."

"(I-is that right...? Just as well, then. But it sure was surprising... Maybe give me a little warning next time...)"

Darkness's consciousness had surfaced, meaning the attack must have weakened Vanir's hold over her.

"Hey, Aqua! A general of the Demon King is possessing Darkness! We're up against a Devil! This kind of thing's your specialty, right?!"

"A-a general of the Demon King?!"

Sena, watching from afar, responded even before Aqua did.

Aqua knitted her brow in annoyance and walked up to Darkness. She abruptly held her nose.

"Yuck! That smell! This is definitely the stench of a Devil! Unclean, Darkness! Unclean!"

"(Whaaa—?! I—I don't think I smell that bad...?!)"

Tears beaded in her eyes behind the mask.

"Ha-ha-ha-ha-ha... **(Kazuma, give me a sniff. Let me know if**

I stink!) Bwa-ha-ha-ha-ha, bwaaaa-ha-ha-ha-ha-ha! (And even on the off chance I do, it's only because we were just running all over a dungeon.) That's enough out of you! This is my moment of truth, and you shall be silent!"

The additional scolding from Vanir only made the tears bigger.

"Bwa-ha-ha-ha! First, allow me to greet you, O Priest who bears the same name as that repugnant and notorious water goddess. I am Vanir! Duke of Hell and general of the Demon King. Vanir, the Great Devil!"

Maybe Vanir had to work to get all those words out of his mouth, because Darkness seemed to be the one with control of the body. The whole time Vanir was making his grand proclamation, her body was kicking rocks disinterestedly.

Wait a second. Had he just called Aqua a "Priest who bears the same name as the water goddess"?

So he *did* know what she really was.

"Hitting me with demon-exorcism magic before you've even introduced yourself—quite a greeting! Bwa-ha-ha-ha-ha! This is why nobody likes the Axis Church! Have you no sense of etiquette?"

"As if! You're nothing but a Devil; what's etiquette got to do with it? You're even worse than undead, and they go against the laws of the gods! But you Devils are just parasites who need human animosity to live! Pfft-hee-hee-hee!"

Then both of them fell silent for a second…

"*Sacred High Exorcism!*"

"As if!"

Aqua had tried to take Vanir by surprise, but he dodged to the side.

"Aww, Darkness! Why'd you dodge? Just hold still, please!"

"(Even if you ask me to do that, my body just—!)"

As Aqua and Vanir set to battling, Sena and Megumin came over to me.

"Kazuma! Kazuma! What's going on here?! Why is Darkness wearing that mask? It's not fair! I want a mask, too! Such a mask stirs the heart of a member of the Crimson Magic Clan!"

"Stuff it! And don't be stupid. Darkness's body is possessed by one of the Demon King's generals. That mask is his true body—think you can do anything about it?"

"Mr. Satou, how in the world did this happen? I've seen that creature on wanted posters. It's Vanir, general of the Demon King, a Devil said to possess great powers of foreknowledge and prophecy, seeing all. What is such a serious threat doing here?!"

Sena was pale as the grave and seemed near the end of her rope.

"He came to find out who defeated the Demon King's other general Beldia. He's got a few more unpleasant things in store, too, but that can wait. For now, I used the seal you gave me to trap him inside Darkness's body."

Sena's jaw nearly hit the ground.

"Trapped him?! Inside your friend's body?! You're just—! You are simply—!"

"…It would appear we find ourselves in a difficult way. That Devil seems able to survive Aqua's exorcism magic. It may be precisely because he is in Darkness's body. Darkness is a Crusader, a holy Knight who serves the gods. She has an especially strong defense against Light magic. Let us remove the seal and set that monster free for the time being."

After listening to Megumin, I observed Vanir, who was busy dodging Aqua's magic.

He made good use of Darkness's normally klutzy body, easily avoiding Aqua's attacks despite being in heavy armor.

Geez, and here I'd thought shutting him up inside Darkness would make it easier to beat him!

I'd had no idea her body had so much latent potential.

"Set him free? As long as he's trapped in Darkness's body, he can only attack with her sword, but he said something about having a death-ray attack or something. Letting him out would probably make him a lot more dangerous."

Somewhere along the line, the other adventurers had joined in the battle, trying to hold Vanir still so Aqua's magic could do its work.

"Th-that is troubling… At this rate…"

"It d-doesn't look good for us, huh…?"

I followed Megumin's gaze to the ongoing battle again…

"Damn! Who knew Darkness had this in her?!"

"I can't hit her! She just parries everything! And she's got some serious attacks—and so fast! We're lucky she's not going all out, or we'd be done for!"

"Bwa-ha-ha-ha-ha-ha! This body is quite capable! Strong muscles and great endurance! And to top it off, it readily resists that noxious divine magic! **(Ooh… I hate to be causing so much trouble for my fellow adventurers, but I am somehow happy to realize I can hold them all off…)**"

Well, gee, I was glad *someone* was happy.

"Come on, Darkness! Hold still already! We're trying to help you! Don't you want our help? Could it be that you secretly kind of enjoy beating up on the adventurers who usually make fun of you?"

"**(N-n-no, I don't!)** Bwa-ha-ha-ha-ha-ha-ha-ha! Cubs and fledglings, all of you! Don't be shy—test yourselves against me!"

Vanir's taunt didn't help Darkness's case much. The adventurers around her looked more and more threatening.

"Darkness! You think you're all that just because a couple of your attacks hit something?!"

"Here I always thought you had it more together than anyone else in Kazuma's party! And now you…!"

"Surround her! Everyone circle up on this quack Crusader!"

"**(I-I'm not the one who taunted y—)** Bwa-ha-ha-ha-ha-ha-haaa! Not even a swarm of you small fries would be a match for me! **(Ahhhhh…)**"

Vanir spoke in Darkness's voice, so the adventurers weren't sure whether it was Darkness or the demon cackling at them. They just got angrier and angrier at Darkness, until they started aiming their insults at her instead of Vanir.

"I cannot stand to see Darkness so vigorously slandered when she is merely being controlled by the enemy! Is there nothing we can do?!" Megumin tugged hard on my sleeve.

I looked at the battlefield. There Darkness was, overpowering a crowd of adventurers under a relentless torrent of put-downs.

"(Oh... Those I normally converse with so happily now look at me with such scorn...!) You feel...happy? What is going on?"

....

"I don't know. She seems to be having a pretty good time."

"S-still, we must help her! Don't you have any ideas?!"

Megumin could ask as many times as she wanted. But in her current state, Darkness was a lot to handle.

The reality was, I didn't have a good way to bring down that Devil. Even Aqua's magic barely had any effect. What was I supposed to do...?

"Will you just give already?! I'm getting awfully tired of you!"

"You think you are weary? Human wave tactics—a dirty trick! Don't think I will waste my time with you lot forever just because I have said I won't kill anyone!"

The battle between Aqua and Vanir continued.

The adventurers had realized that Aqua was Vanir's target, so they formed a wall to protect her. Aqua kept flinging exorcism magic from behind them, but neither combatant showed any sign of winning.

Vanir, though, finally crushed the precarious balance.

He must have been getting used to Darkness's body, because he hefted her massive sword easily and began to smack away the adventurers' weapons.

If nothing else, Darkness was probably leagues ahead of her opponents in sheer strength and endurance. Combined with the battle experience the Devil had collected over a vast lifetime and the agility he granted her, the formerly quack Crusader was taking on ten people and more at a time.

"Hey, is it just me or does she look kind of happy today? Sort of radiant..."

"Cut the chatter and help me... Huh?!"

One of the adventurers finally failed to block Vanir's attack and took a great sideward sweep of Darkness's sword. The battle line began to crumble.

Megumin let out a little yelp at the sight.

"Bwa-ha-ha-ha-ha-ha-ha! The time to exact my payment has come, O my old enemy! And I shall collect it with the hand of your own friend. What could bring me greater joy?!"

"Hey, hey, Darkness! I believe in you! You're stronger than some Devil, right? Y-you're okay in there, right? Darkness! Can you hear me?!" Aqua called out as she danced farther and farther back, but there was no answer from Darkness.

Now that the delicate balance between Vanir and the adventurers had been decisively upset, it was only a matter of time before he reached the back row and started targeting Aqua directly.

"Mr. Satou, are you not going to join them in battle? That Priest and that possessed Crusader are both your friends, aren't they?! Are you just going to leave them there?!"

Sena sounded absolutely at her wit's end, but what did she want me to do?

"Well, as you know, my class is Adventurer. Everyone out there is stronger than me, and they're getting their butts kicked. How exactly do you think I could help?"

"Why, you—! You impossible man...!"

Sena's face twisted in horror as she drew away from me. Meanwhile, one adventurer after another was being rendered powerless.

"K-Kazuma! Does this count as a crisis? Isn't it pretty much the worst crisis we've been in?!" Aqua called out, on the verge of tears. Beside me, Megumin held tight to her staff and turned to me anxiously.

Well, she could look all she liked. I was still just too weak...!

Face pale, Sena watched another adventurer take a knockout blow, and I could feel her eyes on me, too.

I wanted to take this opportunity to lecture the official. To point out how I hadn't caused this, how I was a victim who got dragged into these things.

...Geez. And they say I've got good Luck. Look what I get caught up in. Some Luck, I said to myself.

"Kazuma! Kazumaaaaa!"

It was Aqua's cries for help that finally pushed me over the edge.

"...I guess I've got no choooooiceeeee!"

More than a little desperately, I drew my sword and charged in, hoping that if my Luck was really as good as all that, everything would work out somehow.

9

Darkness had completely succumbed to Vanir.

"Bwa-ha-ha-ha-ha-ha! Bwaaaaa-ha-ha-ha-ha! Are you prepared, ancient foe of mine? Even I did not foresee that the day of your destruction would come here, in a place like this! ...What is it, boy who is the weakest of all the adventurers here? I see all that you are. Shall I then offer a prophecy?"

Vanir spoke as I faced down Darkness.

"I say to you, who seeks peace and stability, do not overthink it and simply turn a blind eye to this scene. Your great Luck is rendered null by the immense Unluckiness of your friends. Good fortune will come from changing your party members, which I suggest for your own safety. If you do so...!"

As Vanir blathered, I wordlessly swung my sword at his mask.

He dodged it easily. I didn't know what I was expecting.

"Boy whose own life is most important to him, what brought on this change of heart? Whatever you do will not avail you. Desist, and I shall give you a Vanir doll and a mask that matches my own. I advise you to take them and go home."

"N-no thanks... Hey, Darkness, what are you doing in there, anyway? Are you just going to let any Devil who comes along dominate you like this? I didn't know you were such a pushover."

At my taunts, Vanir responded:

"Bwa-ha-ha-ha-ha-ha! It is useless. As you can see, I have already— **(Why, you...! Who's a pushover?! And he's not dominating me! I'm just really enjoying the emotional turmoil of being under this Devil's thumb...!)** So your words cannot reach...your... Hmm. I had not expected such iron will. In all the eons I have lived, I have never encountered one I was unable to control."

Naturally, our test-of-endurance-loving Crusader was still conscious and well in there.

"All right, Darkness, listen up. I'm going to take the seal off his mask. Then I need you to get back control of yourself. Just for a second is plenty. Pull off the mask and throw it away. Then..."

Once Darkness was rid of it, Aqua could handle the rest.

But Vanir must have been able to read those thoughts, too.

"Hmph. Not a terrible strategy, but you have one problem. How are you, a weakling, going to reach this seal when I can deploy my host's full strength? It turns out I'm quite happy to fight my old enemy like this. I may let you break the seal...*after* I'm done with her. **(Hrm, I admit I'm disappointed to hear you underestimate me. Right now I could take on the world!)**"

Suddenly, Vanir said...

"Y-you fool. Are you even now prepared to stand against me?"

All around us lay the unconscious adventurers who'd taken the blunt side of Vanir's great sword.

And there was Aqua, casting restorative magic on them as Vanir and I squared off. She came over and stood behind me.

"Kazuma, I've got your back! With my support magic, you can take down that Devil just like a real hero!"

Easy for her to say.

"Heh-heh! I've got a pretty good streak of Luck myself. All right, Kazuma. It is time for you to awaken the power within you. You don't have to hold back anymore. Take back Darkness from that Devil!"

Easy for Megumin, who had joined us, to say.

So what was this power I had within me?

For that matter, why did Aqua and Megumin think I could face down Vanir head-on and get that seal?

Vanir took up a stance.

"Bwa-ha-ha-ha! Shall you force me to yield? **(You think)** you can take this **(seal)**? I'd like to **(see you tr—)** Shut up, shut up! Those are my lines!"

"You were both so unhappy about that seal earlier. You want it off or not?"

While I jumped into their argument, Aqua prepared her exorcism magic.

"You are planning something, boy. The shining aura from that despicable creature behind you prevents me from seeing exactly what. But I know you do not mean to cross swords with me... Hmm. Some kind of skill, then? **(It's Steal! That's his favorite trick!)**"

"Wh-what the hell is wrong with you, giving away my ideas!"

She sounded so proud of herself, too. Vanir smirked at me.

"Kazuma, my magic's ready!"

"Great, leave the rest to me! All right, Darkness, here we go! How about another bet? Just like at the training grounds. If I win, I'll add something absolutely unbelievable to that 'awful demand' you already owe me. If you win, you can do whatever you want!"

"(Ahh! To m-mention that h-here...!) H-hey, you! Don't be distracted by that boy's sweet nothings! Show no weakness—bring your heart to bear! Raise your magical power; prepare yourself to resist Steal—!"

Vanir's hold on the conflicted Darkness weakened as her body came to a stop.

Behind me, I suddenly heard Megumin begin to chant Explosion.

I whipped around and found her focused on the dungeon entrance.

The adventurers who had gone underground with us were dashing out, Vanir's dolls hot on their heels.

Vanir had noticed the same thing. The eyes of his mask glowed weirdly, and the dolls pouring out of the dungeon ran pell-mell straight at us.

They were going to take out Megumin.

"All right! It's on, Vanir! And Darkness, you fight back—keep him from moving!"

And then I reached out toward his mask...!

"If you think the Steal of a mere Adventurer will prevail against me, you are profoundly mistaken! To those who resist, I show no mer—"

"Kindle!!"

The spell incanted at the top of my voice wasn't Steal but the fire-starting Kindle.

There was no special need for me to Steal the tag or remove it by hand. Burning it off would do just fine...!

"...Bwa! Bwa-ha-ha-ha-ha! Bwaaaa-ha-ha-ha-ha-ha! **(Ahhh! No fair, Kazuma! You suck!)** I must say I am somewhat impressed, boy! It is rare for anyone to deceive the all-seeing Devil!"

The tag stuck to his mask burned away, leaving nothing to connect Vanir and Darkness.

"Okay, Darkness, show us what you're made of! Rip off that mask!"

The Crusader grabbed the mask and...

"(…! I… I can't take it off…!)"

Vanir was still fighting to keep the mask stuck to her face.

And his dolls were still heading for us with murder in their eyes.

The adventurers who had come out of the dungeon formed a wall between them and us. They seemed to have intuited that we were fighting a boss monster and tried to hold off the smaller enemies.

"Kazumaaa! What now? Can I go ahead and use my magic?" Aqua called.

"No, wait, the mask is still attached to Darkness! If you use your spell now, her defense will just—"

But then…

"(Don't worry about me. Do it.)"

Darkness spoke briefly, her hand still on the mask.

Do it? But it wouldn't have any effect…

"(If Aqua's magic won't work, then… Don't worry about me. Explode me and the mask.)"

Wait…

What did she just say?

"You idiot! I don't care how tough you are, you can't survive Explosion!"

"(Only one way to find out!) Now, there's no need to rush. Let us talk."

At Darkness's words, Vanir finally sounded like he was starting to sweat.

Behind me, Megumin had finished preparing her spell.

"(Aqua! If I get the mask off, don't hesitate! Use your exorcism magic!) Well, this has been fun. How about we call today a draw? **(If I don't, then use Explosion…!)** A draw with the Duke of Hell, a general of the Demon King. Quite an achievement, I'd say!"

"I—I hear you, Darkness! When you get rid of that dumb thing, I'll be right on it!"

Aqua watched the mask, hardly blinking, ready to fire off her exorcism at any moment.

"Kazuma, Darkness is not in her right mind! Even she cannot withstand this spell!"

Megumin was about to burst into tears.

Everyone—the dolls that had been heading our way until just a moment ago, Sena, and the other adventurers—kept their distance from Darkness, frozen.

And in the middle of it all...

"(...Hey, Vanir. We didn't have long together, but I kind of enjoyed it. So...I want to give you a choice. You can get off me and be purified out of existence. Or we can be blown up together. Take your pick.)"

"Get destroyed or get destroyed"? It didn't seem like much of a choice to me.

"...I am a Devil," Vanir said grimly, "one of the enemies of the gods. Never shall I let one of them purify me. Bwa-ha-ha-ha... In a strange way, I am meeting my end exactly how I wished. I quite enjoyed possessing you."

Explosion it was, then.

Hearing this, Darkness and the mask took a few steps away from us.

"(All right, Megumin!)" Darkness demanded harshly. Megumin gave a small shake of her head, not able to bring herself to do it...

Sena took in the entire scene with a vacant stare. I patted her on the shoulder.

"If anything goes wrong, I want you to testify that I gave the order. I'll take full responsibility. Again."

Sena nodded, her face white, and swallowed heavily.

Our Crusader was the toughest around.

The toughest in all Axel.

"Megumin, do it!"
I said the words. A moment passed.

And then a massive explosion rocked the field in front of the dungeon.

Epilogue

Epilogue 1 —Aqua—

A while after the battle with that weird demon...
...Kazuma and I were summoned to the Adventurers Guild.

Geez... Kazuma. That Kazuma.

How does he get us into one potentially deadly situation after another like this? If I ever see another general of the Demon King, it'll be too soon. If only we could have a boring day once in a while.

Sure, I want to hurry up and get back to Heaven, but somehow it's been nothing but hard times since we got to this world.

"...It's weird. It's like you have these great talents, but they're all for things that are totally pointless," Kazuma muttered as I drew a picture with water from my glass.

"Well, of course. Just who do you think I am?"

For someone who could control water at will, this was merely...

"If you called yourself the goddess of artists, maybe someone would actually believe you."

I was tempted to fling a holy fist right at that dumb mouth of his. But I remembered my immense dignity and refrained.

It was definitely my dignity that kept me from doing it and not my fear of how he might get me back.

Because I'm not afraid of that. Not at all.

Kazuma has to struggle every day with the problems Megumin causes and with Darkness's nonsense. I at least can try to be nice to him. Everyone else in the party is an irresponsible child. As a goddess, I have to watch over them.

"...Hey. What are you thinking? Something weird, I'll bet. I see that pitying look. I hate that look."

Here I am being the most grown-up person in the room, and look what he accuses me of. Is he drinking enough milk? I've heard a lack of calcium makes a person irritable.

But I'm sure he'll learn to be more forgiving, starting today.

Because the reason we were called here is...

Epilogue 2 —Megumin—

I'm afraid I was not much help this time around.

I do cause Kazuma trouble on a daily basis—even if not as much as Aqua or Darkness—so I thought this one time, maybe I could do as he asked.

As the rational thinker in this party, it behooves me to be the most collected.

On the table, my familiar, Chomusuke, showed her affection for Kazuma. Perhaps he'd endeared himself to her by feeding her back at home.

"...I don't get it. This thing seems really fond of me. But it won't even go near Aqua. Maybe it's true what they say about animals being able to tell who's a good person."

"I was just thinking how sorry I feel for you with all the problems you have to solve every day. I was going to show how magnanimous I can be by cutting you some slack. But I can't quite ignore what I just heard. It sounded to me like you said that despite all my holiness I am somehow not a good person."

"Yeah. That's exactly what I'm saying."

Chomusuke came running to me to avoid the fight brewing between Kazuma and Aqua. I picked her up and put her on my shoulder, where she always sat.

In a corner of the Guild, Yunyun, who was supposed to help me clear Kazuma's name, sat eating by herself.

She didn't have to. It was time for her to stop getting so caught up in our so-called rivalry and come join us.

I would have to thank her later. Admittedly, Kazuma had done a fine job on his own of convincing everyone he wasn't one of the Demon King's spies. But she had helped in the background.

"Errgh... I can't take any more..."

The mutter came from the seat across from Kazuma.

Darkness collapsed over the table, quaking, her face red.

Adventurers of every stripe had been calling out to her for some time now, and with every shout she grew redder.

She was the oldest of our party members but perhaps the least worldly. She tried to act cool, but it was actually quite simple to get a rise out of her. Those factors together made it intensely tempting to tease her from time to time.

...All right. I rose from my seat and approached her...

Epilogue 3 —**Darkness**—

Oh my gods.

How did this happen?

"How long are you going to keep babbling?! Do you realize you're responsible for more of the things that I'm on trial for than anyone else?

From most to least troublesome, the order goes: you, Megumin, Darkness! If you've finally got that through your thick skull, then go sit in the corner and count the specks of dust on the wall or something until I've got my award!"

"Waaaaaaah! How could you be so cruel, Kazuma?! It's not like I cause problems deliberately! With the flood damage from our battle with Beldia, the spirit barrier around the graveyard that caused all those hauntings—I was just trying to do what was best!"

"Pardon me, but I was of the belief that *I* was the least troublesome."

I leaned on the table with my head in my hands, watching the three of them argue out of the corner of my eye.

Suddenly, someone called from behind me.

"Hey there, Lalatina! That's your name, isn't it? Cute!"

I trembled.

"Lalatina, sweetheart, we've got to get you some clothes that are as cute as your name! I'll help you pick some out!"

I trembled a little more.

"'Lalatina,' huh? Sounds all…high-class and cultured."

Aww, gimme a break…!

We'd gotten through the whole mess with Lord Alderp, but now I had a new problem…

I raised my head, tears in my eyes, and glared at the source of all this teasing from the other adventurers.

"Ooh, what's with the scary face, Lalatina? It doesn't suit someone with such a sweet name."

"Grrrrrr…!"

I could feel my face grow hot right up to my ears, but I gritted my teeth and bore Kazuma's taunt.

He had promised after he bested me in our duel that he would do something so awful it would make me weep…and he'd delivered.

Hrr, curse me! To lose my nerve at the last minute, when I'd been so close to victory…!

Old Alderp, for his part, hadn't said anything after all that had taken place. But he was a stubborn one, and I seriously doubted I'd heard the last of him.

"Ooh, looks like they're starting. Catch you in a few...*Lalatina*!"

I grabbed a wooden cup nearby and flung it at Kazuma as he stood up.

Epilogue 4 —**Kazuma**—

"Adventurer Sir Kazuma Satou." I stood at the front counter of the Guild, the intent gaze of every adventurer in the room fixed on me. "I hereby present you with this award and a letter of gratitude from the town. In addition, I offer my profound apologies for suspecting you in any ill capacity."

With that, I accepted the letter of gratitude from Sena, who gave me a deep bow of her head.

It was a week after our battle with Vanir.

We had been cleared of any suspicion of being spies for the Demon King on the logic that if we were working for him, we would never have gone so far as to defeat one of his generals, up to and including how we put our lives on the line.

Sena, after watching the battle firsthand, had arranged for me to be cleared of the sedition charge and to receive my due reward for my role in defeating Destroyer—even if it was a bit later than everyone else's.

For me, just being out from under the threat of the death penalty was practically reward enough. And I was very grateful for the thought that I might actually be able to repay our debts.

We had been summoned to the Guild today, since Darkness's wounds had finally healed.

"And to the noblewoman Lalatina Ford Dustiness. Your act of self-sacrifice in this matter was beyond reproach. In respect of the honor you have done the Dustiness name, the royal family sends you a letter of their gratitude, as well as a full set of the finest armor money can buy to replace that which you lost in battle."

The Knights approached from a respectful distance, bearing a new set of armor for Darkness, who was beet red and trembling.

Megumin's Explosion had vanquished the masked Devil Vanir.

Darkness had been left in a crater, with near-fatal wounds and without her precious armor.

Aqua had nursed her back to health, leading us here today, but...

"Congrats, Lalatina!" someone shouted. Darkness twitched.

"Yeah, way to go, Lalatina!"

"That's our Lalatina for you!"

"Lalatina! You're so cute! Lalatina!"

As one person after another called out to her with her real name, Darkness covered her face with both hands—blushing up to her ears—and leaned on the table again.

"This...this humiliation is not the kind of awful thing I was hoping for," she muttered weakly, keeping her head down.

I'd said I would do something so bad she would weep.

All I'd done was keep my promise...

"But Darkness, I think Lalatina is a really cute name! I'll chew out Kazuma later for spreading it around as a prank. But you should try to have a little more pride in the name Lalatina!"

Aqua, completely well-intentioned, was oblivious to the fact that she was only twisting the knife.

Megumin had come over to enjoy the show and shook with suppressed laughter. Darkness's shoulders were shaking for an entirely different reason. The Arch-wizard gave her a little pat. *There, there.*

In keeping with my promise to do something so awful it would make Darkness weep, I had let everyone know her real name.

Now every adventurer who walked by teased her about it, but they would let up in due course.

"Now, to continue. In the matter of Mr. Satou's reward." Sena's words brought silence to the chattering in the Guild. "Adventurer Kazuma Satou and party. You made immense contributions to the defeat of Mobile Fortress Destroyer and were essential to our success in the battle with the Demon King's general Vanir. In accordance with this…"

The intense, somber expression Sena had worn when she came with my indictment had vanished, replaced with a soft, gentle smile.

"…minus your outstanding debt and the reparations for Lord Alderp's mansion…"

She pulled out a piece of paper.

"…you are presented the amount of forty million eris. Congratulations on your achievements!"

She handed me a bulging sack. Wild applause spread through the Guild as I accepted it. Adventurers shouted in celebration and called out that I should treat them.

The mood in the Guild Hall was jubilant.

I left it to Aqua—goddess of parties—and Megumin to handle the situation, while Darkness got to her feet and exited the Guild with me.

Our debt had finally been settled.

Yet Darkness and I didn't find it very comforting.

…There was somewhere we had to go now.

There was someone we had to tell about the death of Vanir, general of the Demon King.

Vanir had told us he'd come to this town to see a friend.

A friend who ran a junky little store and somehow managed to be penniless no matter how hard she worked…

That could only be his fellow general—Wiz.

In other words, we had killed an old friend of hers.

He had been after Aqua, and as adventurers, we sort of had an obligation to deal with him. But that was cold comfort now.

*   *   *

We were at the corner of a back road that didn't see many visitors, in front of a store with a sign boasting WIZ'S MAGICAL ITEM SHOPPE.

"Kazuma. Let me tell Wiz about this one. Vanir and I wreaked havoc together in the same body, even if it was just for a while. And though I can't agree with his taunts about humans, I didn't think he was so bad... Even if he was kind of obsessed with getting revenge on Aqua. Maybe it's not becoming for a Crusader in the service of Our Lady Eris to say this, but... Well, I didn't hate him."

The whole time she spoke, Darkness gazed into the distance.

Wait. "We wreaked havoc together"? Geez. I thought she looked like she was having an awfully good time taking out those adventurers.

In any case, I pushed open the front door and entered the shop.

"Welcome!"

A chipper voice greeted me. I could picture the smile on Wiz's face, and my heart ached.

No sooner had I come in than I realized Wiz had a new employee, someone else wearing the shop's characteristic apron.

The new person was tallish.

He was incredibly cheerful, and his lips were twisted into a big smile...!

"It's you! Welcome! Young woman who was standing outside the store speaking as if ashamed, there is something I want to tell you. I gather you don't hate me—but we Devils lack gender, so I'm afraid I can't respond to your blush-inducing confession... Ooh, a most bitter embarrassment, how delectable! What's wrong? Why are you in the fetal position? Did you really think I'd been destroyed?! Bwa-ha-ha-ha-ha-ha-ha!"

The masked employee acted as if there was nothing unusual about his being there.

He patted Darkness on the shoulder reassuringly as she sat on the floor of the shop with her face in her knees and her cheeks red, trembling. That was when Wiz poked her head out from a back room.

"Oh, Mr. Kazuma, welcome! I heard how you defeated Mr. Vanir and convinced everyone you weren't a spy. Congratulations! Now all that's left is your debt, right? But don't worry, Mr. Vanir here is very talented at earning money…"

I held up one hand to stop the merry flood of words.

"You're right that my name's been cleared. But what's with this guy? He seems pretty lively for someone who took a direct hit from Explosion. He shouldn't even be here, should he? There isn't a scratch on him!"

Vanir seemed genuinely surprised by my question.

"What do you mean? Even I could hardly expect to weather a blast like that without a scratch. Here, take a closer look at my mask."

He pointed to his face as he spoke.

I leaned in close and saw a Roman numeral II.

"That explosion cost me one of my lives, so this indicates that I am the second Vanir."

"Get out."

My retort provoked calming murmurs from Wiz.

"Mr. Vanir has wanted to quit being a general of the Demon King's army for some time now. It seems that, having been destroyed once, he came back again in order to pursue his dream. He has already ceased supporting the spirit barrier around the Demon King's castle. So he's perfectly harmless now."

Wiz smiled the whole time she spoke, perhaps happy to have been reunited with her old friend.

Harmless, though…? Hmm…

Maybe I'd better get Aqua in here to destroy him one more time.

Just as I was mulling over the possibility…

"You, man who comes from a land far beyond. You, man who seeks to defeat the Demon King though he has no talents and no strength.

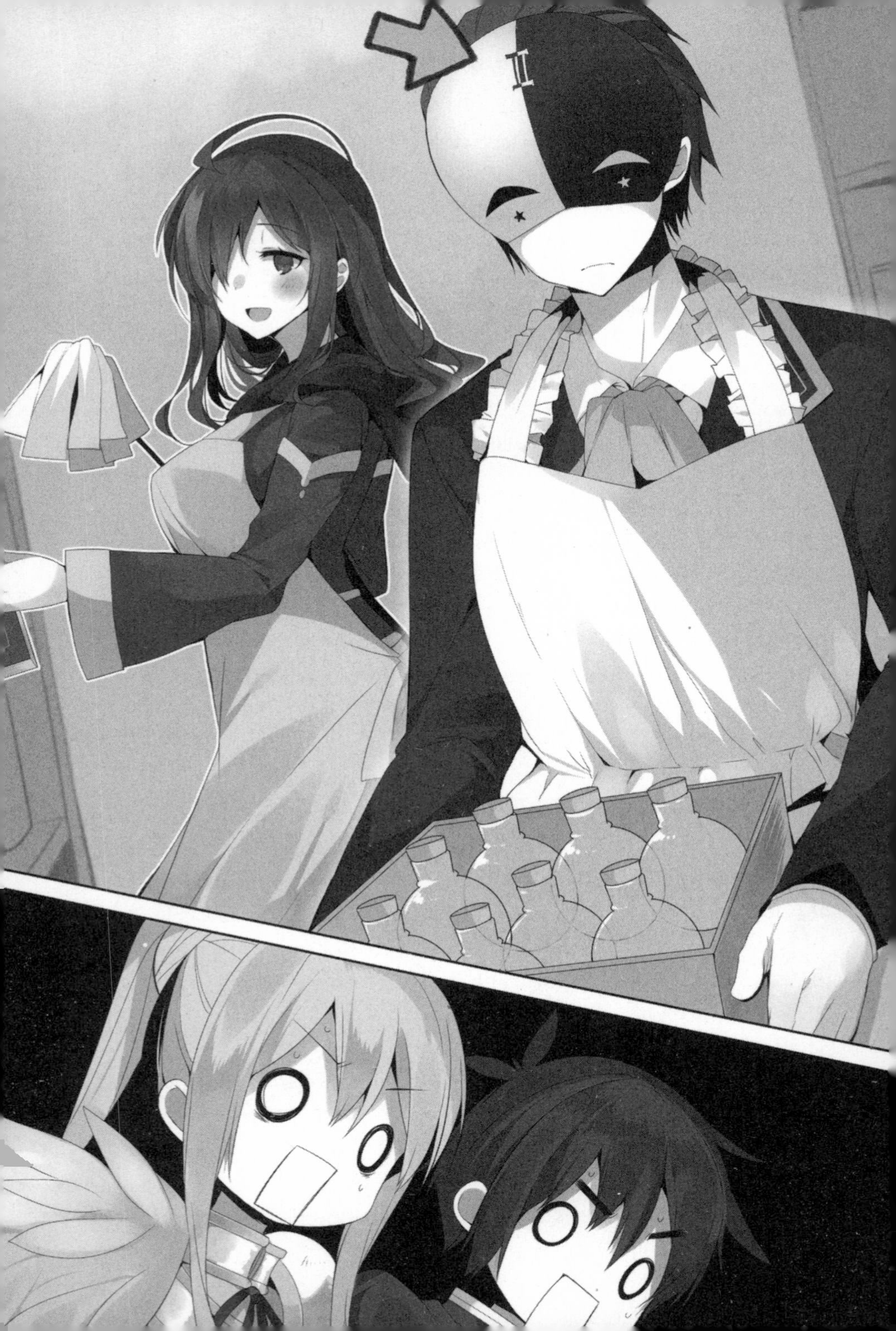

The all-seeing Devil prophesies. In the not-too-distant future, you and the young woman curled up and blubbering on the floor there will encounter a trial most difficult to overcome. The trial will be great; it will make you keenly aware of your own powerlessness. Until that time, good fortune will come of our cooperation in business... I've got some good ideas. Want to hear them?"

Vanir's face scrunched up into a pleasant smile, even though everything coming out of his mouth sounded like trouble.

FIN.

Afterword

Wooooooo! Volume threeeeeeeee!

Thankfully, Volume 3 is out…for better or worse.

Now that I've made it this far, some things are starting to feel more real to me.

I keep expecting to wake up saying, "So it was all a dream…" I was so worried I might be imagining the whole thing that I put copies of Volumes 1 and 2 under my pillow. At this rate, I won't need an actual pillow much longer.

In fact, before I knew it, there were translated editions overseas. The book has been translated into several other languages and is already on sale.

I wonder what those translations are like. I use a lot of weird words and strange turns of phrase.

If I may say so, I'm not always even sure my Japanese makes a whole lot of sense. I hope it's not causing too much trouble for the people who have to translate it.

I get it, I get it. I'd better start using more proper Japanese.

I get it, but I'm not gonna do it. I just mean I hear you.

The other day: I headed to the bookstore planning to do them the service of pulling my books a centimeter out from the shelf so they would stand out. When I got there, I found someone standing in the store, reading a copy of *Konosuba*, Volume 1.

While I was busy being totally thrown by this turn of events, the person took the book up to the register, and I found myself making a little bow of thanks in their direction.

I watched someone buy a copy of my book. It sends tingles down my spine.

You know how in Japan it's rude to point the bottoms of your feet at somebody? I realized I have readers all over the country, meaning that when I go to sleep, my feet must inevitably be pointed at some of them. So starting tonight, I'm going to sleep standing up.

…No, I'm not. Sorry. It's just not possible.

All right, enough random chitchat. Let's talk about the book.

Volume 3 introduced everyone's favorite government prosecutor. You can expect to see much more of her in the future.

Personally, I'm considering having her association with Kazuma send her straight off the professional rails, after which she will lead a fallen life. Or not.

I would feel sorry for her if she got stuck dealing with every problem the main characters caused from here on out.

I just realized all the characters in this story are kind of pathetic.

No! Surely by the end, they'll…!

Well, I'll do my best to keep you interested until the end.

As I mentioned in the last book, a spin-off series featuring Megumin is currently being serialized on the Sneaker Bunko home page. Please feel free to have a look! If you fill out a questionnaire as well, it would make this author very happy.

As ever, I had to lean on a lot of people to make this volume possible.

Frankly, I would like to make fewer typos and usage mistakes.

I'm very sorry. I promise I'll try to do better next time.

My dear Kurone Mishima, thank you for another volume's worth of wonderful illustrations.

To everyone in the editorial department and everyone involved in the production of the book, thank you so much. It's thanks to all of you that Volume 3 made it to publication. No, really.

Maybe, as an author, I could learn to cause fewer problems some of the time. I need to grow up a little before I give my editor a heart attack.

...I'll try.

......Well, I'll *try* to try.

On that note, it looks like Volume 4 will come out a little early.

Ahh, how grateful I am...!

I'll give writing it my all, so I would be thrilled if you would consider picking it up.

"I got a girlfriend around the same time I bought this book."

"On a lark, I bought ten lottery tickets along with this book. I won three hundred yen!"

"I wove several copies of this book together and used it as a bulletproof vest. It brought me home alive from the battlefield."

I have...not...had many testimonials such as these.

If you got just a few minutes' enjoyment from reading the book, I'll be perfectly happy.

So, to all those who labored in the production of this volume, and to those who read it—my deepest thanks!

Natsume Akatsuki

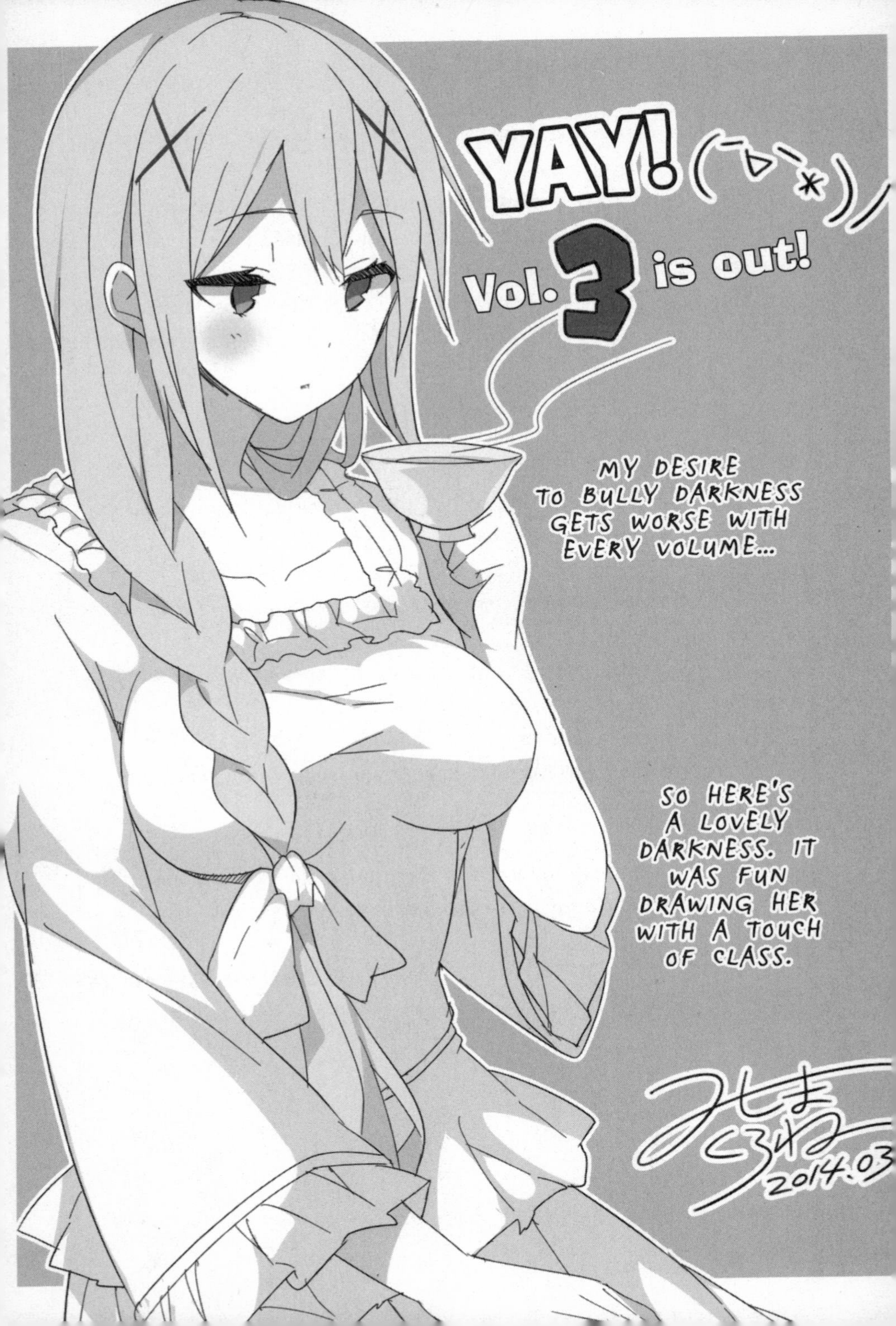
YAY!
Vol. 3 is out!
MY DESIRE TO BULLY DARKNESS GETS WORSE WITH EVERY VOLUME...
SO HERE'S A LOVELY DARKNESS. IT WAS FUN DRAWING HER WITH A TOUCH OF CLASS.
みしま くろね 2014.03

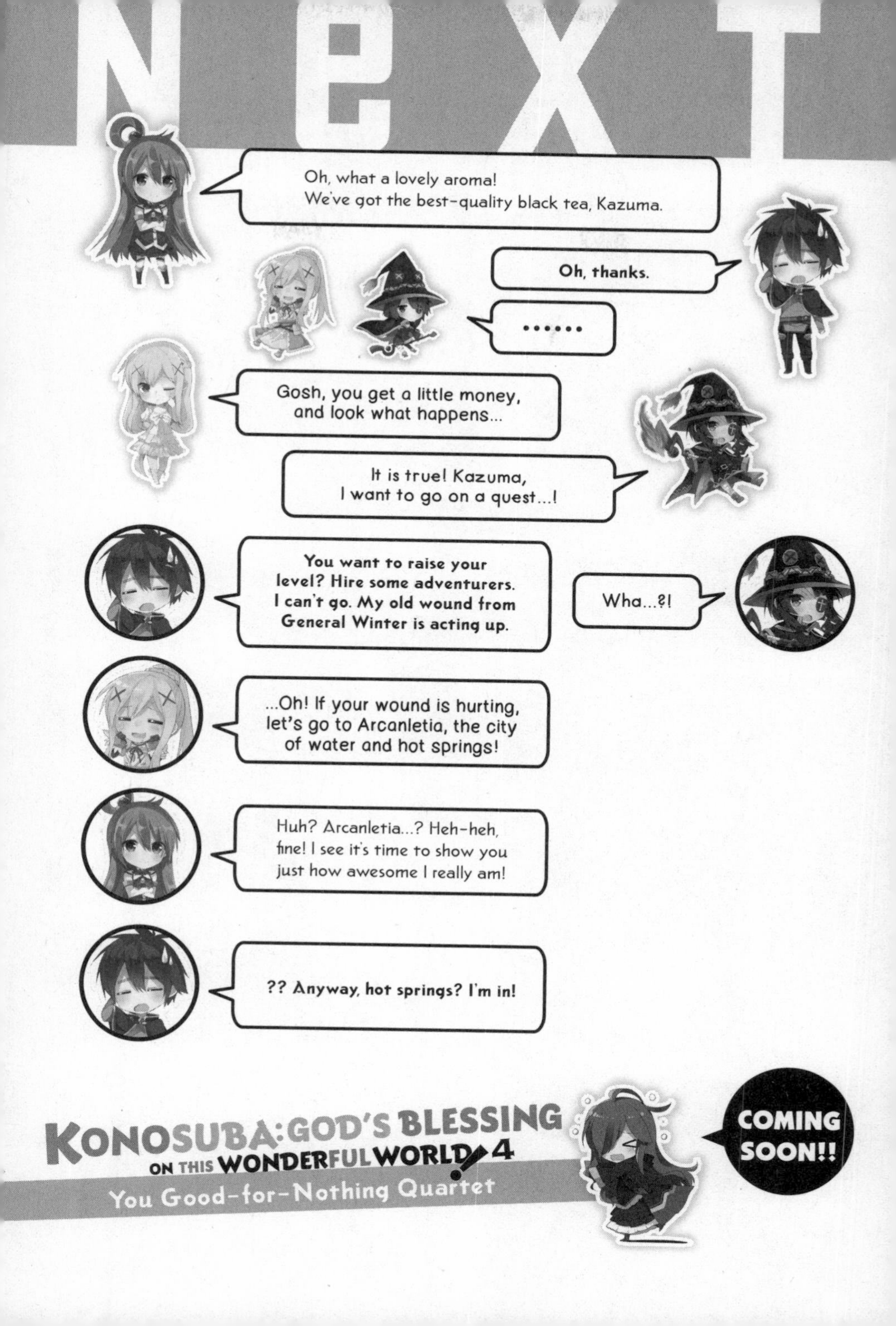
NEXT
Oh, what a lovely aroma! We've got the best-quality black tea, Kazuma.
Oh, thanks.
......
Gosh, you get a little money, and look what happens...
It is true! Kazuma, I want to go on a quest...!
You want to raise your level? Hire some adventurers. I can't go. My old wound from General Winter is acting up.
Wha...?!
...Oh! If your wound is hurting, let's go to Arcanletia, the city of water and hot springs!
Huh? Arcanletia...? Heh-heh, fine! I see it's time to show you just how awesome I really am!
?? Anyway, hot springs? I'm in!
KONOSUBA: GOD'S BLESSING ON THIS WONDERFUL WORLD! 4
You Good-for-Nothing Quartet
COMING SOON!!

HAVE YOU BEEN TURNED ON TO LIGHT NOVELS YET?

IN STORES NOW!

SWORD ART ONLINE, VOL. 1–11
SWORD ART ONLINE, PROGRESSIVE 1–4

The chart-topping light novel series that spawned the explosively popular anime and manga adaptations!

MANGA ADAPTATION AVAILABLE NOW!

SWORD ART ONLINE © Reki Kawahara ILLUSTRATION: abec
KADOKAWA CORPORATION ASCII MEDIA WORKS

ACCEL WORLD, VOL. 1–10

Prepare to accelerate with an action-packed cyber-thriller from the bestselling author of *Sword Art Online*.

MANGA ADAPTATION AVAILABLE NOW!

ACCEL WORLD © Reki Kawahara ILLUSTRATION: HIMA
KADOKAWA CORPORATION ASCII MEDIA WORKS

SPICE AND WOLF, VOL. 1–18

A disgruntled goddess joins a traveling merchant in this light novel series that inspired the *New York Times* bestselling manga.

MANGA ADAPTATION AVAILABLE NOW!

SPICE AND WOLF © Isuna Hasekura ILLUSTRATION: Jyuu Ayakura
KADOKAWA CORPORATION ASCII MEDIA WORKS